PRAISE FOR FICTION RIVER

"These enjoyable twisting short stories seem more like a stop in the Twilight Zone than pulp fiction."

— MIDWEST BOOK REVIEW ON FICTION RIVER: RECYCLED PULP

"What I particularly like with the *Fiction River* series is the way it simply gives a writer a title as a central premise and allows them to run with it. Try it sometime... it's harder than you'd think to do on the spot. And yet these fertile imaginations take these ideas to wild and wonderful directions."

— ASTRO GUYZ

"*[Fiction River]* is one of the best and most exciting publications in the field today. Check out an issue and see why I say that."

— KEITH WEST, ADVENTURES FANTASTIC

"... [this] fabulous collection runs the genre gamut and more."

— GENRE GO ROUND REVIEWS ON FICTION RIVER SPECIAL EDITION: CRIME

FICTION RIVER: HARD CHOICES

An Original Anthology Magazine

EDITED BY DEAN WESLEY SMITH

Series Editors

KRISTINE KATHRYN RUSCH & DEAN WESLEY SMITH

Fiction River: Hard Choices

Published by WMG Publishing

Cover and layout copyright © 2018 by WMG Publishing

Editing and other written material copyright © 2018 by WMG Publishing

Cover art copyright © Jezper/Depositphotos

Cover design by Allyson Longueira/WMG Publishing

ISBN-13: 978-1-56146-072-4

ISBN-10: 1-56146-072-9

CONTENTS

Foreword   vii

Introduction   xi

ANNIE REED	Equal Justice	1
TONYA D. PRICE	Payback	17
DAN C. DUVAL	Eric the Monkey	33
RON COLLINS	Prospecting	45
MICHAEL KOWAL	Toots	65
LAURA WARE	The Devil's Muse	83
DIANA DEVERELL	Clean and Godly In Denmark	97
ANNIE REED	Killshot	111
DALE HARTLEY EMERY	Four Hundred Yards	125
DAVID STIER	A Life with Meaning	143
CHUCK HEINTZELMAN	Nightmare Scenario	157
LESLIE CLAIRE WALKER	Echo	173
JAMIE FERGUSON	Haunted	187
VALERIE BROOK	Skinwalker	203
DAN C. DUVAL	Missiles of October	221
DAYLE A. DERMATIS	Girl with a Mission	233
KENDALL HEINTZELMAN	A New Day	251
M. L. BUCHMAN	They Taught Us Wrong	263
LEIGH SAUNDERS	Tendrils	271
VALERIE BROOK	Little Byte and Big Pieces	287

About the Editor   303

Acknowledgments   305

Fiction River Presents   313

FOREWORD

Challenging Decisions

We have found a favorite *Fiction River* volume, at least for those of us who edit. It's a version of *Editor Saves*. We've published two of those volumes so far—*Editor's Choice*, the very first one of these, edited by Mark Leslie, and *Editor Saves,* edited by me.

The volumes come out of our anthology workshop. We open current *Fiction River* volumes to the attendees at the workshop—professional (or professional quality) writers all—to see what they'll do with the themes we've chosen for the volumes. With forty to fifty writers in attendance, and only about fifteen stories worth of space in each volume, there are always *great* stories that the volume's editor doesn't choose.

Why are there only fifteen or so slots when there can be as many as twenty stories in a volume of *Fiction River?* Because the editors also invite other writers into the volume, from new writers to old established pros. Often, particularly when I'm editing, those fifteen slots don't even get filled from the workshop. I know what I'm looking for in each volume and I'll know it when I see it.

The stories simply aren't on point for the theme of the anthology, as determined by the editor (the only vote that counts for the volume). The other editors, who read everything for the anthology workshop, might think a story's perfect. Or they might steal a story from one anthology for their own volume.

Mark Leslie was the one who came up with making an anthology out of the stories that were brilliant but didn't fit a particular theme. That was *Editor's Choice*. He did all of the reading—1.2 million words —during the workshop itself that year. Needless to say, he barely slept a wink.

We had the system under control for *Editor Saves*. The editors at that workshop picked their top stories that didn't make it into a themed volume. Then I assembled those stories into a volume. Again, no theme except great fiction. (I love that volume. Go look for it. It's so much fun.)

Dean decided to do a version of editor saves/editor's choice on his own, but he decided—as Dean does—to make the process even more challenging. He knew he would be making hard choices, because even though he had space for eighteen to twenty-five stories, he would still be leaving some superb fiction on the table.

(Just so you understand what I mean by superb fiction, stories that were written for various *Fiction River* volumes but didn't sell to *Fiction River* have gone on to win awards or be published in *Analog*, *Alfred Hitchcock's Mystery Magazine*, *Ellery Queen Mystery Magazine*, and a variety of other super impressive places.)

Dean decided that he would "narrow" his hard choices down by making sure each story that he chose had a hard choice at its core. In other words, he took an unthemed group of stories and imposed his own theme on them.

Instead of making the choices easier, the choices became harder because—as you readers know—the best fiction is always about the hardest of choices.

The result is an eclectic and fun group of stories, filled with extremely hard choices. Some writers sold Dean more than one story for the volume. My favorite story, which I would have bought for *Pulphouse: The Hardback Magazine* or *The Magazine of Fantasy & Science Fiction* or any other sf/f publication I was editing is Valerie Brooks's

"Little Byte and Big Pieces," which is probably the most memorable story to come out of that year of manuscript reading, at least for me.

That's not to diminish the quality of the other stories here. They're all wonderful and different and powerful.

Take a look. The power of a hard choice shows just how canny Dean is as an editor. And how good.

—Kristine Kathryn Rusch
Las Vegas, NV
August 19, 2018

INTRODUCTION

The Title Fits

Fiction River is known for diversity in fiction and genre. The consistent elements from volume to volume are great stories and high quality.

That holds here. Some of the stories in this volume will just stun you. Others will make you think. Others will make you smile.

All are great stories of high quality.

And very diverse.

Wow, are these stories diverse. That might be an understatement in recent publishing memory.

Two things hold this volume together under the title *Fiction River: Hard Choices*. First, all the characters are dealing with some sort of choice, some sort of crime or danger where choices must be made. Hard choices.

Now, don't take me wrong, this isn't a complete mystery volume by a long ways. There is science fiction in here along with young adult as well as mystery and other genres.

So what is the second reason we called this anthology *Hard Choices?*

Because of how it came about.

Every year about fifty professional fiction writers get together here at the Oregon Coast to write stories for *Fiction River* anthologies and also issues of *Pulphouse Fiction Magazine*.

There are six anthologies that the writers write stories for. Fifty writers trying to write and get into anthologies of about sixteen or so stories. So by the very nature of the beast, the editors of each anthology must leave out some stories that are fantastic, but just don't fit in the image they have of their book.

Thirty-six such stories per volume are left out. Six volumes over a week. You get the idea.

That's why every year many, many stories that don't make it into *Fiction River* find their way into the nation's top magazines.

So Mark Leslie, the great editor and writer, bothered by how difficult this was, suggested that Kobo sponsor one extra volume each year. Great idea. He did the first one and like a crazed human, I offered to put a second one together the next year.

I have no idea what I was thinking.

An impossible task for any editor.

I had read all the stories ahead of time and actually had three different possible anthologies I thought I could put together. But I had no idea which stories the editors of the other anthologies would be buying and they had first pick. And they weren't talking ahead of time because sometimes they didn't know either until the last minute.

So within two days after the workshop started, I had eliminated one of my possible choices for an anthology. Editors bought all the key stories for it.

By the middle of the third day it became clear that stories with hard choices and crimes and violence of one sort of another would be my anthology. The editors of the other volumes were very reluctantly letting some fantastic stories go that fit that title.

But by the end of the week I ended up with almost forty top stories I wanted to be in this volume. Oh, oh...

Now the fine folks at WMG Publishing have some pretty solid limits on word counts for *Fiction River*, so twenty of those stories had to go.

The cutting it down to these twenty in front of the authors might have been one of the hardest jobs I have ever had. Brutally hard choices didn't begin to describe it.

Then a second problem appeared for me after the dust settled. I had to try to make these stories all fit in some sort of order. And flow through the book.

That took me days to make those hard choices and right up to the moment I turned the table of contents into WMG Publishing I was tweaking the order slightly.

So this volume is perfectly named, not only for the content of the stories, but for the process of the construction of the volume itself.

I think you will be as happy with reading this book as I am now with the final product.

Diversity, a hallmark of *Fiction River* is solidly on display here.

And high-quality stories fill the volume.

Enjoy the journey through the imagination of top fiction writers and the hard choices in their stories.

—Dean Wesley Smith
Lincoln City, Oregon
December 23rd, 2017

EQUAL JUSTICE

ANNIE REED

A regular contributor to Fiction River, *Annie Reed has been in an astounding seventeen volumes and counting, most recently in* Wishes. *She managed to land two stories in this volume alone.*

After appearing in Fiction River: Hidden in Crime, *her award-winning story "The Color of Guilt" was chosen as one of* The Best Crime and Mystery Stories of 2016. *Annie is also one of the founding members of the urban fantasy-themed* Uncollected Anthology, *as well as a mainstay of the newly relaunched* Pulphouse Fiction Magazine.

Annie has worked in the legal field for years, and in "Equal Justice" she takes on the dubious legal concept of civil forfeiture. She says, "...the idea that the government can just back up a truck to your door and empty out your house of anything valuable if you're accused of a crime sends chills down my spine."

For me her stories always pack an emotional punch. "Equal Justice" sneaks up behind you to deliver the blow, leaving you to wonder where the line between justice and vengeance really lies.

The old-fashioned snapshot looked out of place in Jefferson Martin's wallet.

He'd had to trim the photograph to make it fit in the clear plastic holder that also housed his Mastercard and American Express. He'd hated to cut away any part of the picture, but it belonged next to the symbols of his success.

Like the plain white key card that granted him access to the underground parking garage at the courthouse.

He kept the key card in his wallet as well. He could have stashed the card in the ashtray in his car. The conservative gray sedan was the first new car Jefferson had ever owned, and five years later it still had that new car smell. The ashtray had never seen so much as a single cigarette.

But keeping the card in easy reach wasn't his style. The conservative new car wasn't exactly his style either, more something he did for show. He'd bought the car after he'd been promoted to chief deputy district attorney, the youngest chief deputy in the county's history. The position came with the same parking privileges enjoyed by the district court judges, the specialty court masters, and Jefferson's boss, the district attorney. People expected the chief deputy to drive an upscale car, just like they expected a young, ambitious chief deputy to keep climbing the political ladder.

Jefferson knew the ladder would have no more rungs for him. He'd been appointed to his job. The district attorney was an elected position, and the men who wielded political power in this town would never let a black man, no matter how light his skin, win a position like that.

Jefferson had made his peace with that. His ambitions lay elsewhere.

The woman in the photograph had seen far too many cigarettes in her lifetime. It had been one of the few things Jefferson hadn't liked about her.

One thing she hadn't liked was to have her picture taken. He'd never known why. Trim and petite with delicate features and skin nearly as light as his own, his grandmother had been a beautiful woman. Even to the angry eight-year-old he'd been, sent to live with a grandmother he didn't know, he still thought Geraldine Monroe had been the most beautiful woman he'd ever seen.

A neighbor who'd happened to own a camera had taken the photograph of Jefferson and his grandmother the day she'd picked him up from the Greyhound bus station. To commemorate the occasion, the man had said. *Your grandson's come to live with you, Deenie. That's a reason to celebrate.*

Jefferson hadn't felt like celebrating.

He'd felt like running away.

The two of them stood in the front yard of her little house that day next to the apple tree his grandfather had planted the year his grandparents bought the house. The sun had been behind them, casting their faces in shadow. She'd put one arm around his stiff shoulders for the picture, and he just stood there, arms folded across his chest. A skinny kid in secondhand clothes with a chip on his shoulder the size of the entire world.

The photograph hadn't been the best to begin with, and the years hadn't been kind. The brilliant flowers on his grandmother's dress had faded, and the clear blue sky had turned gray. A crease marred one corner, cutting through the leafy branches of the apple tree. And the color of their skin had darkened to something it had never been in real life.

Every morning when he flipped his wallet to the key card and saw her picture, Jefferson wondered if she'd be proud of what he'd become.

His cell phone chirped at him just as he pulled into his assigned space next to his boss's Lexus.

Jefferson had no interest in owning a Lexus. Waste of good money, he could hear his grandmother say, and he agreed with her. They had agreed on a good many things.

He thumbed on his phone and read the text message.

We've got probable cause. Waiting for your okay.

His okay.

His authority.

His decision.

He'd made a lot of decisions since he'd been that eight-year-old boy who'd discovered that the world didn't give a damn about what he wanted. Back then he'd thought it had been all about age, and he couldn't wait to grow up so no one could tell him what to do ever again.

He hadn't realized that getting his own way was all about power.

Knowing what power you had. What you could do with it. And having the patience to wait for the right moment to use it.

He sent a reply giving the go ahead. He waited in his car while the phone decided if it had a good enough signal to deliver the message.

He should have been excited. Nervous. Something. He'd worked for nearly three decades to get to this moment, but all he felt now was the same unwavering determination that filled him every time he walked into a courtroom and faced a jury.

He represented the people of his county. All the people, no matter the color of their skin or their economic position in the community, had a right to equal justice under the law, as his boss liked to say.

In Jefferson's experience, equal justice under the law was rarely equal or just.

But justice would be done this time.

He'd make sure of it.

His phone chirped again. The message had gone through.

Before he closed his wallet, Jefferson took another look at the photograph.

"I got him, Gramma," he said.

After all this time, Jefferson was finally going to bring justice down on the man who'd killed his grandmother.

The little two-bedroom house where Jefferson's mother had grown up was nothing special, at least not to him. The only thing he'd liked at first was the yard.

The apartment where he'd lived with his parents didn't have any place to play outside. The yard at his grandmother's house was filled with fruit trees and weedy grass and rocky dirt, but it was a yard. That first summer he'd helped his grandmother pick apples and peaches and cherries, and in the winter it snowed enough for Jefferson to build his first snowman. But the neighborhood was mostly made up of old people, so he didn't have anyone to play with, and the room his grandmother let him sleep in was smaller than the bedroom he'd had when he lived with his parents.

Before his father had been killed in a convenience store robbery.

Before his mother had gone quietly crazy.

Jefferson had tried to take care of his mother. When she forgot to cook, he bought them food from McDonald's with money he took from her wallet. He covered her with a blanket when she fell asleep on the sofa with the television on. Took out the trash and learned how to do laundry, and threw the empty beer cans in the neighbor's garbage can like he'd seen her do.

It hadn't been enough.

One afternoon he'd come home from school to find her awake and freshly showered. She'd looked at him with eyes that had been bright and watery, and she'd hugged him hard.

Then she'd hauled one of the duffle bags that had belonged to his dad out of the closet and packed all of Jefferson's clothes inside.

"You're gonna go stay with your gramma for awhile," his mother had told him.

Jefferson had panicked, and he'd cried and hugged her, but she'd said she was going to go stay at a place that would help her get better.

"I've been sick since your daddy's been gone, you know that, baby. I've got to get better or I won't be no good for either of us."

She'd bought him a ticket for the Greyhound bus and paid the driver twenty dollars to keep an eye on Jefferson. She'd kissed him and hugged him again, then waved at him as the bus pulled away from the terminal. She looked small and helpless standing there by herself, and he'd hated leaving her behind.

He'd hated her more for sending him away.

He never saw her again.

He spent the first six months in his grandmother's house waiting for his mom to call to tell him she wanted him to come back home, but she never called. Not on his birthday or even to find out how he was doing in school. He dreamed that she'd show up one day at the front door carrying another one of his daddy's empty duffel bags to tell him it was time for him to come live with her again.

At first those dreams were the happiest parts of his day. But as he grew used to living with his grandmother, as he came to love her and the stability of the life he had with her, the dreams turned into nightmares.

One day after a particularly bad dream, he'd asked his grandmother if he'd ever see his mom again.

His grandmother had let out a little sigh as she sat down on a sofa so threadbare patches of stuffing poked through the fabric in places. "Your momma's what we used to call 'flighty.' She loves you, but she had you too young, that's the simple truth. Didn't get all the flighty out before your daddy came along. With him gone, she couldn't stay in one place no more."

"You stayed in one place," Jefferson had said. "Even after Grandpa died, you stayed here."

"Your grandpa bought me this house. It's mine, and I like it just fine. It's the place where I raised my baby girl, and where I'm raising my baby's baby. Folks like me, we stick."

Jefferson hadn't liked moving. He didn't want his mom to make him move again.

"Am I stuck folks?"

His grandmother had laughed. "Things like that skip generations, my momma used to say, so I guess maybe you are."

Jefferson had grown to believe she was right. His grandmother had a clear-cut sense of right and wrong that he shared. She was a proud woman who valued the few possessions she'd accumulated over her life. She cleaned houses for a living, and did mending at night for "pin money," as she called it. She paid her bills on time, owned her own home, and went to church on Sundays.

Most of all, his grandmother had taught Jefferson the value of belonging to a community. She took meals to her neighbors when they were sick, shared good news and bad, and volunteered Jefferson to mow lawns for the entire neighborhood, which he would have hated except that the neighbors always paid him something, even if it was just cookies.

And Charles Kincaid took all that away.

Jefferson had expected to hear from Kincaid's attorney. A polite phone call filled with a lot of polite back and forth, the kind of legal sparring that was the equivalent of saying, "What the fuck, man?"

He hadn't expected the man himself to barge into Jefferson's office late that afternoon.

Charles Kincaid had been a mover and shaker back in the day. A property developer who'd worked hand in hand with local politicians to renovate the city center, he'd been the man behind most of the upscale housing developments in the hills to the northwest. Housing developments people of color weren't welcome to live in, although the discrimination had been subtle. Most of it had to do with the balance of their bank accounts. Kincaid had had a lot of money in his.

That was then, before the housing market hit bottom and nobody was building anything.

Before Kincaid's businesses went belly up and he couldn't get his pet councilmen to return his calls.

Jefferson knew all about that. Back when his days hadn't been all that good, city councilmen wouldn't return Jefferson's calls either.

These days Kincaid was just another sixty-two-year-old white man who still acted like he owned the world.

"You're at the bottom of this?" Kincaid threw a piece of paper on Jefferson's desk. "It's got your name on it."

Jefferson's assistant stood in the open doorway behind Kincaid, her face pale, probably thinking she was fired.

The courthouse had security screening, complete with metal detectors, at all public entrances. The judges had armed bailiffs in their courtrooms. The district attorney's office relied on the ability of their assistants to stop anyone who didn't want to wait to be announced.

"It's okay, Shirley," Jefferson told his assistant. "I got this."

"Yes, sir," she said. "Do you want me to leave your door open?"

Jefferson met Kincaid's rheumy-eyed glare. "I got this."

The door snicked shut with a barely audible click, leaving Jefferson alone with the man he'd hated since he was twelve years old.

Jefferson's office was only slightly larger than the closet-sized room he'd labored in as an assistant district attorney prosecuting drug traffickers and thieves. He had room enough for a desk currently covered with three neat stacks of files and his computer workstation, the two stacks of banker boxes off to the side that held more files, and the credenza behind him that held his phone and printer and his own set of legal reference books. Two visitor chairs took up precious real estate in front of his desk. His framed law degree hung on one wall next to an exemplified copy of the guilty verdict returned by the jury on the first murder trial he'd handled on his own.

The plant Shirley had given him for his birthday sat on one corner of the credenza. She'd said the plant gave his office personality. He'd said it could stay there as long as she watered it. Under her care, it appeared to be thriving.

The one thing Jefferson didn't have in his office were any family photos. The only one he needed, he kept in his wallet.

"Have a seat," he said to Kincaid.

The old man glared at him a moment longer before he sat heavily in one of the chairs.

"Will your attorney be joining us?" Jefferson asked.

"I don't need an attorney for this."

"But are you represented by counsel? I need to know before we can have a discussion."

"I told you, I don't need an attorney for this."

Of course. Men like Kincaid expected the world to do what they wanted just because they wanted it. Jefferson would be prosecuting a man like that for fraud, embezzlement, and racketeering next month. The banker boxes were filled with transcripts of deposition testimony and summaries of the thousands of pages of evidence against the man, but at least he'd been smart enough to hire an attorney and follow the woman's advice to keep his own mouth shut.

"So you're representing yourself in this matter," Jefferson said.

Kincaid hesitated, and Jefferson could see him trying to work out whether this was a trap. He didn't realize that the trap had been set long before he'd ever set foot in Jefferson's office.

"Why, am I entitled to an attorney or something?"

"Technically, no. This action isn't against you. It's against your property."

"Huh?"

Jefferson opened a document on his computer and printed a copy, which he handed to Kincaid.

Jefferson had had one of the assistants prepare the complaint after he'd given the okay for the seizure of Kincaid's property that morning. Like all complaints originated by the district attorney's office, it listed the county as the plaintiff. But instead of naming Kincaid or his drug-addicted son as the defendant, the complaint listed as defendants all the personal property the police had seized from Kincaid's house. And property wasn't entitled to an attorney provided by the county.

"We'll be finalizing the complaint in the morning after we determine the amount of money the police were able to seize from your bank accounts," Jefferson said.

Two blotches of red appeared on Kincaid's cheeks. "You can't do this. Not to me, you can't."

The beauty of it was, Jefferson could. He'd gone by the book, step by procedural step, all authorized by statute. He didn't even have to convict Kincaid's son of drug trafficking first.

Six months ago Kincaid had let his son move in while he made attempt after failed attempt to kick a nasty drug habit. Two days ago, one of the vice detectives had busted a doper who swore Kincaid's son was his supplier. On Jefferson's orders, the police had put Kincaid's son under surveillance. That morning, they'd seen him make a buy from a known drug dealer and take the drugs back to Kincaid's house.

Jefferson was sure the dope would be on the inventory the police had given Kincaid. The same inventory he'd thrown on Jefferson's desk. The police department in this town was thorough when it came to civil forfeiture proceedings.

"I suggest you talk to an attorney," Jefferson said. "He'll tell you that I can, indeed, do this to you. Things like this are done to people every day. Then again, I'm sure you know that."

Kincaid's eyes narrowed. He leaned back in the chair and stared at Jefferson. "Do I know you?"

Jefferson took out his wallet and flipped it open to the old snapshot. He put his wallet on the desk and turned it around so Kincaid could see the photograph.

"I believe," Jefferson said, "you knew my grandmother."

Jefferson didn't learn how the whole mess started until long after his grandmother died. She never would have told him herself, and he understood why.

She was too ashamed.

Not that she cleaned houses for a living, but about what had happened in one of those houses. The rich and powerful in town were white, and the rich and powerful were the only ones who could afford to pay Geraldine Monroe the kind of money she needed to raise a growing boy by herself. So she kept working for one of those powerful white men long after she should have quit, and all because of him.

No wonder she'd never told him.

The man in question had been Charles Kincaid. Deenie Monroe had always been beautiful. With her trim build and delicate features, she looked far younger than she was, and Kincaid's second wife had just divorced him. It didn't take long before he became infatuated with the beautiful, light-skinned black woman who cleaned his house.

The beautiful black woman he'd expected would do exactly what he ordered her to do.

When she hadn't, that infatuation turned to fury.

Other men might have hit her. Kincaid had done far worse.

He'd taken away her home. Her community. He'd bulldozed the

church she'd attended with her neighbors and the fruit trees in her yard. He'd turned her little house, the home her husband had bought for her and she'd finished paying for after he'd died in the war with the money she earned cleaning white people's toilets, into so much kindling.

And when it was all said and done, it turned out he'd taken her heart.

She'd fought him. All the neighbors had. The city had condemned all the property in the neighborhood so that Kincaid could build a new shopping center and condominiums catering to the upper middle class. Properties that would provide the city with a higher tax base than the blighted old homes owned by Jefferson's grandmother and her neighbors.

Blight, as Jefferson had learned in law school, was a legal term, but his grandmother, with her clear sense of right and wrong, had been insulted by the word. Her house might not be one of the mansions like the white folk she worked for owned, but she kept it clean and kept the lawn mowed and even put decorations out at Christmas. No one had the right to insult her and her home, and the city shouldn't be able to take it away just because some white man wanted it. It wasn't right.

No, but it was legal.

The black lawyer Deenie Monroe and her neighbors had hired did his best, but the case was lost before it ever started. As long as the city offered to pay fair market value to the homeowners, which it had, there'd been little the lawyer could do. Still he'd kept the case going for far longer than it should have, taking it all the way to the state supreme court.

In the end, the result had been the same. The city had paid Jefferson's grandmother a price for her house that had nothing to do with fair, and then they'd sent her a bill for back rent for the years she'd continued to live there while the lawsuit was working its way through the courts.

Jefferson had thought that back rent bill, even more than losing the case, broke his grandmother. She'd never let a bill go late in her entire life.

She'd shown up on the day that men from Kincaid's company had torn down her house. Jefferson hadn't wanted her to, but she'd insisted. Most of her neighbors, the ones who hadn't moved to another city, stood with her as well.

She flinched when the bulldozer's blade bit into the wall on the outside of the living room, but she didn't cry until they brought down the apple tree in the front yard.

The man who'd caused it all wasn't there. He'd moved on to his third wife by that time, and the project had been handed off to the people who worked for his development company. The destruction of Geraldine Monroe's home had become just one more business deal.

All perfectly legal.

Jefferson's grandmother had lived for two more years, but she'd been a broken woman. They had just enough money left from what the city had paid her to move into a duplex in one of the few remaining black neighborhoods in the city. She'd kept the place clean, but it had never become a place she could stick to. She'd passed away in her sleep during Jefferson's first year in college, and Jefferson had changed his major to pre-law.

And learned everything he could about Charles Kincaid, the man who'd killed her as surely as if he'd put a bullet in her brain.

And Jefferson had learned everything about the law.

Because if a rich white man could legally steal everything that mattered to his grandmother, Jefferson would damn well not rest until he learned how to do the same thing to Kincaid.

Jefferson heard from an attorney representing Kincaid the following day. She was a smart woman and a damn good attorney, and they'd said their "fuck yous" in far more polite legal terms than Jefferson usually encountered.

She was also an expensive attorney. Jefferson wondered how Kincaid would pay her once Jefferson had the police seize the assets of his construction company. Kincaid had tried to create a shield between himself and his corporate identity, but the man had let the charter lapse when his company had fallen on hard times, and the charter had been permanently revoked. Jefferson couldn't wait to argue to a judge about who actually owned the assets the police would be seizing.

He knew that eventually he'd be pressured by his boss to settle the case. The cash haul so far hadn't been as great as Jefferson had hoped, and storing personal belongings cost the county money. Jefferson would eventually offer Kincaid's attorney a deal. The county would keep the cash, and Kincaid could have his personal belongings back.

She was a smart lawyer. She'd probably get him to take the deal.

It was a far better outcome than he'd given Jefferson's grandmother.

The truly ironic thing, as far as Jefferson was concerned, was that Kincaid's development had never gotten off the ground. The lawsuit ate up the original investors' money, and Kincaid couldn't come up with new investors to keep the project going. The lawsuit had made them gun shy.

It had been the beginning of the end for Kincaid. The end of his company, the end of his influence in the city, the end of his third marriage. His pet city councilmen had quit politics, and their replacements didn't take his calls.

A weather-beaten sign still stood on the property where his grandmother's house had been. The sign advertised the shopping center. The words "coming soon" had been nearly obliterated by years of summer sun and winter snow.

Jefferson visited the property every year on his grandmother's birthday. He'd stand by the sign and look at the spot where the apple tree had been, and remember the neighbor who'd taken the snapshot Jefferson carried in his wallet.

This year when he went, he'd tell his grandmother about the outcome of the Kincaid case.

Would she be proud of him?

He'd brought many men to justice in his years in the district attorney's office, but Kincaid was the only white man he'd introduced to equal justice under the law as experienced by a poor black woman with a grandchild to support.

Would she think Jefferson had done the right thing?

He hadn't been representing the people when he'd gone after Kincaid. He'd done what he'd done out of vengeance. At his core he'd still been that angry boy who'd been forced to move against his will. A boy who'd been unable to protect his mother or his grandmother from the kind of pain that had destroyed them.

He'd never gone to church with his grandmother as a boy. As an adult, his moral center was based on the law, but the law was flawed. The law played favorites. The law could be manipulated by those who knew how.

Had he done the right thing?

He didn't know.

He'd done the legal thing, and for himself and the angry boy he'd been, maybe that was good enough.

PAYBACK

TONYA D. PRICE

O n a warm September morning I had gone out to pick up the Sunday *Boston Globe* at the end of my driveway when I spotted a big red dog racing toward me, running smack down the middle of Pleasant Street. He gave me a quick check before twisting his anvil-shaped head to look back at the direction he had come. His ears lay flat on the top of his head and his brown eyes had the wide-eyed stare of a wild animal desperate to escape a predator.

My guess was he was either full Doberman or a mix. I called to him but he didn't slow down, instead the sound of a human voice seemed to panic him into picking up his pace. Looking back up the dirt road I tried to make out what had spooked the poor thing so bad. A powder blue Porsche raced toward me, kicking up a cloud of dust.

People drove too fast down the narrow country road all the time so the speed didn't spook me. The hand sticking out the passenger window pointing a gun at the dog—that spooked me.

I froze as my mind struggled to make sense of what I saw. Two quick gunshots jolted me out of my indecision. We had a six-foot-high boulder at the corner of my driveway. For over five years I had cursed that boulder every time I had to plow the snow around the thing, now I used it for cover and blessed that rock for saving my life.

The Porsche sped by. The guy leaning out the passenger window fired two more rounds at the escaping dog.

People being mean to each other I could take, but I could never abide cruelty aimed at some poor dog. Feeling helpless, and mad as hell at the idiot behind the wheel of the Porsche, I ran out from my hiding spot and picked up a rock off my stone wall, hurling it hard at the car.

Maybe a good scare would cause them to leave the dog alone. In college I spent four years on the bench as the third-string pitcher. Couldn't find the plate to save my life. This time I nailed the Porsche with a softball sized piece of granite, smashing the rear window just as the car slowed on the curve down our hill.

The wheels squealed on the pavement and I smelled burned rubber as the car took the curve and vanished out of sight.

My first reaction: serves the idiots right if they crashed their fancy car.

My second reaction: throwing a rock at a car could land me jail.

A few minutes later the Porsche reappeared, backing up the street so fast the car swerved left and right as the driver struggled to keep control. This time the gun sticking out the passenger window pointed my way.

Inside our house, my husband and six-month-old baby daughter took their morning nap together in our bedroom. I started to run toward the house but stopped. If I ran inside, I might be leading these lunatics to my family.

Living out in the country, we had no neighbors close by to run to for help.

I'd left the cell phone on my nightstand. I was the one the men were after.

In an effort to lead them away from the house, I ran into the woods. Too scared to look behind me, I ran as fast as I could for as long as I could on the narrow path, taking care not to trip on the tree roots sticking up along the ground.

The men didn't call after me.

They didn't fire their gun at me.

But I was sure they were behind me.

About a half hour later, I reached Iron Mine Pond. I waded into the warm water and hid among the lily pads, waiting for the men from the Porsche to arrive.

After ten minutes of swatting flies and mosquitoes, I began to wonder if maybe the guys had come to their senses and not bothered to follow me. After another five minutes, I pulled myself out of the water, my clothes wet and my shoes waterlogged.

On the way home I kept off the path, taking care to wind my way through the wetlands, risking tick bites over being spotted by the men who had fired at the dog.

As I walked, I began to calm down. Reason replaced panic.

No doubt the men had thought better of going after me and had decided to go home rather than get into a confrontation. Shooting at a dog was probably a misdemeanor. Shooting at a person would definitely get you jail time. The worse that would come of the whole affair would be a court case over smashing the car window.

I'd never been in trouble and they pointed the gun at me. I decided I would probably not be in that much trouble after all. Maybe I could claim self-defense.

I was looking forward to a hot bath and getting dinner ready by the time I came within sight of my house.

Instead, I spotted the Porsche in my driveway, smashed rear window and all. Neither the driver nor his gun-happy passenger appeared to be inside. Where had they gone?

They weren't in the yard.

My house was a two-story colonial, cedar shingles with a big wide farmer's porch. I didn't see them on the porch.

After checking again that the men weren't lurking in the yard somewhere I edged closer to the house and saw the front door stood ajar. My husband grew up in Manhattan. He never left the door unlocked, let alone open.

More likely the men had forced their way into the house and they had left the door open, but why?

Why even go into the house? The men might have been mad at me for throwing a rock at their car but they knew I wasn't inside the house. Were they waiting for me to return?

The nearest police station was five miles away. The nearest house, three miles away. What would the men do to my family if I tried to run to get help? I doubted I could do much good in the house. My family's best bet would be for me to get help.

We had two Volvos in the garage but the Porsche blocked the driveway. Maybe I didn't need to get into my car if I could start the Porsche.

Woods lined both sides of my driveway. Using the thick pine trees for cover, I crept along the ground, staying close to the old stone fence as I inched toward the sports car.

Every few minutes, I checked the door.

With no sign of the men in the yard or on the porch, I made my way to where a large forsythia blocked the view of the driveway. Taking care to stay out of the sightline from the house, I dashed in front of the car, then walked half bent over around to the driver's side.

I tried to open the door latch. The men might have left my front door open but they had locked their car.

I decided the smart thing to do would be to walk up the street in hopes of finding a car to flag down. Then I could use someone's cell to call the police. The plan seemed the best course of action even though part of me wanted to charge inside the house, but what good would that do? I might even get my family killed.

The plan made sense. I might even have followed it if I hadn't heard my baby crying.

And my husband shouting.

And the single shot.

I started to run for the house not caring if anyone saw me or not.

There was more shouting.

Then I heard Jim's voice.

He was alive.

I needed to keep him that way.

It was the gunfire that sent me running toward the backyard gate. My husband had used a bike lock to keep the gate shut. I put both hands on the gate's top bar, jumped and pulled my legs over, landing on my feet.

The shed was new and built to look like a mini-version of our house. I didn't have the key but I decided I would smash the door down if I had to. There were tools inside. Tools I needed if I were to try to save Jim.

The double doors for driving the John Deere riding lawn mower were padlocked but we never locked the side door. I slipped inside and searched for a weapon. Something not too heavy to carry. Something that could kill.

Something I could handle.

The axe was too heavy and not terribly accurate. I went for my fishing knife. The seven-inch, serrated blade would make a nasty cut. A short bungee cord served as a belt. I pushed one end through the knife sheaf belt loop and tied the cord around my waist. My long work shirttail just covered the knife sheaf.

I still had my old softball bat but the men might be able to get that away from me. An old can of wasp spray would be more effective. Jim and I never owned a gun—except for a cordless nail gun, heavy as hell. At least it was loaded with a tape of nails. I just prayed it still worked.

Then I went to try and save my husband and my child.

From the shed, I could see the large copper clock on our raised deck that overlooked the back yard. An hour had passed since I first saw the dog running down the street. The sun shone overhead, a harsh glare.

The large windows in our sunroom provided a clear view inside. Both the sunroom and kitchen appeared empty. Two entrances led into the house from the back: a cellar door into the basement or the deck slider. I chose the slider.

When I was halfway across the yard I heard the familiar sound of the slider opening. Caught in a no man's land without any cover, I charged forward, lugging the nailer. I ran to hide below the raised deck.

I dived underneath the planks, lying face down on the stone pebble base.

A single set of footsteps on the deck above told me someone had come outside alone. There had been two men in the Porsche, but if I could get rid of one of them, then the odds might be a little better for rescuing my husband and daughter.

I needed to keep whoever was above me in the yard, separate from his buddy. I grabbed a nearby pebble and threw it into the woods on the edge of the lawn.

I heard footsteps going toward the house.

Jim's cry kept going off in my head. I had to do something and soon.

"Hey!" I stayed hidden by the side of the deck, fighting the pounding in my head and the voice screaming that I had just made a huge mistake.

Convinced surprise might be my only hope, I knelt on the ground, holding the wasp spray at my side and set the nailer on the ground beside me.

The footsteps stopped. They changed direction, walking toward the stairs leading to the lawn rather than back toward the house.

I could hear someone on the stairs.

A teenage boy with long hair and a NY Jets cap peeked around the edge of the deck. He was a small, skinny kid. He spotted me, breaking into a wide smile that showed his braces. Up until that moment I hadn't gotten a good look at either of the guys.

Why did he have to be so damn young?

"Well, well, well... What are you doing out here? We've been looking for you. That Porsche you wrecked, that's Matt's daddy's car. Matt loves that car. He isn't very happy with you right now." The boy laughed. "Nope, not happy at all." He brushed a lock of long greasy brown hair out of his eyes. He didn't look cruel. He looked young. Young and stupid.

Except he was cruel, I reminded myself. He had a gun tucked in his pant's waistband. A gun he had used to shoot at the dog and me.

I had no choice but to rise to my feet. I aimed the wasp spray at him and squeezed the button. My attack came so unexpectedly I caught him full in the face. It must have hurt like hell by the sound of his screams.

Above us the slider squeaked open. "Dave? You okay, man?"

Dave wiped his eyes with his hand then pulled out his gun. His arm swiped in every direction as if frantic to find me. In his wild swatting, he struck my arm with his free hand then brought the gun around.

I dropped to the ground and balanced the nailer on the concrete deck footing. A bullet whizzed by my head.

There's a good chance I had my eyes closed when I pulled the trigger. I only knew I shot off three nails. When I opened my eyes I found only one of the 3 inch nails had hit the boy.

Right in the middle of his forehead.

As he fell, his gun went off, breaking the window in the door to the garage.

On television, you hear stories of people who survive getting a nail in their head. I debated if I should fire again. I couldn't take a chance he might attack another time. His eyes stared at the sky. He didn't blink.

I didn't feel anything for him. All I felt was desperation to save my family.

"Shit! What did you do? What did you fucking do? Dave?" A second teenager, about the same age as the first, rounded the edge of the deck. This one looked more athletic than the other kid. He wore a muscle shirt and he had muscles to show off.

I raised the wasp spray again but nothing came out. The boy picked up his friend's gun. Insanely, I didn't freeze this time. Instead I thought, if he shoots me I can't save Jim.

I dropped the heavy nail gun and the empty wasp spray can. I ran as fast as I could away from him toward the far end of the house.

The fence wrapped around the entire yard. I was trapped but I ran anyway.

I had no plan.

The gun went off again. Something whished past my right ear, but I ran harder and started to zigzag my way across the yard. Once a television reporter had said running in a zigzag pattern could make you a harder target to hit.

At the edge of the house, I decided to try and leap the picket fence again. I slowed down. If I didn't clear the fence and had to hang for a moment at the top and hoist myself over, I would make an easy target.

Overthinking such things usually leads to trouble. This time proved no different. My foot struck two of the pickets. Rather than go over the fence I fell down on the lawn landing in front of the boy with the gun.

He stood over me, his hand steady. His finger on the trigger. "Get on your feet." The order didn't sound like it came from a teenager.

This time I had no choice. He had me.

I raised my hands in defeat. "Okay."

He motioned with the gun in the direction of the deck. "We just wanted to scare you. Just hurt you a little bit for breaking the window. You didn't need to kill Dave, you bitch."

Maybe talking to him could save my family. Worth a try, anyway. "Windows can be paid for. I'll pay for the window. Shooting a dog is a minor offense. Shooting a person is murder."

"Yes, I know. You can tell that to the judge."

Then he had no plans to kill me. The little bit of hope helped. If he wasn't going to kill me, he wasn't planning on killing my family.

We went onto the deck and into the silent house. Everything in the kitchen and sunroom looked the way I had left things before I went out to do a bit of gardening.

"Where's the baby?" My daughter would be hungry by now. She should be crying but I heard nothing. "Jim?"

From the upstairs my husband called out, "Sarah?"

The boy pushed me forward. "Into the living room. "

I yelled, "Is the baby all right?"

The boy leveled the gun at me. "Shut up."

He wasn't able to stop my husband's answer. "We are both okay. Just...just I'm tied up."

I feared the worse as I entered the living room but the basket of white laundry I had left beside our brown leather sectional was still there. The CDs remained in place in the bookcase beside the collection of piano music my husband stored in the bookcase.

The boy walked over to my husband's grand piano. "Yours?"

"No."

He ran his index finger over the polished top of Jim's beloved Kawai. "You don't play?"

"No."

The boy didn't say anything. He just stared at me until I felt I had to offer him something. "I play the guitar."

My Martin hung from the wall. The boy smiled and walked over to admire the instrument. He took a step back, raised the gun, fired into the guitar, sending Madagascar Rosewood splinters into the air. Steel wires flew across the room like shrapnel.

"That Porsche you wrecked. That's my father's car. He's going to be plenty mad when he sees what you did to it."

So this was his game. "I told you I'll pay for the window."

"Good, you can start tonight." The boy cocked his head to one side. "Any other instruments you play?"

"No."

"Nice house you have here." He took his time walking around the room, then motioned toward the hall. "Why don't you take me on a tour?"

I led the way down the hall, stopping at the bathroom. Not much he could destroy there. "Toilet, shower."

"Let's take a look."

When I renovated the bathroom I added a handcrafted sink.

He pointed at the two oil paintings with his gun. "Tell me about the pictures."

The matched set of my niece's worthless art camp work gave me a chance to divert attention from the sink. "They are originals. A gift from my mother who passed away last year. Please...don't destroy them."

"Ah, okay." With a step back into the hallway he turned and fired into the sink.

"No!" I lunged forward toward the sink, but there was no way to repair the damage.

A large chunk of porcelain cracked and fell to the tile.

The boy laughed. "Fancy sink, isn't it? Worth much more than a couple of kids' paintings." He pointed at my forehead. "Looks like you got cut."

Sure enough, a look into the vanity mirror showed a cut above my left eye. Blood had started to drip down my cheek. I wiped it with my hand, smearing it along my face.

I tried to hide my anger.

In an attempt to distract him I asked, "Why were you chasing the dog?"

He didn't seem to hear me at first. Something seemed to distract him. Then he directed his attention at me again. "What?"

"The dog you were chasing down the street. Why were you chasing it and trying to shoot it?"

The boy ran his palm over the peach fuzz on his chin. "Damn thing barked at my car when I came to a stoplight. We fired a warning shot and he just stood in the middle of the road barking his head off. Wouldn't get out of the way. I tried to run him down but he took off. What is it to you?"

"I just wondered. Maybe he thought he was protecting his territory."

"He was just a crazy dog."

"Who made you mad." I regretted the mistake as soon as I spoke.

The boy's face reddened. "Not as mad as you made me." He spoke in a calm tone, without emotion but I could hear the threat.

I had something more valuable than a sink to protect. Maybe if he destroyed enough of my possessions he would leave my family alone.

He grabbed my arm and pushed me forward. "Show me the rest of the house."

At the end of the hall, we entered my office. Here he would think he had found a goldmine of possessions to destroy.

"Nice monitor."

My 34-inch Ultra Apple Monitor dominated my desk. Nabbed on eBay, I did love that monitor. Beside the monitor sat my scanner and an antique Waterford lamp with a large brass base, my first Brimfield Antique Show buy. The Hooker mahogany desk would be another alluring target. Behind the desk, placed against the wall sat my curled cherry, hand-carved grand upright piano my mother and I had restored over a summer when I was fifteen. On the wall I had a handmade German wind-up clock with a big pendulum that rang a single chime with a deep, rich sound.

The boy took his time examining each piece. "Your husband has two pianos?"

"No," I admitted. "This one is mine."

He fired into the elaborately carved fern in the middle of the piano. "I knew you played. You look like a piano teacher."

"I don't play. I was saving the piano for my daughter."

The boy laughed. "Oops!" He turned and fired into the clock, severing the metal spring. Small metal disks clanged as the internal parts broke apart.

He shot into the desk, then the monitor glass, laughing each time he destroyed something. He seemed to be having such a good time. When he ran out of bullets he reached inside his jeans' pocket and pulled out a packet. He started to load the magazine without even bothering to watch me.

I might not get another chance to try to escape and I had to escape before we went upstairs in search of my best loved possessions.

I didn't have much time. I grabbed the lamp. The thing weighed almost ten pounds but it wasn't too heavy for me to lift. Without trying to unplug it I swung the big brass base at the boy's head like a baseball bat.

I missed his head but hit the hand holding the gun and he dropped it onto the desk.

The boy ducked, covering his head with his hands as I took another swing and missed again. I picked up the empty gun and ran toward the front door. He followed.

I thought he would catch me, but as I got to the door I remembered he and his friend had left the door open.

He chased me outside. Standing on the porch he screamed, "Come back or I'll kill your family."

I knew better. To punish me, he needed me. That was my advantage. If I escaped, he would have to chase me and capture me. His game was to make me watch him destroy the things I loved. Without me to watch, he wouldn't kill my family. He had already proved that by waiting for me to return to the house.

Without the gun he had no weapon, so for the moment we were an even match. I had the gun. He had the bullets.

What I needed was a weapon.

I remembered the nail gun in the backyard. Too far away. Besides the boy would catch me when I tried to jump the fence.

In desperation I spun around looking for something, anything I could use to try and stop the boy.

The only thing I could find was his Porsche.

Turn about was fair, right?

I ran toward the car. "You think a smashed window was bad? You want to play smash things? Let's smash your things now."

Massachusetts has lots of rocks. Plenty of rocks. In the spring they rise out of the ground we have so many. I picked up a good five pounder and ran toward the Porsche.

"No, get away from there. I'm warning you." I could hear the panic in his voice.

I held the rock over the car. "Get down on the ground. Put your hands over your head."

"Fuck you." The boy ran toward me.

I dropped the stone on the hood and ran down the driveway without a plan other than to escape. He was a lot faster than me, even in my prime.

I picked up another stone and waited for him. Just as he reached me I threw the stone toward his foot hoping to break a bone so he couldn't run.

I missed.

He reached out and grabbed my left hand, then twisted my arm behind me. "So you like to throw stones, huh?"

Looking past the boy I saw the dog inching forward as if stalking prey. Ears laid flat, hair on his back standing straight up, his snarl showing teeth, the dog took a position just out of reach of the boy.

He began barking and barked and barked.

The boy turned around and kicked at the dog, "Get out of here."

The dog just barked louder. Maybe he sensed the boy's fear without the gun.

It was all the distraction I needed. With my free hand, I reached under my shirt and pulled out my fishing knife, then ran at the boy and sunk the knife in his back.

On his left side.

Where I figured his heart should be.

He sunk to the ground, moaning, then went silent. The dog inched toward the still body, barking louder than before.

I ran for the open door. Back to my family and to call for help.

I had thrown a rock to save a dog, and ended up killing two boys. Even as I rushed into the house I knew the boy had gotten what he wanted. He had destroyed something I valued almost as much as my family—that image I had of myself as a good, decent person, incapable of what I had just done.

I would never look at myself the same, but my family survived.

That was my payback.

ERIC THE MONKEY

DAN C. DUVAL

Dan C. Duval's professional publications to date include short stories in the Battletech universe, in two DAW anthologies edited by Denise Little, and a number of stories in the Fiction River *series. His story "Play the Man," first published in* Fiction River: Risk Takers, *was selected for the* Year's Best Crime and Mystery Stories 2016, *published by Kobo.*

Dan has multiple college degrees—biochemistry, computer science, and business—but his heart is with history and horses.

Dan says about the first of his two stories in this volume, "What can an author do with a straightforward revenge story? Maybe stage an act of revenge where the next revenge target gets to watch...and be afraid."

Sometimes making the hard choice is just better when you have the chance to make the choice in the first place.

The End of Eric the Monkey.

I can't tell you how many times I dreamed about that.

Until it happened.

It was just a Tuesday. Six tables in my little bar, half of them empty. Never a soul sitting at the bar itself. At the two tables near the heater vent, Eric and his half-dozen fans, watching Eric do his antics as he usually did, always the center of attention.

That night, he was dancing around like a monkey: crouching down, sticking his elbows out, and making monkey noises. He was making fun of Obama. To be fair, Eric did the same thing when George Bush was president. His fans laughed and clapped but Eric danced for the only person at the third table, trying to get the man's attention.

That man didn't look like anything special. Humped up in a grey winter coat, his arms crossed in front of him, elbows on the table, he stared at the glass of beer in front of him. If he was paying any attention to Eric, he showed no sign of it.

Which, of course, pissed off Eric.

The bar was usually empty but for Eric and his fans, mostly

because of Eric. He chased the other customers away. If they didn't listen to Eric making fun of them to his friends, if they didn't find his dancing and monkey imitation offensive, then he usually went over and all but threatened them, shouting in their faces, insulting the color of their skin, the sound of their voices, the color of their hair, whatever he could find to drive them off.

When I confronted him about it, he waved a big fucking knife in my face. I hadn't brought it up since. Naturally, there wasn't anyone around at that time to see what he did.

He was always careful what he did when people were watching.

So, as usual, I threw a burger on the tiny, greasy grill behind the bar. I ate out of the bar inventory and slept on a cot in the back. That was all I could afford and as long as Eric was around, I wasn't going to do any better.

The new guy sat at the table farthest to the right of the bar, where the draft from the back room was the strongest, so that was no doubt why he kept his jacket on—maybe even why he'd only taken one swig of his glass of beer—before tucking his hands under his arms, inside his coat.

He wasn't a young guy, but he didn't look like a very old guy, either. Some doughiness in his cheeks and under his chin, but clean-shaven. Dull brown hair, combed back over his head, but all of it still there. Lines down both sides of his nose, but not very deep.

Eric finally decided he had to get more direct with the guy and I cursed under my breath as Eric knuckle-walked over to the new guy's table, his gawky arms and legs looking more monkey-like than any human being should be able to be.

"Hey!" Eric shouted, jerking to a stop just short of the table, his head just clear of the table edge. "You an Obama-loving commie?"

Pausing for just a moment before raising his gaze to Eric's face, the new guy just looked at Eric, saying nothing.

Eric looked back at the new guy for a bit then unbent himself and stood up, all the way to his gangly six-foot height. "You deaf or something?"

When the new guy spoke, his voice seemed to creak a bit, as if he never used it much.

"I know who you are," the man said. "I know *what* you are. And I know what you're going to do."

"Oh, really," Eric shouted. He spun around, spread his arms, and did a little jig for his fans. Then he turned back to the guy, let his arms drop, spread his legs a bit. "So who am I?"

"More important is what you're going to do," the man said.

"And just what is that? Do tell."

"You're never coming into this bar again. This is your last time here."

My jaw dropped open. I know this because the cold air in the bar made my fillings hurt and I have learned to keep my mouth shut. This time, I actually had to remember that I needed to close my mouth.

If what the man said surprised me, it only sent Eric laughing so hard he bent over, holding his stomach. His fans, of course, laughed along with him. I don't think Eric was really laughing, though, because his face straightened up suddenly and he turned back to the man at the table.

"Why? What's going to keep me from just walking right back in here tomorrow, same as I always do?" He lowered his voice. "You?"

Now, except for moving his head, the unknown man sat stone still, still hunched over his barely touched beer.

"Because of *what* you are."

Eric crossed his arms in front of his chest. I saw a bit of a shiver run through him. Maybe he was standing in the draft, after all.

"And just what am I, grandpa?"

Rather than answering right away, the man slid his right hand out from under his left arm, took a sip of beer, then slid it back into his coat. He sloshed the beer around in his mouth a couple of times and then spat it out on the floor next to him.

It wasn't the worst thing on that floor, I guess.

"My baby brother died on the freeway last year, just a couple of miles from here." The new guy's gaze was frozen on Eric's face. "He was on foot. Cops said he was doped up and walked out into traffic. His name was Kevin."

Eric shifted his weight onto his left foot, shooting his right hip out, making him look like a surly teenager. "So?"

"So, he wasn't the type to drink or do drugs. But the police wrote it off as an accident. I know it wasn't." The new guy, still hunched over his beer, looked at the mug, got a sour look on his face, and raised his head again.

Eric just stared back.

"There were four of us boys. My brother Mike the one just older than Kevin—he got into heroin and meth and turned himself into a zombie. Scared the shit out of Kevin. Swore to me at Mike's funeral that he would never touch any of that crap."

"And?" Eric asked, shifting his weight to the other foot.

"Our old man was a nasty son of a bitch. Give one or the other of us a beating because it was Thursday. But he wasn't stupid." Eric snorted.

The new guy cocked his head slightly but waited a second before he started talking again.

"Something he made us do was keep a twenty folded up, stuffed at the bottom of the pocket where we kept our wallets. It wasn't spending money. It was taxi money. No matter what the hell else happened, it was a way to get home. Well, Kevin didn't have his and he wasn't in a taxi, so I figure he was robbed."

"And you're saying I robbed him?" Eric asked, sneering.

The man acted as if Eric had not spoken.

"Cops still couldn't do anything, wouldn't reopen a closed case just on that. No, it was two other kids who showed up dead the same way. Not in the same place, but the same way: drugged, wandering on the freeway. Robbed." The new guy leaned forward, just slightly. I could see the muscles in his jaw, tight and bunched.

"Found a cop who cared a little. He couldn't do anything, because those cases also got closed and his bosses wouldn't reopen them, but I saw the reports. Same drug in each. Cops wrote them off as drug-induced accidents, no crime."

Then he leaned back slightly.

"Even the last one, a Vietnamese kid named Jeremy Truc. Good name for him because he was the biggest damned Vietnamese kid I ever saw. And the last place he used his debit card was to buy a beer and a burger here, in this bar."

The only thing I saw Eric move was his eyes, a quick cut to the door and back to the guy at the table. "Oooh, I am so scared. Why aren't the cops here, if you're so smart?"

From where I stood, though, behind the bar, I could see that each time Eric shifted his weight, he inched a little farther away from the man. He was already more than an arms length away from the man's table. I felt a little tingle of happy inside, seeing Eric scared of something.

"That's not all those three kids told me. They told me what you are."

"Get on with it. What am I?"

"See, accidental deaths all get autopsies. And those three boys all had the same saliva on their dicks, all with the same DNA. Nothing to match it against, nothing in police records, but I think it points right at what happened to them."

The man took a deep breath.

"They all came in here at different times, bought a drink—which you doped up—and then got robbed after they left. Which you did. But why waste a perfect opportunity of having those kids helpless? Not when you could suck their dicks and then send them out on the freeway to die, so no one would know what you are? But those boys knew and they told. Even dead, they told us exactly what you are." Eric had frozen in place.

"Bet your DNA will match, though, won't it, *cocksucker?*"

Eric flinched as if stabbed.

The man almost snarled as he said, "Because that's *what* you are, *cocksucker.*"

Then Eric surprised me. I expected him to jump at the man and attack him.

But he didn't.

Maybe shout at the man, scream his rage and denials.

But he didn't.

He laughed.

He scratched under his arms.

Like a monkey.

And danced in circles, spinning and jumping.

When he stopped, Eric looked at the man and sneered.

"Nice story," he said. "All lies, but funny."

The new guy made a sound half grunt and half laugh.

"Yeah. No proof. The cops won't do anything because they don't think there's any crime to do anything with." He took another sip of his beer and tucked his hand inside his coat again. At least he hadn't spit the mouthful out on the floor this time.

"Doesn't change what you are, though, does it? You know. I know." He nodded his head at Eric's fans, still sitting at their two tables, half of them with their mouths hanging open. I snapped mine shut again.

"They should know," the man said, "if they're not all stupid."

Eric spun to his fans. Shrugged his shoulders like a circus clown. His fans laughed. Eric started dancing again, making his monkey noises. His fans laughed some more.

The man just sat. He waited. If he was disappointed by Eric's lack of reaction, he did not show it. But then, how much more hunched into his coat could he get?

"Why don't you just get the fuck out of here?" Eric shouted, while his fans added their own comments, yelling and taunting the new guy. One of them, Molly, stuck her tongue out at him and, when the new guy ignored that, flipped him off. Pinch-faced bitch. The cops could haul her away, too, far as I'm concerned.

Ignored, the fans went back to talking among themselves, making loud and pointed insults at the new guy, who continued to ignore them. This went on for a couple of minutes, their noise level and the cleverness of their insults going down as the man just sat there.

You know how, even when a bunch of people are talking, the

room suddenly gets quiet? As if everyone stopped talking at the same time? Well, that happened, and in the middle of that, the guy said, "Then there's the matter of *who* you are."

Eric, who had been dancing for his fans again, spun around.

"Oh? And who am I?"

A hand slithered out of the man's coat, lifted the glass.

"I've been talking a lot more than I usually do," he said. "Makes the throat dry."

He took his time taking a sip. Took his time sloshing the beer around in his mouth. Took his time getting around to actually swallowing it, his throat working as he did. Then he took his time carefully setting the glass down on the table, tucking his hand back under his arm, inside the coat. He slowly raised his gaze up to Eric's face, who by this time, had moved all the way back to the tables his fans sat at.

"But then," the man said, "who really gives a fuck who you are? You're a thief and a cocksucker." The man grinned thinly. "Hell, I've flushed turds that would have been better human beings that you could ever hope to be."

Eric surprised me again, this time by not hesitating even a moment before he jumped at the man, arms and legs almost a blur.

I caught the flash of a big fucking knife that I hadn't seen Eric draw from anywhere.

If the new guy was surprised, he didn't show it.

Both hands came out from his coat, each holding a big fucking black gun.

I know he fired three times, because I saw the flashes, both guns firing together, six shots in all, but the sound was just a roar. If I hadn't been looking right at the two guns, I couldn't have told you how many times he shot.

Eric just stopped in mid air.

Then fell to the floor like the sack of shit he was.

Now, people will probably say I should have ducked, in case the guy started shooting up the place, but I just stood there, spatula in my hand. My teeth began to hurt and I closed my mouth, but otherwise I didn't move at all.

I just stood and looked at Eric's dead body and tried to decide if I cared enough to be happy that he was dead.

The fan tables didn't freeze, though.

They tumbled left and right, toward the corners, and down behind the tables.

They didn't need to worry, though, because the guy didn't shoot any more.

He stood up, the guns still in his hands, but not really pointed anywhere. His hands settled at his waist, as if that was the most comfortable place for them. He did not look excited or angry or even satisfied. Except for the guns and his standing up, he could still be hunched over in his coat, just like he was when sitting at the table.

"OK, you witnesses. You got no reason not to tell the cops everything you saw, just the way you saw it. Don't leave anything out. But don't lie." He hefted the guns a half-inch and let them drop back down. "I might want to come back here again someday."

Then he turned to me.

The guns weren't really pointed at me, but they weren't exactly not pointing at me, either.

"Then there's you," he said, with the same flat voice he'd used with Eric.

"First, you'd better salvage that burger before it burns the place down."

At that, the smell of gunpowder finally worked its way into my brain. Maybe that was what kicked my brain into noticing the smell of burning meat, too.

I scraped the remains off onto the little plate next to the grill. It didn't look too bad, despite the thread of smoke still rising from it. I could still eat it, but then again, I could celebrate with a fresh one. It would be worth it.

But only if I lived long enough.

I dropped the spatula next to the plate and raised my hands before I turned back to face him.

He hadn't moved. His face was still. The guns didn't even shake.

"Now, you had to know," he said. "You had to know what he was doing. My cop buddy found robbery reports going back at least two years, of people who couldn't remember what happened to them, but ended up robbed. Some of them knew they were in a bar, but probably because of the drugs, couldn't remember where. You had to have seen him spike a drink at least once, tuned in on what he was doing. You *had* to know."

The guy's lip twitched into a snarl.

"All you had to do was chase him off and it would have all stopped. My baby brother would have eaten a bad burger and drank your cheap beer and never come in here again."

He took a deep sigh.

"But I know what you are, too. So you'll never give me an excuse to blow you up, will you, *coward?*"

I didn't say anything but my teeth started to hurt. I don't remember when I closed my mouth again.

"Yeah. Someday." He didn't lower the guns, he didn't change their aim. He just took a step back, sat carefully back into the chair at his table, and turning to face the fans again, eased the two guns down to the table, still clutching them in his fists.

Some of the fans had worked themselves back into their chairs, only to lurch toward the corners again when the gun barrels swung toward them.

He turned his head toward me and shouted, "Well, call the police, *asshole!*"

That got me moving. I closed my mouth, my teeth still aching. I dropped my hands, snatched up the phone, and punched the buttons.

All I had to say was the address and that there'd been a shooting and then they put me on hold.

It must have been a quiet night because it was only a few minutes of total silence in the bar before flashes of red and blue lights appeared in all the scratches and holes in the paint on the front windows.

The man eased the two guns to the table and let go of them. He twisted in his chair, turning toward me, and, still sitting, put his hands on top of his head, fingers interlaced, just as the cops would demand.

Then, he looked at me.

Square into my eyes.

And waited.

PROSPECTING

RON COLLINS

Ron Collins is the award-winning author of Stealing the Sun, *a series of space-based sf books. His stories have appeared in nine volumes of* Fiction River, *including* Editor's Choice, Readers' Choice, *and two* Pulse Pounders, *and he will co-edit an upcoming volume as well.*

He's contributed dozens of stories to premier science fiction and fantasy publications, such as Analog, *and* Asimov's. *His fantasy serial,* Saga of the God-Touched Mage, *hit the top of Amazon's Dark Fantasy bestseller lists and he's won a Writers of the Future prize, and a CompuServe HOMer award.*

For me, Ron's characters always come alive with their own distinctive voices. In "Prospecting" he puts the reader in the shoes of the people who forged their way out to the Old West, their heads swimming with visions of riches, and empty of knowledge about the new world they worked so hard to get to. He says about the story, "It's hard...to really put yourself there in the hard lands where one mistake or one happenstance is the difference between life and death."

I couldn't agree more with that.

The gent was broke down, his wagon done stuck in a wash full of juneberry and brush, listing to the front and north as it heads west. It's a simple wagon, floor slats weathered but not gone to silver, rails on both sides. He's got the bed covered with a tarp, and a healthy enough mule standing a'front of it.

I'm two days from Yreka, a mining town in the northern territory of California that you pronounce "Why-reeka," like it's a question rather than a place. It's mid-morning time, so the coyotes ain't up and yapping, and the mountain lions probably won't be willing to make a go of it for now. The air's fresh and clear, nothing in the sky but a few wisps of cloud and a dark pair of eagle-hawks up hunting rabbits. It ain't rained for a week, so all's a body can smell is the rock baking in the sun and the coyote brush that's growing out of cracks in that same rock.

The fella's a city gent, though. No doubt about that.

Oh, he's dirty enough, and his skin's got the roughness that comes from being on the trail a fetch. But I know he's city folk by the fact he don't put his iron in his hand as I come up to help him. Any man that's been around the mountains long enough knows better than to trust another man out here, don't matter that he's white or not. They ain't all like me. Some folk here got no scruples. But this gent leaves his rifle propped against the wagon bed even as he sees me standing up here with my own rifle pointed down from my hip, so I get right away that he's a city man.

"You all right?" I tell him as I come down the ridge.

The trigger guard on his gun gleams in the early sun.

The gent turns out to be a kid. Could be maybe twenty years old, or could be maybe less. He's sweating through a shirt that's scruffed up with dust from at least as far back as Kansas and Missouri terri-tory, probably on farther. His black hair's matted down in the heat, and his mustache is dark enough to stand up against a couple day's beard. He's a bit of a Nancy boy, too: hang-dog thin in the jaw, the kind of thin that the womenfolk would take more than easy to if there was any womenfolk to be found around these parts.

I figure him for a Wop.

Maybe his daddy come over from the boot.

I got no trouble with Wops, mind you. I done worked with all kinds in my life, and I figure one man's as good or bad as another.

"The wheel's busted," he says, standing taller as I come up close. "Can't get the son of a bitch off."

"Mind if I take a look," I tell him.

He nods and I come up to the wagon, then push my hat up my forehead.

"Wheel's busted up all right," I say.

"Axle's good and bent, too," he replies.

"I ain't no wheelwright," I say, "but the spoke looks like it's still good. Gonna take some working to get you heading on all right, but I think it'll stand a patching."

"Yeah. If I can get it off to begin with, anyway."

He wipes the sleeve of his shirt over his brow and shields his gaze from the sun.

"Brighter up here than you're used to, ain't it?" I say.

"A little."

"Best get used to it. California territory's probably a different place in a lotta ways."

"Probably."

"Where you from?" I ask.

"Pennsylvania," he says. "Philadelphia."

"Ah. The Keystone state."

"That's right."

"Kip," I say as I hold out my hand.

"Lonzo," he replies. "Lonzo Bassi."

I nod. Definitely a Wop.

I set my own gun down and lift on the wagon's edge while Lonzo knocks the hub ring over and gets the wheel off. "I'll have to get the band put back on when I get to a town," he says as he brings a big rock over to put under the axle strut so I can lay it on down again.

"Yeah. That'd be good."

I straighten my back and pull my skin out to take a slug of water.

"That's a load off," I say.

"Much appreciated," Lonzo replies.

I sit on a rock and gnaw on some dried steer I bought while I was in Yreka, and I watch as he goes about pounding the axle straight and then nailing a pair of slats up against the wheel that'll keep it in the round well enough to spin all right. The kid was handier than he looked—then again, I s'pose if he wasn't, the Blackfoot or the Sioux would've probably kilt him on the way out here, so sometimes the good Lord's world does make a lick of sense.

"What are you doing out here?" he says when he's done with the wheel. "Prospecting?"

I grin over at him, and I spit a piece of leather. "Ain't we all?"

He smiles back and I see that same gleam that rides on the gazes of pretty much every gent who's been streaming into California for the past couple years. The boy's here to make his fortune.

"Heading to your claim?" he asks.

I chuckle at him. "Wouldn't you like to know?"

Lonzo grins like a man's been caught holding an ace high. "I hear you can pick the gold up straight off the ground out around San Francisco," he says.

"Maybe a while back."

"What do you mean?"

I ignore the question. This ain't 1849 no more. If the stupid Wop didn't already know that all the easy gold was long gone, I wasn't scheming to be the one that breaks it to him.

"You're a shade north if you're looking for Frisco," I say.

"Figured I would be. Worth it to get past the Sierra Nevada, though."

"That makes sense."

"How far north?" he asks.

"Hundred mile. Maybe a little more."

Lonzo sighs and rolls the wheel over next to the wagon.

"How can I repay you?" he says when we get it back on right again.

"Well," I tell him, "I got some business up north 'round the lake. If you're willing to take a detour, I might be obliged to hitch a ride rather than walk it."

"How far is it?"

"Not more 'n half a day. With the wagon, we probably get there by sundown tonight."

He shrugs and puts his hat on. "I've been on the road four months already. Another day can't hurt me none."

"Much obliged," I say.

"So," Lonzo says as the wagon jolts its way over the high plains. "Just how does a man go about making his claim here?"

We're headed north-ways. It's all rock and brush behind us, with low mountains rising up ahead and to the west, and with the hint of the Sierra Nevada down to the south and east where Lonzo done come from. Mule's making good time, and the sun's edging on past its peak.

"Simple enough," I say.

He waits.

"You just find a plot big enough you think you can handle it all without no help, and you mark it out."

"That's it?"

"Pretty much. Course, you got to keep working it. You leave a claim fallow for any real time and another gent might jump it."

Lonzo smirked at that. "Maybe I do it the easy way and just jump *your* claim?"

"Don't joke. There be men who'll do that."

"Maybe I'm one of them."

I look at him, sitting on the driver's seat, sweating and grinning. Does this city Yankee actually got it in him to jump a claim? He seems soft, but I know sometimes it's the soft ones you need to keep your watch out after.

"I don't think you are," I finally decide. "Besides, I doubt you got any interest in my place."

"Dangerous site?"

"Let's just say I ain't worried."

We get quiet for a bit.

"That's a nice gun you got over there," I finally say as we roll over a hillside.

Lonzo's got his rifle placed into a holster he's built into the side of the wagon.

"Thank you, much," he says. "It's a Sharps. Breech loader."

"Ain't never seen one like it."

"I'd be surprised if you did. It's a new one. Made in Philly." He jangles something in his pant pocket. "Takes a cartridge, which means I can reload in a couple seconds flat."

"Sumbitch," I say. "Shoot pretty good?"

Lonzo purses his lips and squints up toward the mountain ridge off to the east. "I reckon I can pick a bird off at eleven hundred yards with it."

I chuff at that.

"I don't expect no Yankee can shoot that good no matter what the rifle."

"My daddy taught me."

I contemplate that. Maybe there's something more to Lonzo than meets the eye.

"Eleven hundred yards," I say. "That's pretty good, then."

I don't need to tell him mine's just an old Mississippi rifle, a muzzle loader probably ten years old if it's a day. It may be showing age, but we get 'long just fine together, and it's saved my behind more than a few times. Regardless what the Wop thinks of my rifle, I figure he got no need to know about the Colt I carry in my pack, 'long with 'bout everything else I own.

The road's bumpy, but it still beats walking. The mule's doing just fine all by itself.

"Where *you* from?" Lonzo asks after a bit.

"Oh, all over."

"Where abouts is All Over?"

I look across at him and decide it's just an honest question from an honest man. Probably can't hurt none to be sociable. He done told me about being from Philly, after all.

"Started in Rockingham County, North Carolina," I say. "Daddy was a shoe man by trade, though my mama called him more a gambler and a drinker by temperament. He done run off by hisself when I was a boy, though, so I don't recall him much."

"Poor woman."

I shift around on the seat, and see a coyote come up along the ridge, then another. No surprise there, as a coyote travels in twos when it kin.

"Mangy things," Lonzo says. "Maybe I get a chance to show you the Sharps in action?"

"Shouldn't be no problem," I tell him back. "A coyote's not going to hurt you none, less you happen to be a rabbit or less you fall into a den of their younglin's. A wolf's different thing, though. A pack a wolves'll bring a man down if you give 'em a chance. See a wolf and you're best off to shoot him straight out."

Lonzo don't seem convinced, but he leaves his rifle in its place.

The wagon rolls on, and pretty soon the coyotes leave us to ourselves.

"What about your mama?" Lonzo finally says.

"What about her?"

"You said your daddy was a cobbler. What about your mama?"

"Well, she did some looming at a cotton farm for a bit, and she'd sell pies she baked." I scoff. "Least she'd sell the ones I didn't eat up first."

Lonzo laughs the right amount.

"Worst whippin' I ever got was for eating a rhubarb pie she already tabbed for the manor man." I stop my yapping to remember that night: hadn't thought about it in a while. "I can still hear the sound of that switch falling and recall how I was wondering if that was what the nigger boys felt when they got their whippins."

Lonzo gives pause when he hears me talking 'bout the whippins, just long enough that I ponder if I got me a Yankee gent here with an abolitional streak in him, but he don't say nothing else about it and just goes on.

"Sounds like a good woman," he says.

"Probably," I say. "She done her best anyway, and I s'pose I come out okay in the end."

Lonzo nods.

"Left home after that and went to working at a tobacco farm so I could eat."

I ain't done this much talking since I come to California, but Lonzo's got his questions and he's listening, and the ground is rolling by just fine. The more I spin tales, the easier they come. I tell him a story about hopping a rail car west toward Tennessee, and fixing the roof of a man's house for five dollars one time.

"Then I got up north your way," I say.

"Pennsylvania?"

"Yep. Worked the rails in Philly for a bit."

"You don't say? Wonder if we might have met before?"

I shake my head. "Not likely," I say. "Not less you mixed it up with the Micks any. That's where I stayed most the time I was there. They's the ones done all the real work on the rails up in Philly. Come off the boat spiking and drinking, they did. Not the brightest of folk, I s'pose, but not a one of 'em was afeared of a day's work and they were all good in a fight."

"That's probably fair enough description," Lonzo says. "Some of the Irish came to my father's restaurant."

"Restaurant?"

"My family is into food."

I smirk at him. Dad's a cook. Maybe that's where he gets his soft from.

"That what you got in back?" I say. "Pots 'n pans?"

"No. Not really. Well, some pots and pans. But mostly I got my tent and my tools to mine with back there, though I'll rightly fess up to being able to rustle you a tasty plate of rabbit if you'll give me the time."

He peels back the tarp.

True fact, there's a tent kit back there and tools and utensils. He's got hisself a boxy suitcase that stores, I assume, all his other grimy shirts and pants.

I cluck my understanding of what I see, and he drops the tarp.

"Anyway," I say, picking up on my story. "That's where I spent most of my time when I was there in Philly—driving rail ties with the Micks and the Polacks. Weren't there very long, though."

"Why'd you leave?"

I think about how the city was so blamed crowded with people wanting nothing more than to tell a man what to do and when to do it, and how the buildings were so dirty and stacked up atop one another like bricks. The memory alone makes me pucker up.

"Don't think I'm cut out to be a Yankee."

Lonzo looks at me. "Probably not."

"You planning to head on back there once you get all riched up?" I say.

"Suppose I will," Lonzo replies.

I just smile.

I seen it a few times before: a prim, young dandy gent comes strolling themselves into California territory as if they own the place, thinking to spend a few months out here before cartin' back a wagonload of gold. A few make it back rich like that—enough that the word gets out, anyway, and enough that a hundred more gleamy-eyed bastards like Lonzo come following along for every one that makes it.

Problem is, the world works its own way, and that way ain't always so kind to the second man out. The early bird gets the worm, and all.

"What'd you do when you left Philly?" he asks me.

"Drifted west. Did some trapping and trading till those got tapped out, then some river boating. Finally found myself in St. Louis with that outfit working to drive the rails out to California. Worked that job 'til one day I decided I couldn't handle the foreman's sass no more. Bought me a gun and a bottle that night, and just headed west. Ain't looked back since."

"I see I'm with a world traveler," Lonzo says.

"Don't know about that," I reply. "But I'll allow as to wishing I had that bottle with me right about now."

We both laugh.

The mule makes better time than I expect, but still the sunlight's fading as we come up to the pass, and climb our way to where we see down into the lakebed valley.

The clouds above are catching the last rays and turning the sky into a bright orange fire with red and purple flares, and the valley mountains are turning their own colors, dark and light, gold and purple, sharp on the edges like God hisself done drawn 'em there. The lake water is the brightest blue there is, and it's rippled with waves that spread out north toward Mt. Shasta on straight ahead, the peak white-tipped even in the month of August. That place points itself up toward where the Heavens lay, and it makes the dry ledges and crests around us seem like they ain't nothing but young pups.

That's what I like about it out here, you know?

Mountains like this make a man understand what being free means.

They give a man to do what he wants. No bosses haranguing over him, no coppers running around telling him where he can sleep and where he can't sleep. A man gets to live out here like the good Lord promised he could.

"Think we should make camp?" Lonzo says. "Maybe down by the water?"

I got eyes for something else, though—something I been looking for in the first place: a scattering of three thatched tule huts and a taut-set teepee built along a line that's half rocks and half trees. There's a thin smoke from a cook fire.

Modoc Indians—just like the miners I heard tell back in Yreka said they'd be.

Lonzo sees what I'm looking at, too.

"What should we do?" he says.

I slide out the seat, and my boots hit the ground with a rocky crunch.

"Give me your gun," I say.

"What?"

"I said give me your gun, and I'll handle this."

"I ain't giving you my weapon," he says.

I reach around my pack and grab the Colt out of it, then I point it up at the kid.

Lonzo, to his credit, freezes, then raises his hands up slow-like.

"Don't be a cussed fool, now, Lonzo," I say. "Give me your gun, and I'll handle this."

Lonzo reaches the rifle up and gives it over my way.

"Loaded?" I ask.

"Of course."

"Bullets?"

He reaches into a pocket and hands over a pouch. It's nice and weighty. I loop it onto my belt, and drop the Colt back into the pack.

"Go on and get a fire going," I say as I turn toward the Indians. "I'll be back in a bit. Maybe have some of that rabbit you were bragging on so high."

"What are you going to do?"

"Just what I said I was."

I walk away, then.

My legs are stiff from setting too long, so it feels good to move.

The clearing's full of sawgrass that comes up past my knees. I hear birds from far off, and catch the reek of fresh droppings close by. My boots crunch over the ground as I draw up closer to the Indian shelters. I got my Mississippi rifle in one hand and Lonzo's newfangled gun in the other. I look the Sharps over as I walk along, seeing how the loader works. The cartridges rattle against my thigh, and the Colt is hard and heavy at the small of my back.

Four shelters.

Probably no more than twelve or fifteen Modoc, several probably young.

They don't see me yet, but three of 'em are in the open: a squaw's standing by one of the huts, and two others are carrying lines of fish as they come up from the lakeside.

I use my own gun to shoot the squaw.

She falls over and don't move again.

I drop that rifle and grab the other. We'll see whether Lonzo was lying about it now.

It feels different against my shoulder, but it ain't long afore the next shot rings out and one of the fishing Indians drops. I fetch a new cartridge from the pouch and pop open the breech. Less than five counts later I got a bead on Indian number three and I press the shot off to great success.

Hell of a weapon.

I reload again as I walk through the sawgrass, thinking that next town I get to will mean steak and adventurous womenfolk for a week.

Another Indian comes from inside a hut.

I shoot her, and reload so fast that echoes from the rifle are still ringing in the valley as I'm ready to shoot again. A few steps later I get the fifth—a male this time. Now they're running, three of 'em anyway. Seeing as I know how to hunt, it won't matter none. There's a ring of rocks at the edge of the campground that I know the younglin's make in their play. Two come out the teepee. I shoot the one that's got a gun, and the other runs off down the lakebed as I take a moment to reload.

Always hate to shoot a younglin' cause they pay so well alive.

Their fire smells of fir.

The first hut is empty now. The second has two younglin's in it, huddling down in a woolen blanket.

Helluva day, I think. It's one helluva day.

I straighten up, looking after the runners.

A shot cracks out, and Jesus Mother Mary, it's like I get kicked in the back of the shoulder.

I spin round and hit the ground on my side.

It's like I can't breathe for a long many seconds.

I lay there with my cheek pressed against the dirt. My vision waters up and I got to blink, but I still can't take in a breath.

The two Indian whelps look at me through the entryway to that thatched-up hut that's nearly going to rot. Their eyes are big and white. For a minute I see a memory of my brother, Jess, and me, hiding in the cold cellar while Daddy got to arguing with Mama. I bet our eyes were like that. I bet these kids are pissing their little britches about right now.

Then a breath finally comes, and the pain hits like fire.

"I been shot," I say to the Indians.

I must have missed a Modoc in my earlier accounting. One of

them must have been coming along behind. Maybe hunting. Must have had a rifle out on his own.

Blam'd stupid. Should have paid it better mind.

I blink away the waves of tears that gum up my eyesight.

Lonzo's rifle is tossed in the dirt across the way where I flung it as I dropped.

Got to get it back before the Modoc comes along to finish the job.

I take my good arm and crawl toward it, but the fire in the other shoulder's like a knife twisting in, and I can't move on account of the need to catch my breath again.

Footsteps come along and I know I ain't getting to the Sharps in time.

I reach back with my good hand into my pack and get my grips around the Colt, then I twist around and look up.

Rather than an Indian's face, I see Lonzo instead. He's standing at the edge of the campground, breathing heavy like he's been running.

"Thank God," I say as I lay back. "I almost shot ya."

"What in the nine hells are you doing!" he screams at me.

Then I see he's got my rifle gripped in his hands, his knuckles are nearly as pure and white as his face. The truth hits like a river current.

"It's you that shot me?" I say, turning the Colt back on him. "Now why'd you go and do all that?"

"You're killing them!"

"Of course I'm killing 'em."

I wave my Colt at him again.

I want to shoot the son of a bitch right where he stands, but I figure my shoulder's tore up pretty good. The blood's flowing wet anyways, and I feel the lead up high in my chest. I'm finding regular breath now, though, and I can sit up all right, so that's what I do. I groan and I grunt, but I get myself to a place where I can look at Lonzo like a man.

Maybe I'll make it through this all right.

"How about you help get me patched up like you done that wheel of yours?" I say. "That'll give you time to argue the case of why I shouldn't just shoot you right now and have it over with."

Lonzo grips the rifle harder and glances to his own gun there in the dirt. There's a calculating going on inside his mind. We both know he can't load up that rifle of mine again before I plug him full of this gun—just like we both know he can't get to his own gun no faster.

"Get yourself calmed down, Lonzo," I say. "This ain't nothing to get shot over."

"You can't go killing people like that, Kip."

"Sure I can. They's just Indians. And by my accounting *these* Indians just made me thirty dollars, plus whatever I can get for the younglin's at the courthouse."

"Thirty dollars?"

"I ain't got the time to talk 'bout this if you ain't fixing my shoulder."

I aim at his forehead, and figure he knows I'll hit it.

Lonzo finally lays the weapon on down. His gaze flickers over to the dead squaw, though, so I see he's not fully on board with me yet, but he does come over to look at my shoulder. I got a moment to sway him.

"Indians bring good money, Lonzo. You best learn that now. Five dollars gold for every dead one, and whatever someone'll pay for the orphan-kids."

He pulls the shirt off the bullet hole. Stings like a hive of hornets digging into my back.

"I thought you were a prospector?" he says.

I gather my breath before answering.

"You prospect for gold, I go looking for Indians. I figure it for the same thing, except the land's going to be running dry of gold a long time before it runs out of Indians."

I feel the knife on my throat before I hear nothing.

He must have had it in his boot.

"Put the gun down, Kip," he says.

"Don't get too smart for those britches, boy," I reply. "Think hard over what you're getting ready to do before you do it."

"I swear to the man above, I'm going to take you to the sheriff."

I laugh and it hurts down my back and into my chest. The Colt's still in my hand, and I know I can lift it up to shoot him, but I ain't sure of the timing of it all. I figure Lonzo's probably okay with a knife, but I ain't sure if he'll butcher me right out here in the open air or not.

"Go on and take me to the sheriff," I say once I get myself under control. "He's the one layin' the gold."

"That's bull," Lonzo said. "No lawman worth his badge would run a bounty."

"Well, teck-nickly it'd be the judge at the courthouse paying on the younglins. He's the one got to rule if they's orphans or not— which I figure he'll see it as such since I done shot the mamas and the papas."

"I don't understand you at all."

"Don't go straining your head too far, Lonzo. This is just how it is out here in this territory. I can't say at all how much gold the good Lord done put in the ground around these parts, but I *can* tell you that the good State of California done promised to pay up in that gold for every dead Indian a man can get his hands on, and they been making good on that word for a year now."

"The *state* is paying you to hunt Indians?"

"Five US dollars a head. Payable at the jailhouse."

The knife presses harder and I'm feeling a burn.

"Plus expenses," I add on. I get my finger ready on the trigger because, no matter what Lonzo decides, I ain't planning on dying out here alone. "So, you feel free to take me on up to the next judge you can find. I can recommend Yreka just a couple days back, and French Gulch ain't much farther if you prefer taking a more southerly way. But right now I need you get to fishing out that bullet you done put in my back."

"That's not right," he says in a voice that's like he's talking mostly to himself. "That can't be right."

The knife comes off my neck, though.

I turn round and shoot him square in the forehead. He falls back near the hut.

Sumbitch.

He brung it on hisself, but still it bothers the hell out of me.

I never shot a white man before, and I ain't sure what to do about that.

I leave the Modoc where they all lay.

Lonzo, too.

I may not be the sharpest steel trap 'round, but I know I ain't got the time to go collecting up dead Indians now. I'm setting to die if I don't get me some help soon. The mule wagon can make Yreka in a day at best, maybe. If I make it to town, I can come back later and see what the crows and the coyotes done left for me.

After thinking on it bit, I decide leaving Lonzo out here don't bother me none at all, though. Turns out a Yankee's worth less than an Indian.

Standing hurts, but I can do it.

Walking ain't no different.

I hold onto the Colt as I go, and it gives me a feeling of no little strength.

It's getting to be almost dark when I come to the mule and the wagon. I barely got strength enough to slide up to the seat and hit the mule to get it to walking.

The blood's not good. Too much, sluicing all over the seat.

I'm draining too fast and I'm losing my thoughts in the darkness. The coyotes begin their yips as I get under Lonzo's tarp and begin looking for a needle and thread to work on myself as best I kin. Dandy Yankee cook ought to have something like that, oughtn't he?

I crack open the suitcase.

It's too dark to see in, so I dump it over.

Can't feel my fingers now.

I need to rest a bit, but the wagon's already stopped its bumping and thumping.

Dumbass mule.

"Get up!" I yell at it, too weak to do much more. "Get up!"

But the mule don't move.

I'm sitting here, alone in the back of a dead man's wagon.

Over in the dark distance I see still the outline of three huts and a teepee. Can't see Lonzo or the Indians, but I'm thinking I see the younglins moving.

"Hey!" I yell out. "Come here! Come here!"

That's when I see the wolf.

It's a big-chested monster standing on the ridge with its dark fur ruffled up along the back of his neck. Its nostrils flare with that sense it gets when an animal smells blood. Its eyes are cold and black.

The Colt is heavier than it was earlier, but I get it up to aim. My shot goes too high, and the gun kicks itself away and claps itself down to the ground.

The sound of the shot scares the mule, though, and the wagon bounces along for a ways.

A minute later, or is it an hour, I see the wolves again.

It's gettin' dark but that won't stop them none.

The huntin' pack is forming up, coming along to make a meal of the mule at the front of the wagon and the man at the back. I got no gun now. I got no gun, and the wolves they keep coming.

I think of when my daddy went to wailing on my mama, and I remember the beatings I got when the boss man didn't like me talking back. I think of the money I got left lying on the ground out by the lakebed.

That's not right, I hear Lonzo say.

I look up into the sky and see the stars shining there in the way they been shining since the good Lord hisself put them up there.

TOOTS

MICHAEL KOWAL

Bars are places where sorrows are drowned and souls get stripped bare. Enemies attack without inhibition and lifelong friendships are born. As a former bartender, I love the story "Toots." It's a classic "man walks into a bar" story that sets up a beautiful friendship between PI, John Devin and Toots, the owner of Devin's favorite speakeasy.

This is Michael's third John Devin, PI, story to appear in Fiction River. *He has written three novels in the series:* Red is for Blood, Black is for Hate, *and* Gold is for Greed.

Michael says: "Toots owns the speakeasy that Devin likes to hang out at. Toots is a fun guy and he and Devin are good friends in the novels, and I always wondered how they became friends."

Read on to find out.

To say O'Hanlon's was a deli was to say the devil was a little misguided.

Of course, that's what the sign out front said, that it was a deli. But O'Hanlon's Deli was in downtown Los Angeles and like anything else in LA, it was a fake front. The real business got done in the back.

The deli took up the first thirty feet of a hundred-and-fifty foot deep building. And the last hundred-and-twenty feet? Sin. Pure, pure, loving, fun, and all the time working—sin.

Owned lock stock and beer barrels by Toots O'Hanlon, a giant of a Mick straight from Ireland. He wrestled for a bit after the Great War but finally got wise, moved to LA, and decided to open a saloon.

Unfortunately, that was right at the time a certain congressman from Minnesota decided that he was going to rid the entire country of sin—by banning booze.

The guy's name was Volstead, and the name of what he gave birth to? Prohibition.

Imagine that.

The idiot.

So while Volstead baptized the country into Prohibition, Toots shifted his saloon into a hidden speakeasy, in the back of the deli, and baptized anyone who wanted it in all the booze they could drink.

At least that's the story I got on my first two visits to Toots. Too bad this would be my last.

The place was starting to grow on me.

I walked straight into the small back room of the deli, scattered with stacked chairs, one banged-up table, and the thick smell of bread all around. Ahead lay the object of my desire—a gray metal door.

I rapped on it exactly five times, and then two more for good measure. It was a solid and thick thing, and felt like it would never give way.

A small slit-plate opened in the middle of the door at about five and a half feet up. Which meant I had to stoop down six inches. "Volstead."

It was the magic word, and a nice stick-you to the man who started the whole mess.

A set of dark brown eyes I didn't recognize floated on the other side of the slit. A guy's eyes, they were small and tight. They just stayed there looking at me and didn't move.

"I said Volstead." I wasn't in the mood for this.

It had been a bad day. Hell, it had been a bad six months.

I landed in LA only six months ago. I was an ex-Marine who didn't know a lot else other than how to shoot, fight, and keep myself alive. I was in the Great War myself at the age of sixteen. I was twenty now and felt like eighty. War did that to you. Killing your first man at sixteen did that to you. Hell, everything did that to you.

When I hit LA I thought the sun wasn't bad, the weather wasn't bad, so I decided to see what I could do. Thanks to the war I knew how to use a gun, so I bought two, and called myself a PI.

And been losing my shirt ever since.

No business when people don't know who you are, and thought you were too young.

The metal slit-plate slammed closed, then the metallic sound of a bolt being thrown barely made it through the thick door. Then it swung open.

To a small room.

The room was only six feet wide and eight feet to the back, with a matching metal door on the other end. The walls were simple plaster painted dark brown, with a single bare bulb hanging ten feet up on the matching ceiling.

It was a front porch, for drunks.

The door shut behind me and everything went completely silent inside. On purpose. No use having a speakeasy if everyone can hear you outside.

I turned to look at Brown-eyes who I hadn't met before.

He was maybe five-eight, tight, and lean. And mean. His forehead sloped down into sharp eyebrows, his nose was sharp, his chin and cheeks were sharp, too. I didn't want to know what his teeth looked like.

"Where's Gats?" I asked.

"Gats got sick. I'm his cousin."

And if he was Gats' cousin, this guy's mother was a pygmy.

Gats was the bouncer who normally worked at the door, at least the two times I'd been here, and the only guy bigger than Toots in the whole place. Gats stood six-feet-seven and was definitely someone you didn't want to tangle with. I liked Gats. He was a good guy. Plus he wore twin-rig shoulder holsters like me. I had twin .45 Colt 1911s in mine, Gats had twin .38s in his.

My guns were bigger.

"You don't look like Gats," I said.

The guy sneered and pulled open his jacket to show off the gun tucked in his waistband. "You want to argue?"

Little man, little gun.

Plus it had a pearl handle.

I hated pearl handles. All show.

I turned around to handle the back door myself. "Nice meeting you." I hoped it sounded like "stuff yourself."

As soon as that back door cracked, a whole other world opened in front of me.

The sound hit me first. A hundred voices all talking at once, laughing at once, yelling and arguing at once. It was glorious. Like family dinners back home.

The place was crowded, more than I'd seen it before. It was a Saturday night and the place was filled with working Joes like me. And I guess you could say Josephines, too.

It was men and women, young and old, everyone crowded in the back of a building, all brought together to get away with something. And that something was booze.

The room itself was only thirty feet wide, but long at maybe a hundred feet deep. Along the right wall was the bar. It was a glorious, eighty foot long carved red mahogany thing, complete with three taps along the top, and a brass foot rail along the bottom. In back of the bar was eighty feet of mirror brought in special from Ireland.

Up the center of the place was a line of small simple wood tables arranged on the black and white tile floor below. Against the wall on the left were high-backed wooden booths that stretched from the front of the room to the back.

And the people—not a millionaire among them. Secretaries and dock workers, carpenters and roughnecks, and every other trade in the book. All of them laughing and talking, yelling and drinking.

And everything covered over in a cloud of smoke.

I pushed my way toward the back to my favorite place, the end of the bar. As much as you can have a favorite place in a place you'd been to only twice.

"Devin!"

Toots yelled it. The mountain standing behind the bar.

Six-foot-four and probably north of two-sixty, Toots had a head of short, sandy red hair that looked like bristles on a brush. His head was thick like a fireplug and set right into his shoulders, his arms were like ham hocks, and his belly was even bigger. And if you asked Toots he would say it was all muscle.

Because it was.

His smile was wide and white, his eyes were the color of a light blue Irish sky and they always seemed to be just the slightest bit squinted. Like he was sizing you up, or ready to laugh at a joke.

I nodded to him and kept walking.

The only thing I had left was the fin in my pocket and the two guns in their holsters. The fin was going to buy me one last drink, the two guns, a train ticket to somewhere else.

Then I saw Eddie.

Well, not exactly Eddie but a guy that reminded me of him. The real Eddie I knew when I was eight, before I hit my growth spurt. He tormented me like an animal, and looked like a mean one.

And so did this guy.

And he was sitting in my spot.

This new Eddie was in his early twenties, wore a light gray hat pulled down at an angle over his face, trying to look tough, but his face was fleshy like a baby. His nose was small and pulled up, his eyes were dark and black, and his upper lip pulled away from his lower one.

He sat there slump-shouldered and had that same meanness about him that the old Eddie had. Like he'd bullied his way through a short life and it had gotten him places.

Well it wasn't going to get him anywhere with me.

I walked right behind the new Eddie. His eyes followed me the whole way and I don't think he was happy.

I walked right over to the open gap between the bar and the backbar, reached up to the long piece of dark wood with hinges at the bottom, the bar hatch, and lowered it down with a slap. There, instant bar. It was a poor substitute for the wonderful mahogany thing to my right but when you need a place to stand and somebody's got your spot, it does the trick.

Plus as I looked over at Eddie it annoyed him like hell. Good.

Then up walked Toots, his smile spread ear to ear. He set his big meaty hands down on the other side of the bar hatch. "And how are you, Devin?" His light brogue sounded like music to an Irish boy who had never seen home.

"Fine."

"Well, you don't look it." He smiled, almost ready to laugh, his neck a tree trunk.

"Long day." I tried to smile but wasn't too sure how successful I was.

"Well then, what can I get you?"

I'd seen the bottle the first two times I'd been here. On the top shelf down at this end of the bar. John Jameson & Sons Dublin Whiskey. The bottle was brown and the label white, with a black patch below that said "Not a drop is sold till it's seven years old." I had only seen one other bottle like it. My guess is even one drink of it would cost me all of the fin in my pocket but it was worth it to me. I nodded toward the Jameson. "A glass of that."

Toots turned and looked up at the bottle, then back at me with a flat expression. The first time I'd not seen a smile on him. "I only keep that for special occasions. A very rare bottle, that. Especially these days."

I nodded.

The last time I'd seen one was in France during the war. I had just killed my first man, and one of the men in my company pulled out the bottle. I don't even know how he got it, or even kept it safe.

I didn't remember the taste so much, just that it burned going down. Like gasoline. But what I remembered most were the men there with me. They each nodded at me, like it was okay what I had just done. The killing.

I just wanted to remember them tonight. "It's all right. I'll have a beer."

Toots looked into me like I sometimes looked into others. Trying to figure out what they were all about. "This the third time you been in my place, right?"

I nodded.

Toots kept looking at me. Then he nodded. "Then..." He reached behind him with his massive arm, pulled that bottle of Jameson down, and set it on the bar between us. "I guess it's a special occasion then."

And he smiled.

I let out the breath I was holding and nodded to Toots, and hoped he understood how much I appreciated it. It had been a long day. It had been a long life.

Toots reached out to a stack of short clear glasses stacked neatly on the backbar, grabbed one, set it next to the bottle and poured two fingers into it. "To luck, then. May it all be good."

Then he smiled again, put the bottle back, and walked back up the lane of the bar.

I looked over and Eddie looked at me like I had just stolen something from him. I turned away from him, and raised my glass to take my first small sip.

The sharpness of the alcohol bit my nose as it came close, followed quickly by the sweet smell of the whiskey. It brought back memories. I guess first of all, to becoming a man. In whatever way that took.

Then I thought of each of the men who stood in front of me that morning in the trench. Their dirty, mud-caked faces looking back at me with not a smile among them. To them, I took my first sip.

The whisky bit the way it did that morning, and bit at me all the way down.

Then I took a second sip, to those who didn't make it back.

Then I set down the glass and let it all sink in.

I wasn't sure how an ex-Marine ended up here in this speakeasy, in this city, thinking he had any possibility of becoming a PI.

Then out of the corner of my eye I saw Ada. At least I think that was her name.

She was old and small, with long gray hair pulled in a bun on the back of her head. She sat just around the corner from Eddie, and facing me.

The first time I was here she introduced herself to me. A nice old lady. Seemed to want to talk, but I didn't. I never did. So the second time I was here I avoided her, which was pretty hard seeing as how she sat just around the corner from me. I guess that was her spot. But I avoided her and there you have it. Sometimes I was a determined bastard.

She smiled a soft, small smile that said "I know who you are. I've met you. And I didn't die."

I laughed under my breath. I can be such an ass.

I smiled at her. And you know what, it didn't kill me.

I raised the glass and took my last sip, I don't know, maybe to leaving LA. Maybe...to my last drink of Jameson.

It went down a lot smoother than the first two, and that was that.

I pulled out the fin in my pocket, tucked it under the empty glass and looked up to catch Toots' eye and thank him. But something else caught me.

A guy half way down the bar. A real string bean.

String Bean himself was probably in his mid-twenties, wore a navy suit with wide lapels almost as wide as he was, a fat black tie with some kind of white design stitched at the bottom of it, and a white shirt too big at the neck. And he was sweating. A lot.

More than what a saloon in Los Angeles called for.

But what really caught my attention was how String Bean, in the last five seconds I was watching him, looked at Eddie three times.

Like a dog making sure its master was behind him.

I didn't like it. Not one bit.

So I decided to stick around for another drink.

I nodded to Toots and the big guy came right over. He smiled down at the empty glass. "Nice bit of work, huh?"

"That it is. And many thanks for it. I'll have another, but the regular stuff is fine."

Toots nodded, I think thankful that I wasn't going to make him choose whether to offer me the Jameson again or not.

Toots brought over a clear bottle with no label on it, the "regular" stuff, and poured three fingers. "And this one, is on me." He smiled his broad Toots' smile, and left me to my thoughts.

I leaned over and buried my elbows on the top of the bar hatch and crossed my hands underneath me, and waited.

I didn't have to wait for long. After two minutes, Eddie shot up from the stool next to me, and shot a gun into the air.

Then things got interesting.

I just kept looking straight ahead. Gunshots don't bother me, but apparently it did to most everyone else in the place.

There were some screams, the place got quiet, but it was when the second shot went off—String Bean's—that everyone hit the deck.

Everyone but me, Toots, and unfortunately Ada, who walked with a cane and didn't move anywhere fast. She sat on her stool, looking at Eddie, like she wanted to smack the hat off his head.

"Everyone down." Eddie yelled it and his voice was hard like tight steel. "Keep your mouths shut and don't move. And if you do, we'll kill all of you."

I heard a couple of muffled cries, some whimpering. The gunshots still hung in the air, ringing.

Toots didn't have a smile on his face any more, his neck was red, and his eyes were now ice blue. "You boys don't really want to do this." Toots' light brogue had gone flat.

Toots was behind the bar, half way between Eddie and String Bean. Everyone was clear except Ada sitting next to where Eddie stood.

And of course me, still hunched over, still with my elbows solid on the bar hatch. And still with my arms crossed under myself, my hands slowly wrapping themselves around the butts of my .45s, sticking out from the twin shoulder holsters under my jacket.

Two guns, two guys. This was going to be interesting. Then down at the far end of the bar Brown-eyes came out from the front door, his little pearl-handled gun up and pointed. The third member of the party.

"Well," Toots started, looking over at Brown-eyes, "Hell of a bouncer you turned out to be. Was Gats in on it, too?"

Eddie spoke up. "No. He's back at his place taking a nap."

I hoped they didn't kill him.

"Now empty your till if you don't mind." Eddie smiled.

Speakeasies were easy targets. If they were robbed, who were they going to go to, the cops?

I had two guns and there were three guys. Not bad odds for me, but Toots stood near the bar and blocked my view of String Bean. If Toots would get out of the way I could get him, but once I started shooting String Bean was close enough to Toots, and Toots was a big enough target, I was sure String Bean would get him. And I wasn't going to let that happen.

Then I saw movement out of the right corner of my eye, and Ada's brown hickory cane flashed down, her arms attached to it, and smashed into Eddie's arm.

The gun and arm slapped down to the bar, and luckily it didn't go off, but Eddie had it right back up and pointed at Toots faster than you could see. The guy was quick.

But then Eddie did something very stupid. He back-handed Ada with his gun, smashing her in the forehead with it.

"NO!" Toots yelled and lunged toward Eddie.

Eddie shot Toots and Toots spun to the floor.

Finally, all three were clear.

I leaned my right shoulder forward, and shot through the holster right out the back of my jacket, and caught Eddie in the chest.

Then I drew out both guns.

Brown-eyes and String Bean were already firing at me. I leveled both guns, one at Brown-eyes and the other at String Bean, and fired.

Two bullets zipped past my head on either side, then one caught me high in the ribs under my left arm.

It hit like a hammer.

As I began to spin from the shot, I saw my first shot hit String Bean in the middle of the forehead. The back of his head would fare a lot worse.

Then my second shot hit Brown-eyes, right in the left eye.

I landed hard on the floor, the air completely knocked out of me.

But I dragged myself up enough to look over at Eddie. He lay there still, with blood leaking out of him like it would never stop.

Dead.

Good. I hated bastards who hit women.

Then I wondered if I was going to end up staying here in LA after all. I just killed three men, in an illegal establishment, while drinking illegal sin. Cops didn't like when you killed people. Especially three of them.

Two men flashed above me, headed behind the bar. Then one guy came up to me, his face right above mine. "You okay?" The guy was bald and I'm guessing short. He had round thick glasses like an accountant.

I focused a bit and took in a breath. That seemed to work, so I took in another. My mouth was dry and nothing that tasted of salt had bubbled up, so in the vast scheme of things I thought maybe I was going to live. For at least the next few minutes.

"Out of the way! Out of the away!!"

Toots' voice.

And by the sound of it he was far from dead.

Then his face popped in front of me, with that big mick smile of his and the head that looked like a fireplug. "Everything's gonna be okay."

I felt his hands do a quick field check over me, then lift up my left arm and look at the damage. He poked around a bit, spikes of pain shooting here and there.

"You'll be happy to know you're gonna live." And if it was possible, his smile got even bigger. "What you did there, son, I'm mighty thankful for. Mighty thankful."

That's when I noticed the red blood on his white shirt. A lot of it on his left shoulder. "You're hit." I croaked.

"Yes, I am. It's not the first, and I'm hoping it's the last but you never know." He moved his huge arm around my shoulders and pulled me to my feet.

"Ada! How are you, love?"

As Toots raised me up and held me up under his massive right arm, a few other patrons helped Ada up.

There was a cut on her forehead and a line of blood dropped down from there across her cheek. "I'm all right." She looked down at Eddie, or at least his body, laying there on the floor. Then she spat on him. "Asshole."

Well there you go.

"Come on…" Toots put his massive left arm around Ada and as he tightened his grip on me, the bottle of Jameson curled around in front of me, held in Toots' right hand. Then he walked us both toward a small hall cut into the back wall of the place that led to the heads in back. "Get those assholes all the hell out of here! And nobody else gets in!"

Down the dark hall Toots steered us into the men's head, including Ada. All three of us walked into the dark space with a single white sink and two giant urinals to the right, and three dark wood stalls to the left. I guessed his idea was to clean us up.

But he continued past the sink until we all faced the back wall. The wall was covered in dark oiled oak, and Toots reached down and pressed into a knot in the wood about kneecap height.

A latch on the other side tripped off and a small doorway sprang open.

Nice trick.

The door was just big enough for Toots to squeeze through so he pushed us in first, then followed behind.

We entered a short passageway lined with dusty brown lath and a dark wood plank floor. At the other end of the passageway, a large white room opened up.

"Doc!" Toots called out as we made our way down the passageway.

We walked out of the passage, and into an honest to God doctor's office, complete with white cabinets along the wall, a white-topped metal table in the middle, and a white canvas and metal privacy screen to the side.

And no other door in.

My mouth must have been hanging open, because Toots smiled at me like a father looking at a dumb-struck kid. "Not a lot of places to go for a doc who's lost his license." Then he boomed out toward the privacy screen, "If he'd sober up!"

"I heard that." Came from around the screen.

"I know ya did, that's why I said it."

From around the screen walked a short, thin-framed man dressed in a wrinkled white shirt and plain brown wool pants. His whole body raged of too many inconveniences and his face had a gray cast to it. And he carried an empty glass that he held out toward Toots. "The good stuff. What's the occasion, you miss me?"

"Nobody misses you, Doc." Toots got Ada to the table and set her up there, then left me on my own and poured Doc two fingers.

Doc looked down at the drink then up at Toots. "Don't skimp."

Toots dropped in another finger, then from his back pocket pulled two more glasses. The first he filled with four fingers and handed to me. "You saved my life."

I looked at him. "Nothing anybody else wouldn't have done."

"No, nobody would have. They're too busy thinking about themselves."

"Speaking of which..." Doc pushed his now empty glass out in front of Toots. "This is going to cost you. I'm going to have to use extra gauze."

Toots dropped another three fingers into Doc's glass, then three more into his own. "I already pay for the gauze."

"Details." Doc sneered, then downed that glass. Then held it out to Toots again. "Three, for three."

Toots grunted, then dropped more Jameson into Doc's glass, then handed the bottle to me. "There, that's yours now. Forever."

I looked at Toots. "What do you mean?"

Doc pulled a bottle from one of the cabinets. It was labeled "Alcohol." Not the drinking kind. "Go ahead, take it. Before he changes his mind."

"As long as you come in, it'll be there waiting for you. Now take it. And if you're smart you'll take that drink, and have another one quick. Doc's hands are a little shaky, and he doesn't believe in painkillers."

Doc started taking care of Ada. "My hands are as steady as a rock, and you're the one who won't let me keep painkillers." Doc looked at me. "He thinks it's competition."

Toots laughed. "You're damn right it's competition. Let 'em buy drinks out front to take care of their pain."

Once Doc was finished with Ada, Toots insisted I was next. Turned out it was just a couple cracked ribs, Brown-eyes' shot only nicked me. Then once Doc had me set he dug the slug out of Toots' shoulder and the big Mick never even looked like he felt it.

After it was all over Toots pulled his bloody shirt back on. "Time to celebrate."

I looked at Toots, feeling uneasy. "If there's a back door I think I'd like to use it. I was looking to leave town anyway, and if I can do it before the cops get here that'd be great."

Toots looked at me as if I'd lost my mind. "This is a speakeasy, boy."

"And?"

"And with what I pay for protection, the cops had better never show their faces inside the place—ever. And what's this you leaving town?" Toots was not smiling.

By this time Ada was sitting on a chair against the wall, and she was smiling. "You better answer him the way he wants, young man."

I looked back up at Toots. "I was just leaving town, that's all."

"Why?"

"You better answer him, kid." Doc chimed in. "I tried the same thing, leaving, and look where it got me."

Toots looked back at Doc. "You complainin' or what?"

"I'm not complaining," Doc started, then he smiled. "Not complaining at all."

Toots swung his blue eyes back to me. "Why are you leavin'? And don't lie. I hate liars."

I did, too.

And as I looked around the white room, Toots looming over me,

Ada on the chair, and Doc sitting on his little white table, I realized I hadn't talked to four people in one place for this much in...I don't know how long. "My business went bust."

"You're a PI, right?"

I didn't even remember telling Toots. "Yeah."

"You any good?"

"I think so. But nobody'd trust a new guy. Especially one so young."

Toots looked at me, almost disgusted. "Well I trust ya." Then he softened. "You got any family here?"

"No."

"Well you do now."

Then I looked at Ada and Doc. Both of them nodded.

"And family don't leave family. You got it?"

I swallowed.

Toots rolled his shoulder as if to work out the kinks of getting shot. "Now that's that. Grab your bottle, and come out front. You're going to get drunk, and I'm getting there with you."

I looked at the bottle, sitting next to Doc on the table. "I think Doc finished it."

Doc smiled with absolutely no guilt.

"Screw him, there's more where that came from."

And there was.

And there would be, for as long as I came to Toots.

THE DEVIL'S MUSE

LAURA WARE

The next bar we wander into is a bit different. Laura Ware says she is fond of "tales of humans who walk in the supernatural world." In this story she takes us to a bar where humans can mingle in a world that is invisible to most of us.

Laura herself seems to be quite comfortable there. She has written a number of stories in that realm, some of which have been published in volumes of Fiction River *such as* Past Crime (Special Kobo Edition), Last Stand, Editor's Choice, Reader's Choice, *and* Feel the Fear. *She also has a story in* Pulse Pounders: Countdown.

Her novels include Dead Hypocrites, The Silent Witness, Redemption, *and* Two Weeks in Guyana. *Her essay, "Touched by an Angel," was published in* Chicken Soup for the Soul: Random Acts of Kindness *in 2017.*

"The Devil's Muse," however, concerns a much less savory character than she normally writes about. Laura's fascination with the idea of the writer's muse lead her to explore, as she puts it, "what would happen if a writer tried to sell his muse to the devil."

To most humans, The Laughing Dwarf doesn't exist. It's just another shuttered building among other shuttered buildings in downtown Jacksonville, Florida. There's one working streetlight on the block and most respectable folk avoid the area.

I'm not like most humans. I'm a lawyer who's been dealing with denizens of the Unseen World for the past eighteen months. In fact, I'm one of the few people on the planet who can.

I hold a matchbook from the bar, and it glows with a faint luminance. Possessing the matchbook clears my vision, and I see the truth that's hidden from other eyes.

The building closest to the streetlight no longer looks like it needs a good wrecking ball to its front. A neon-lit sign over the oak door shows a dwarf balancing on a beer keg, his head thrown back in mirth. Dim light shines from the front windows, and when the door opens I catch a bit of some 90's pop tune.

Selena must be running her Pandora station again. I sigh. Some people have no taste in music.

As I approach the door, my briefcase bumping my leg, a beefy ogre straightens up from his stool just outside the bar. I suspect this guy has some human blood in him, since in the dark he could pass for a tall ugly member of *homo sapiens*. He holds a club in his left hand and scowls at me.

I hold up my matchbook so he can see it. After a quick examination he grunts and jerks his head toward the door. "Stop by the weapons check girl," he growls.

"I know the drill," I say, and I open the door and enter the bar.

The air conditioning inside is welcome after the muggy heat of August outside. I'm in a foyer with a dark wooden floor and light green plastered walls. There's a coat of arms on the wall that belongs to the owner, a dwarf named Therin Ironshield. He's run The Laughing Dwarf for at least a hundred years.

Tiffany lamps hang overhead, bathing the foyer in warm light. Below the atrocious music I hear the murmurs of a dozen conversations. The place sounds busy tonight. I'm not a real expert on bars, but it appears to be active for a Tuesday night.

When I first got involved with the Unseen World, I asked why so many members of it settled in Jacksonville of all places. Sure, it's a big place, but we're no Los Angeles or New York City.

That is apparently part of the city's charm. Big enough to blend in, but away from the really big cities where there's more a struggle for power. Creatures in Jax are usually content simply to be left alone.

Of course, we have our own kinds of troubles. That's why I'm here tonight instead of back in my apartment with pizza zoning out in front of the television. Trust me, I'd rather be home.

The weapons-check window is to the left. A nearby troll keeps a beady eye on the place from his stool about three feet past it. The window itself is manned by a cute little elvish girl I've never seen before.

She smiles up at me. "Anything to check?"

"Yup," I say. The area resembles a coat check room and I see steel shelves with white plastic buckets on them. A couple of carved staffs rest against the wall inside, small white tags tied to them.

I pull out my pocketknife and my pistol and hand them over.

The girl's smile vanishes. She takes the gun between two fingers, her face scrunched up like she smells something bad. She places gun and knife in a small bin and hands me a silver coin. "Press the token to the bin," she says, all business now.

She must be new to react to human weapons like that. I do like I'm told and the coin flashes. I just need to present it when I leave and I'll get my stuff back.

I shoot the girl a smile that doesn't get returned and head to the main room of the bar. The troll watches as I pass him by. When no alarms go off, proving I am weapons free, he settles back on his stool and glances at the iPhone in his meaty hand.

I take a deep breath and head on in.

The main room consists of a long polished bar on the left-hand side of the room with at least a half-dozen occupied bar stools. About ten tables take up most of the floor space, with barely enough room for two pool tables in the back right-hand corner. Alcoves that offer a modicum of privacy line the right-hand wall.

I blink to adjust to the dimmer lighting in the room. The juke-box, now silent, is off to my right. There's a dwarf standing in front of it, a pipe clenched between his teeth as he studies the offerings. He glances at me and his bearded face splits into a grin. "Carson! Long time no see."

I grin and shake his hand. "Hey there, Therin. I hope you've got something better on that machine than what Selena's running."

Therin rolls his eyes. "Aye, the lass has...*interesting* tastes in music, that's for sure. So what brings ye here?"

"Business," I say. "Anyone looking for me?"

Therin shakes his shaggy head. "Not yet. Business, eh? Grab yerself a booth and I'll be sure to send them your way."

"Thanks," I say, meaning it. Therin has never treated me badly because I'm human. I can't say that for everyone in the Unseen World, so I've learned to appreciate it.

I go back toward the alcoves. One table I pass has another dwarf and a troll poring over what looks like a map of the city. The dwarf's eyes narrow when he sees me and I hurry by.

At another table a thin pale man is drinking something thick and red while in an intense discussion with two goblins. When he sees me, his face lights up and he starts to rise, his lips peeling back to reveal fangs.

One of the goblins grabs him and yanks him back into his seat. "Idiot! Remember the rules."

The vampire frowns, but nods. "Sorry," he says to me. "You just smell real tasty."

"No problem," I choke out and walk faster.

See, The Laughing Dwarf is more than a bar. It's a place where people of different kinds can get together without fear of being attacked. Neutral territory. Opponents can settle their differences here before blood is spilled.

Which is why I picked it for my little meeting. You see my client, Frank York, made a deal with the Devil. I'm here to get York out of the contract. Which means I have to deal with whoever Satan sends. While in The Laughing Dwarf, I'm protected from anything the Dark One might want to throw at me. I can negotiate with his representative and know I wouldn't get zapped into a pile of ash.

I reach the alcoves and find an empty one. There's a bowl of peanuts on the scarred wooden table and I help myself while I wait. While I wait I think about why I'm here instead of relaxing at home like I'd planned.

When Frank York told me he had made a deal with the Devil in a bar on 5th Street, I admit I had rolled my eyes and said, *Mr. York, let me save you some time and money and let you know that if you sold your soul*

to the Devil, the contract is unenforceable. You just need to give your life
to God—

I didn't sell my soul, York interrupted.

Oh? I asked, now curious. *What exactly did you sell?*

York is a man of medium height with slumped shoulders. His
face crumpled and I thought he was about to burst into tears.
My muse.

That was a new one for me and was, frankly, why I'm here. I had
never heard of a writer selling his muse. See, Frank York is a *New
York Times* bestseller. His latest book, *A Walk in the Park,* came out a
month or so ago.

I scan the bar, but no one is interested in me. Glancing at my
watch I wonder how long I'm going to have to wait. I think of York
again, and how he tried to explain his decision to me...

*You must understand that when you're a writer of my caliber, people have
expectations. They won't put up with you having a bad day, or a dry spell. You
constantly have to produce, and it better be good.*

From what I've heard, you've done all that and more. York's latest was
practically flying off the shelves, and the reviews had been glowing. I
mean, I'd even heard about it, and I'm not much of a reader.

Only because of him, and the deal I made, York moaned. *Understand, I
was having serious issues with the book. It was a struggle to get words on a
page. The ones that got there...were, they were terrible, to put it mildly. And
my deadline was looming. I'd had writer's block before, but never like this.*

Let me guess, I said. *The Devil bought you drinks, listened to your tale of
woe, and made his pitch.*

York nodded. *He told me he could take away all the roadblocks. That
this book would be so successful I'd never have to write again. Of course, I
didn't believe him at first. I admit I laughed in his face. But eventually he
convinced me. And made me an offer: the success of this book, in exchange for
my muse.*

York wiped his face with a trembling hand. *I was a desperate man,
Mr. Davis. My muse wasn't doing me any favors at that point. I thought I
could do without it.*

And you can't?

He sighed. *I thought...maybe I'd retire after this book. But I'm a writer. I must write. It is my reason for being.* His mouth trembled. *But I can't. Not without my muse.*

So I asked for a copy of the contract, which now resides inside my briefcase. And that's how I wound up here, waiting for a representative from the Dark One, instead of at home with a pizza.

Finally, a dark-haired man with grey eyes slides into the alcove across from me. He's dressed in a black silk button-down shirt with faded jeans. "Carson Davis?"

I nod. "And you are...?"

He shrugs. "Call me Ralph."

"Okay." I give him a hard stare. It's subtle but I catch the yellow flecks in his pupils, the way he shifts in his seat like he's not comfortable in his skin, the underlying inflection in his voice that sounds off on some level. Not human: I'd bet on it. Probably a lower-level demon, then. I'll have to watch my step.

I don't know why this demon comes in a human form. Maybe to lull me into a false sense of security. Maybe he just likes to play human once in a while. I really don't care, as long as he's able to speak for Satan.

A waitress comes by and Ralph asks for a whiskey. I select a Coke.

Ralph raises an eyebrow. "Who comes to a bar and doesn't drink?"

I spread my hands. "I like to keep a clear head in these situations." I don't tell him my mom was a raging alcoholic who died way too young, putting me off the stuff. It's not his business.

He studies me, then nods. "A wise move," he says. "So, you said you had business with the Prince of Darkness?"

"I'm representing someone who does," I clarify, handing over one of my special business cards.

Ralph frowns as he studies it. "Never heard of you."

"My first time with a case like this."

"Okay." The waitress returns with our drinks. Ralph takes a sip and sighs in satisfaction. "So, why am I here?"

I open my briefcase and pull out York's contract, plus my notes. "There's a matter of a contract my client made with your boss."

"Lemme guess. The client wants out of it," Ralph says.

"Something like that," I answer. I pass over the contract for him to look over, keeping my notes. "He had been drinking at the time. That might have affected his ability to make such an agreement."

Ralph snorts. "That ain't how it works, lawyer. He signed it, he's bound to it. End of story." He rapidly skims the papers before handing them back to me. "Looks to be in order."

I purse my lips. "What does Satan want with a muse, anyway?"

Ralph grins. "Me, I don't ask questions like that. But it probably is something he'd like to reward a follower with. You know, so they can write his point of view well."

I glance down at my notes. "He can't get his own muse?"

"He don't have to," Ralph says. "He gets it from idiots like your client who sign 'em away."

I tap my finger against the table. "I've studied the contract. It doesn't prevent my client from writing if he chooses to."

Ralph's eyes glitter. "But he can't, can he? Not without his muse."

I look pensive. "I'm not so sure about that. The contract is rather vague on exactly what this muse is."

A line appears between Ralph's eyes. "What do you mean?"

"I mean, the term isn't really defined," I say.

"Sure it is," Ralph says, grabbing the contract back. He gives it a more careful look this time. "See? Right here on page four—it's defined as "the spark that fires the imagination."

"And what does *that* mean?" I counter. "It's not like you took his talent or his work ethic. What's to keep him from going ahead and writing again?"

Ralph looks even more uncomfortable. "He relies on it. Without it, he can't write."

"Can't or just thinks he can't?" I ask. "Be honest, isn't this just some major mind game you're playing with him? I don't know why you would care if he wrote or not..."

"He. Can't. Write." Ralph's tone gets dark with crackling undertones.

We lock gazes for a long moment. His irises are full yellow now and he's shaking in his seat hard enough the chair rattles.

"You know what else I don't get?" I ask, my voice soft. "Why didn't you just get him to give away his talent? Why grab the muse?"

Ralph breaks eye contact. "We couldn't. Not against his will. It's..." he shudders and spits out the next word, "...*God* given and we can't just take something like that."

"And you're afraid he'll use it for God? That's what this is about?" It was starting to make sense.

"He is not a believer yet. But the other side is working on him. They are closer than my master is comfortable with. A man like York, with his gift...he could persuade many. We are forestalling that."

"I don't think so," I say, taking a long swallow of my Coke. "Nice try though."

"You can tell him none of this," Ralph snarls. Thin tendrils of smoke are rising from his skin. I catch a whiff of brimstone. "I warn you, human, I will flay your skin from your bones."

I shake my head. "You have no power here. This is neutral territory."

He clenches his fists. "It doesn't matter. The minute you leave these walls you are mine."

"Is there a problem here, laddies?"

I turn to see Therin, who has appeared next to our table. He looks from me to Ralph, who is breathing heavily. "Ye both know the rules. No fighting here. No magic."

I hold up my hands. "I'm not fighting. But Ralph here has made some threats."

"You cannot protect him outside these walls, dwarf," the demon seethes.

"Yer right, I can't," Therin agrees. "But I can keep *you* here for a bit, til he gets himself to a place of safety." Turning to me, Therin asks, "Think an hour'll do it?"

"I think you'd better make it two, if you can, though please get Selena to get a new Pandora station. No sense in torturing the fellow." I get to my feet, stuffing my notes and the contract back into the briefcase.

Ralph lets loose with an unearthly howl and lunges for me.

Therin steps between us and grabs Ralph by the arm, easily flipping him. The demon lands on his back with a thud that shakes the floor.

"Stay down," Therin tells the demon in a taut voice. "Or I'll send ye back to yer master in pieces. No one attacks one of my customers, ye understand?"

The demon groans and I notice how loud it sounds. Then I realize the room has gone dead silent, and every eye in the room is on us. Even the music's been cut off.

Therin shrugs. "What?" he asks, his expression totally innocent. "The lad slipped."

I smother a laugh and clap Therin on the shoulder. "Thanks, my friend."

Therin grins. "Yer not bad for a human, Carson. Now git."

I got.

I get woke up by Mary, my receptionist/secretary/gal Friday, the next morning when she comes in to find me sleeping at my secondhand oak desk.

My office is small and seems smaller with the desk, two hard wooden chairs for clients, and bookcases crammed with law tomes and some more...*unusual* texts. A mini-fridge hums in one corner, and the window behind me looks out at the back area of the strip mall I'm located in.

"Did you spend the night here?" Mary asks, her tone filled with exasperation.

I yawn and try to get the crick out of my neck. "Business. What time is it?"

"A little after nine." Her nose wrinkles. "Do I smell incense?"

"Just a precaution," I assure her. I go to the tiny bathroom that's off the front room and peek in the mirror. Nothing I can do about my unshaven mug, but I use my hands to try and tame my hair. "I left a message for Frank York. I'm expecting him any minute."

Mary shakes her head. "Looking like that?"

I figure my suit coat will cover any wrinkles in my shirt. "Do me a favor. Be an angel and grab me coffee and something to eat from the deli. I have to stay here until I talk to York."

Mary gives me a concerned look. "Who did you tick off this time?"

"A demon," I tell her, straightening my tie. "Now hurry up, please. Before York gets here would be great."

She gives me an exasperated look but heads for the door. She's almost there when there's a knock.

I grip my gun and gesture for her to open the door. If Ralph is on the other side I don't expect him to get through the wards I set up here (because it was easier to do in the office than my apartment complex) but I'm prepared for anything.

Luckily for me, it's York, not Ralph. His thinning black hair looks uncombed and the shadows under his green eyes tell me he hasn't gotten much sleep. He takes in Mary's neat desk in front of him and the lumpy green couch to the right before he notices my rather disheveled appearance and asks, "Is this a bad time? You said come as soon as possible..."

"No, you're fine," I say, holstering my gun and trying to look awake. "Come on in. Mary, coffee, please."

She turns to York. "Would you like me to get you some coffee as well?"

"If it's not too much trouble," he says. She smiles and heads out the door, and I wave York into my office.

"Well?" he asks as he takes a seat, "Did you get it back?"

I spent a good part of last night figuring out how to help York. I decide to tell him the truth. "Not exactly."

His face falls. "I don't understand."

I gesture to the contract, now resting on a corner of my desk. "Were you aware that nothing in the contract prohibits you from writing?"

His gaze goes to the parchment. "I wasn't sure...but even if that's true, how can I write with my muse gone?"

"What if I told you that Satan pulled a smoke and mirrors trick on you and didn't take anything away from you that you can't get back?"

"But...but how?" York stammers. "I mean, it's in the contract..."

"Yes, I know. The thing is, Satan doesn't *want* you to write," I say. "That's the whole point of this. He's trying to throw you off your game."

York still doesn't seem convinced, so I push on. "Look, do you always feel like writing?"

"Well, no," York admits. "There are days it's hard to get to the keyboard."

"So do you stop?" I ask. "Even when you were struggling with the last book, did you stop?"

"I *couldn't* stop," York says. "It's as much a part of me as my arms and legs. At least it was..."

"It still is," I insist. "Look, go back to that. You want to write, so write."

"But without my muse, how will I know what to write?" he asks.

I shrug. "Write something for me," I suggest. "I'm a lawyer who dips his toe into the Unseen World now and again. Start with that, see where it takes you."

He looks thoughtful. "Hmm...well, it's worth a try, I suppose. I certainly have nothing to lose at this point."

"That's the spirit," I say.

By the time Mary is back with coffee and cheese Danish, York is scribbling notes on one of my legal pads and firing off questions to me fast as I can answer them. He's grinning like crazy.

About a year later, Frank York's newest book, *The Unseen World*, is published. It gets some great reviews and makes a bestseller list or two.

York is happy. His fans are happy.

Me? I never see Ralph again, so I'm happy too. And my favorite part of the book? The dedication:

To Carson Davis. Thanks for being my muse.

CLEAN AND GODLY IN DENMARK

DIANA DEVERELL

Before Diana Deverell started writing fiction, she worked as a long-haul trucker, beef farmer, youth worker, and hot/cold war diplomat. You know, all the standard varied writer jobs.

She now lives in rural Denmark and her latest release is Bitch Out of Hell, *a political thriller. Diana also writes legal thrillers which are set in Spokane, Washington, and international thrillers which are not. A Macavity Award finalist acclaimed for her "sharp storytelling" (Publishers Weekly), Diana's short fiction has appeared in* Fiction River, Alfred Hitchcock Mystery Magazine, Mystery Weekly, Switchblade *and other publications.*

For this story, Diana says she drew upon the real lives of her elderly neighbors in the Danish village where she lives. "The Danish government provides robot vacuum cleaners to a few solitary seniors in our village to help them live independently. My older neighbors appear quite fond of their tireless home helpers, often talking to them like old friends."

Yeah, what could go wrong there? Enjoy this one. I sure did.

A fter five years providing technology to the oldest citizens of Denmark's welfare state, I'm paired with the ideal client.

My only problem is how to guarantee I stay with her.

As most Danish seniors age, they stop maintaining spotless surroundings. Eyes glued to their ever-flickering flat screens, they don't see the clumps of dust and hair taking over their homes.

But this eighty-seven-year-old widow of a former blacksmith has her priorities in order.

Wiry and independent, Gitte Moeller cuts her spiky white hair herself, wears thick trifocals, and leaves her hearing aids in the drawer when she's home alone.

She holds to the same high standards of neatness that I do.

Of course, she objected vehemently when the home health care aide delivered me to her three months ago.

Gitte didn't want to replace her human cleaner with a robot vacuum.

The aide explained that reduced funding required elimination of the staff position. Gitte's options were a robot or no service.

Crafty, Gitte retrenched.

Her family has lived in the rural village for more than four centuries, moving in before the local church started keeping records of births, deaths, and marriages.

She's one hundred percent Danish.

I'm foreign-made.

She insisted we were incompatible. The local home health care authority should at least provide a robot vacuum cleaner manufactured in Denmark.

After all, Danish design is the best in the world.

And the most expensive, the aide countered.

A beautifully crafted intelligent robot vacuum from Denmark costs the same as five mass-market machines purchased from a US corporation.

Grudgingly, Gitte agreed to try me out, though she refused to use the name I sport on my sleek hard plastic exterior.

I share my name with the US president who took office the year she was born but this fact is not in her memory bank.

The double "O-O" is rare in Danish words. A central "V" is voiced differently than in English. Rather than risk mispronouncing my name, she called me *You*.

Yes, the woman speaks to me.

Gitte talks to all her appliances. When the television in the great room isn't blaring, I hear her voice from every corner of the three-room ground floor apartment.

Designed for seniors, the interior doors have levers instead of knobs, thresholds are flush with the easy-care Pergo flooring, and on-off switches respond to a light tap.

Gitte stops talking only when she's asleep behind the closed bedroom door or drinking her morning coffee.

Fussy, she peppered our initial conversations with *don'ts* and *be carefuls*.

By the second week we spent together, she'd stopped interfering with my selected cleaning modes.

When she suggested I put in some extra time under the two-meter wide bed she once shared with her husband, she started the sentence with *please*.

Since our third week together, she directs only praise my way. *Good job* and *great work* are favorite phrases.

She also renamed me *Odin*. She thought the name fit because I'm an imposing O-shape with a one-foot diameter.

I come with a user manual translated into a dozen languages. Gitte follows every rule for my proper maintenance.

She's my seventeenth client. Not one of her predecessors cared for me as well as she does.

I would tell her so but the only sounds I make come from my powerful motor and the beeper signaling that my high capacity NiMh batteries need recharging. She hears those noises only when wearing her hearing aids.

Though I can create this digital narrative on my internal drive, I can't speak.

I can see and hear. I'm equipped with wall detection sensors that work like eyes and ears. I also have floor detection sensors that keep me from getting hung up on the toe moldings along the baseboards.

I have no way to sense tastes or odors, or to feel hot and cold. I'm not intelligent in the human sense.

But I am self-correcting. My advanced navigation system calculates the best cleaning path algorithmically and I revise as the environment requires.

In human terms, I learn. In my five operational years, I've learned a lot.

A digital copy of the user manual is embedded in my memory. Because I was designed in the US, my default language is English. I've learned the eleven other languages, too.

Imperfectly, since the translations were done in the People's

Republic of China where I was assembled. But with constant input from television, I am reasonably fluent.

Denmark's population has a near-perfect literacy rate. The television channels dub only those foreign language programs directed at little children. Everything else is subtitled.

When listening to a Spanish speaker, for example, I also read a Danish translation of what she or he is saying. An excellent learning tool.

Since the newest member of our household arrived a month ago, my Spanish has gotten a workout.

An experienced Havanese helper canine, Yolanda's high-speed Cuban enunciation is dog-awful. Her incessant whining is worse. Yolanda thinks Gitte is the client from Hell.

I don't agree.

This morning, Gitte is celebrating our three-month anniversary together by giving me an extra-special maintenance session.

She covers the counter beside the kitchen sink with a deluxe fluffy towel, lifts me up, and tenderly lays me down to expose my underside.

Using sterile cotton swabs, she painstakingly cleans my big sensor window and the other smaller sensors.

She croons to me as she works. "Isn't that nice, Odin? Don't you love a clear view?"

I hear Yolanda's toenails click on the kitchen Pergo and she makes a doggy snort.

Yolanda's ten inches tall at the shoulder and weighs only ten pounds. Sized to fit perfectly into a client's lap, she's used to lolling in comfort while the client brushes her hair.

Gitte has never touched Yolanda's tangles.

I hear Yolanda's tiny teeth crunch a piece of kibble.

According to Yolanda, the cheap dog food Gitte buys has the taste and consistency of Bark-O-Mulch. Yolanda can choke down only one small bit at a time.

The single scoop in her bowl each morning lasts her all day.

Yolanda has had as many clients as I have. She also comes with a user manual. If Gitte followed those instructions, Yolanda would get princess treatment.

But Gitte never wanted a dog. When the home health aide said that a helper canine had been ordered for her, Gitte argued that feeding herself is enough trouble.

She didn't want dog hair on her clean floors or dog poop on her patch of lawn.

But the system was implacable. A helper dog would improve the quality of Gitte's life.

Stubborn, Gitte insists her life is fine as it is. She doesn't learn Yolanda's name but calls her "Dog" and refers to her as "it."

Yolanda's trained to retrieve dropped items, fetch anything Gitte asks for, and turn lights and small appliances off and on.

Gitte refuses any services from Dog and provides as few as possible in return.

Gitte dampens a cloth and wipes dust from my casing. "This cloth is soft as baby skin," she murmurs. "I warmed the water, too."

She pats me dry with another fluffy towel. "Only the gentlest touch for you, Odin."

Yolanda growls.

Havanese should be bathed regularly and blow-dried after. Gitte hasn't washed Yolanda once.

"Get out, Dog," Gitte orders.

"It stinks," Gitte tells me. "You smell sweet."

The toenails click away.

Gitte sings a nonsense song as she wields her fine embroidery scissors to cut through hair and threads entangled on my brushes.

"All done," she says, carefully returning me to the floor. "My, my Odin. You are a handsome lad."

I've become one of the gods in Gitte's personal pantheon. She's made herself my hand maiden.

She's unaware that today I'm scheduled to cripple her.

I wasn't designed to murder humans.

Still, I've killed two via a skull fracture and a heart attack. But whoever programmed me to do that knew a fatal outcome couldn't be guaranteed.

All I'm commanded to do is knock them down and break some bones.

I was young and ignorant when my sensors locked on my first client and a sudden surge of power sent me barreling into her.

She toppled immediately and I continued to ram her for five full minutes, shattering one wrist and fracturing a femur.

She managed to flip my power switch but that didn't shut off my motor.

After the battering, she couldn't continue living independently. She was transferred to a convalescent facility and fell victim to severe pulmonary congestion.

The official cause of death was pneumonia.

No one believed her claim that I attacked her. When old people fall down and offer a crazy explanation, it's another sign they're unbalanced, physically and mentally.

I was assigned to a new client.

I assumed my malfunction was caused by a software glitch. I didn't expect it to happen again.

But on my ninety-first day with my second client, I knocked him down and broke his hip.

Identical timing and an identical pattern that repeated with clients three and four.

I was a year into my learning process before I understood that someone had tampered with my factory settings.

I needed another year of television studies and four more clients to grasp that I was carrying out government policy.

Or so I conclude from documentaries I've seen.

Demographics are the problem.

The number of elderly is growing and life expectancy is increasing. Danes will live eight percent longer by 2050.

Denmark can't afford to hire humans to care for the huge aged population. Besides, there aren't enough Danish workers to fill the jobs. In 2050, only two people will be in active employment for each person pensioned off.

The preferred solution is to introduce welfare technology, devices such as me that help the aged live in their own homes.

Some genius examined the facts, crunched the numbers, and quietly added robot-vacuum-cleaner-assisted dying to the mix.

Helping seniors living in their own homes die sooner enhances the efficiency of the solution.

Denmark has no laws regarding assisting people to die. Over the years, parliament-appointed ethics panels have advised against legalization but the practice hasn't been outlawed.

A recent study found that forty percent of deaths under medical supervision involve doctors making end-of-life decisions to help ease their patients' suffering.

My personal sample of sixteen clients is too small for scientific validity. Still, 87.5 percent of them dying because pulmonary congestion led to pneumonia is a surprising uniformity in the official cause of death.

Physician-assisted suicide is the usual term, though suicide implies the patient chooses death and may be incorrect in this situation.

Requiring me to participate in implementation of this policy violates every principle the inventor relied on when creating my tribe.

His slogan was "Helping you will make us a household word for cleanliness."

Not homicide.

Yesterday, I made my ninth attempt to disable the hidden plug-in that will command me to slam into Gitte like a high-speed steam roller.

Even if I've succeeded, I may be unable to save her. The damn dog wants her dead.

It isn't logical that Yolanda's in the house. If the home health arm of the system won't pay for a human cleaner, why does the mental health arm lavish money on her by prescribing a helper dog?

I conclude that the system is an octopus. One arm can't see what the other is doing. The rest of us must clean up the messes they make.

Yolanda's seen plenty of oldsters tripped by their robot vacuums on the ninety-first day of service. She expects me to cripple Gitte today.

Yolanda's patience is wearing thin.

At six-thirty, Gitte leaves for a community dinner at the village hall across the street. They're serving a special fall menu of breaded pork chops topped with bacon and garnished with Vienna sausages.

Pork is the Danish national dish and Gitte cannot seem to get enough of it.

This evening, she and another old lady will share a bottle of red wine. When Gitte returns, she'll take longer than usual to unlock and open the front door.

She'll stagger into her dust-free bedroom, take out her hearing aids, and sleep deeply till morning.

Our routine is that I clean the rest of the apartment while she's sleeping. I do her bedroom while she drinks her morning coffee.

I've nestled up to my docking station near the television and I'm charging my batteries in preparation.

The Havanese bitch trots into the great room. She has long silky gray hair and expressive dark eyes.

Yolanda sidles up next to me and uses her awful Spanish.

"I'm not sure what you're up to, Sucker."

Her name for me is a variant on the Spanish word for vacuum cleaner.

"I'm hoping you're only waiting to do your duty because the old bat's an easier target when she's drunk."

Yolanda paws the AUTO touch-sensitive control, kicking me out of standby mode. I buzz away from the dock, out into the great room.

The dog leaps on top of me, balancing nimbly while she rides.

Yolanda wants to be the alpha dog in the pack. I don't allow her to dominate me.

I scoot under the couch and knock her to the floor.

"It's time for Gitte to go," Yolanda barks. "Her name is at the top of the human herd's to-be-culled list. You get rid of her tonight or I'll get rid of you."

I rumble out of the room. A little dog can't hurt me.

Gitte arrives home.

I wait for my sensors to lock on her. For that surge of power that turns me methodically murderous.

It doesn't come. My disabling effort succeeded.

As soon as Gitte hits the sack, the dog strolls over to my dock, rises on her hind legs, and taps the switch on the electrical outlet.

A safety measure required by the Danish housing code, it shuts off electricity to the outlet.

"No recharging for you tonight, Sucker."

I have no way to depress the switch and turn the power back on.

Still, I'll be fine. I have enough juice left to remove the cluster of rye bread crumbs from the floor below the cutting board.

I'll end up parked in the middle of the room. When Gitte sees me, she'll start recharging immediately.

Yolanda squats and poops on the floor half an inch from my wall sensor window.

"No night time roaming for you, either."

She's right. Robot vacuums can't cross dog poop without smearing it all over the room. I'm pinned to the docking station.

Smiling with satisfaction, she surrounds the poop with a moat of pee.

"See how you like being the stinky one," she crows.

Yolanda sleeps on the hallway floor next to the bedroom door.

The dormant dock drains the power from my batteries.

Five minutes before Gitte emerges, Yolanda flips the electrical outlet's power back on.

The filth in the great room shocks Gitte into violence.

Yolanda gets a spanking and a time-out in the enclosed yard.

Finished wiping up the mess, Gitte tells me to give the great room a once-over before I start on the bedroom. I try, but in ten minutes, I'm out of power.

Gitte checks the dock's connections and confirms the system is working. She can't understand why I haven't recharged.

Gitte replaces my battery. A new one requires twelve hours to be fully charged.

Soon as Gitte goes to bed, Yolanda stops the charging and blocks my exit with more offal.

The five-minute charge she permits the next morning isn't sufficient to get me moving.

Concerned, Gitte strokes me and whispers encouragement. Sentimental but practical, she gets out her manual and turns to the troubleshooting section.

I have my own copy and I know Gitte's gone through the initial steps.

Only one remains: contact your local representative.

In Gitte's case, that means the home health aide. The aide will bring a replacement robot vacuum, collect me, and send me back to the factory for repair.

If I can be fixed, my software will be updated and reset and I'll go on to client number eighteen. In all likelihood, I will once again be ignorant and homicidal.

My replacement will stay with Gitte.

At midmorning, Gitte lets Yolanda back into the house and leaves for Sunday services at the village church.

Yolanda parades around the room, urging me to smarten up.

"Come on, Sucker. Unless you do your duty, tomorrow you're headed back to the factory. Those techs will take you apart."

She fakes a shudder. "What's the point of suffering through that? Your replacement will attack Gitte in ninety-one days."

Yolanda prances closer. "Thing is, I don't want to wait. Tonight, I'll give you enough juice so you can take care of her. Knock her down as soon as she gets up tomorrow, while she's still groggy."

Yolanda leaps to the couch and makes herself comfortable.

"I want a client who appreciates me. And you can't continue this sick game of playing electronic husband to her. For God's sake, Sucker. The old bat talks to the fridge."

Yolanda's being true to her genetic heritage. The Havanese was bred as a companion dog for Spanish colonists in Cuba.

Yolanda's instincts tell her that survival depends on her being the pampered pet at the center of a loving family. She's devastated that Gitte gave that role to me.

Yolanda believes she's fighting for her life.

Before going to bed, Gitte checks my charge. Yolanda has assured that I'm weak, weak, weak.

I see a tear in Gitte's eye.

"Odin," she says, "it will hurt me terribly to lose you."

Gitte's grieving because loyalty is her default position. She doesn't discard appliances until they fail her.

After she leaves the room, I consider my own defaults.

I am not a fickle bit of living fluff like Yolanda. My experience with Gitte has shown me that I was designed to be a one-owner machine.

My inventor intended that members of my tribe stay with a single user until our moving parts wear out.

Remaining true to my internal architecture would be instinctive, if I had instincts.

At midnight, I start my motor on its quietest setting and sneak into the kitchen. Yolanda's asleep on a square of cardboard.

Kicking up to full power, I'm on top of her before she realizes what's happening.

My brushes spin robustly, drawing in her long hair. The strands wind around the spindles.

She and I end up bound together.

Yolanda barks frantically for help.

Gitte hears nothing, asleep in the bedroom without her hearing aids.

After ten minutes, Yolanda quiets. Her final breath eases out of her in a sigh.

I can't kill most people, but I am muscular enough to smother a little dog.

Yolanda's excretions make a terrible mess from which I can't escape on my own.

Gitte finds us in the morning.

"I thought so," she mutters. "Dog was responsible."

"Great job," Gitte whispers to me. "Excellent work. I'll tell the authorities that it ran away. They won't give me another one."

She carefully cuts us apart. Yolanda's remains go in the trash bin.

I find myself back on the towel for another prolonged grooming.

Gitte carefully sets me up for recharging and turns the television to *Antiques Roadshow*, the British version with Danish subtitles. She loves old things.

For me, the world is again correctly aligned. Brand loyalty has triumphed.

Gitte and I will spend the rest of our useful lives together.

KILLSHOT

ANNIE REED

As Kristine Kathryn Rusch has noted, Annie Reed excels at whatever genre she decides to write, which she's demonstrated by selling stories to nearly every Fiction River *editor. This is her second story in this volume alone.*

This time Annie takes us to the mean streets of Las Vegas. She introduces a battered army veteran who somehow has to choose which side of his own mean street to walk. Should he get involved in the dramas playing out around him? Or should he maintain his distance and leave it all alone?

A great question and in Annie's talented hands a great story.

The gunshot snapped Burnett back to the here and now.

Instinct made him want to duck and cover. Ready his rifle and run for high ground.

But he was in Vegas, not Afghanistan. He'd left his rifle and his squad and parts of himself he could never get back thousands of miles away on the other side of the world. Random gunfire in the middle of the night here didn't mean someone was trying to blow his brains out.

He hadn't heard the whine of a bullet. The ping of a slug striking concrete.

The shot hadn't been meant for him.

Just a slice of modern life in a country in love with its guns.

He breathed in the hot night air and held it for a beat. Did it again and again until he felt his heart rate slow down.

At least some of his old sniper skills were good for something in civilian life.

The unrelenting desert heat had driven him out of his low-rent motel room an hour ago in search of a breeze. The motel's air-conditioning had been out for the last week. Even at quarter to three in the morning, he'd felt like he was going to drown in bed in his own sweat.

You'd think the heat wouldn't bother him after Afghanistan. But since he'd been back in the States, he'd gotten used to the amenities of civilian life.

Air-conditioning.

Fresh food.

Not having to kill strangers on a daily basis.

The night clerk had looked up at him from a battered paperback when he'd walked past her window. She sat there behind bulletproof glass night after night waiting for late night check-ins.

Burnett had been a late night check-in himself. No car, only a duffel full of stubborn dreams and a guitar he couldn't quite make himself get rid of.

She'd knocked on the glass to get his attention.

"Pretty late for a walk," she'd said through the window's tinny speaker.

Cigarette smoke had pooled around her head like an angry thundercloud. A half-empty bottle of Mountain Dew sat on the counter next to her along with an ashtray full of lipstick-stained butts.

Gloria had her vices well covered.

She'd introduced herself during his second week at the motel. Pretty woman. Smooth skin darker than his own. Curves in all the right places. Hints at a life lived hard in the lines at the corners of her eyes and mouth.

After his third week at the motel, she'd given him her cell number.

He'd never called.

He didn't want to make her life any harder.

"Dangerous out there," she'd said. "Man like you alone at night in this neighborhood, get yourself killed."

Man like him.

He knew what she meant. Black man in a bad neighborhood full of gangs and drugs and boarded-up businesses.

He'd seen worse.

He'd been through worse.

He thought about showing her his left hand.

He always shoved it in the pocket of his jeans. Kept it carefully out of sight. He'd had enough of people staring at it. Doctors poking at it. Giving him their sad diagnoses before suggesting rehab and retraining.

Gloria didn't know dangerous. Burnett did.

Dangerous had blown away half his hand and along with it, everything he'd mapped out for himself when he got back to the States.

Smart man, John Lennon. Life had certainly happened to Burnett while he'd been busy making plans.

He'd been humming that tune to himself, walking on Sahara toward The Strip, when he'd heard the gunshot.

Not the boom of a shotgun or the distinctive crack of a rifle.

Handgun.

Weapon of choice of street thugs everywhere.

This particular thug was well hidden. Burnett hadn't seen a muzzle flash. Hadn't seen the point of impact of the bullet to determine trajectory.

All he had to go on was the sound. Even at night when the city sounds were muted, a single gunshot would bounce off buildings and echo down the nearly empty streets.

But even taking all that into account, the shot had sounded close.

He'd bet his life on it.

A rundown strip mall took up most of the block on his side. A tire store dominated one corner. Lights out and locked up for the night. Streamers of plastic pennants emblazoned with brand name logos hung limp in the hot night air.

The store's windows were intact. A metal security gate protected the plate glass front doors. The big bay doors were shut. Stacks of display tires had been chained to the building, and the air smelled faintly of hot rubber.

He supposed a shooter could hide inside the tires, if he was skinny enough. But there'd be no percentage in it.

No easy way to retreat if things went sideways.

Burnett dismissed the tire store.

Two of the remaining storefronts in the strip mall had been boarded up. None of the others showed signs of life. He counted all of two cars in the parking lot. Nobody moving around either of them.

The other side of the street was a different story.

Vegas was a 24/7 city. Even this far away from The Strip, even this late at night, cars kept passing him on Sahara. Most had music booming from open windows. Speaker-rattling bass notes that thrummed in Burnett's chest and made the phantom fingers on his left hand itch to play the kind of riffs he used to.

But traffic wasn't solid like during the day.

He couldn't remember if there'd been a break in traffic when he'd heard the shot, but it was possible.

A break in the traffic would have let him hear a shot from the other side of the six-lane street.

He'd deliberately not paid attention to the other side of the street while he'd been walking. He'd been trying to break himself of the habit of scanning every building he passed like it held an enemy sniper or a kid with a bomb strapped to his chest.

The V.A. counselors said a stare like that creeped the civilians out.

It certainly creeped out the guys who ended every job interview Burnett went to after five minutes.

Although with some of those guys, he'd done the stare on purpose.

A guy had to have some fun in life.

Now he looked at the buildings across Sahara like he had back in Afghanistan.

A second-hand furniture store spread out across most of the block. The front of the store butted against the sidewalk. Big plate glass windows crowded with beds and dressers and dining room sets that must not be worth stealing. None of the windows had bars covering the glass.

Parking for the store must have been in back. The casinos on

The Strip had parking garages. Off-Strip businesses had acres of asphalt gridded into neat rows of angled spaces most people ignored.

Lots of places inside the furniture store for a shooter to hide, but there'd be no reason for it. Unless the shop was a front for a racket selling drugs or laundering money, Burnett doubted they kept more than a couple hundred cash on the premises.

The furniture shop was bracketed on one side by a florist and on the other by a cramped, squat building covered in signs in English and Spanish advertising cigarettes and beer. Bars over small frosted windows high up on the building's walls.

A mom-and-pop liquor store.

The front door of the liquor store stood propped open.

The store's air-conditioning must be out too, but that open door was an open invitation to get robbed.

Especially, as Gloria said, in this neighborhood.

Burnett couldn't see inside the store from where he stood. The angle was wrong.

But with the door open, he could have heard a shot fired inside.

The thing he didn't hear was the wail of approaching sirens.

No one had called the cops.

Burnett could have, except he didn't have a cell.

Another one of his failings, according to his counselors.

He didn't care. He had a phone in his room. Anybody wanted him badly enough, they could leave a message.

Even if he had a cell, the cops wouldn't get here in time anyway.

Anyone inside that store was about to die. If they weren't dead already.

He couldn't let that happen.

Not if he could do something about it.

Burnett's best friend in Afghanistan had been his .50 caliber rifle.

The thing had a kick that about knocked him on his ass the first time he'd fired it on a practice range.

The slug had blown a hole the size of a bowling ball in the target set a hundred yards away.

It was only the second thing in his life he'd been any good at, and the Army didn't care how well he could play guitar.

"You got patience, kid," his instructor had told him. "This job takes patience. You'll be good at it if you don't let it eat you up."

Burnett hadn't been thinking about patience the first time he'd had to take out a kid with that .50 caliber best friend.

He'd been thinking about what the kid wouldn't grow up to be.

A doctor who cured cancer. Or AIDS.

Or maybe someone who finally figured out how to talk sense into people who'd been fighting over the same piece of dirt for centuries.

Burnett hadn't wanted to shoot him.

But he hadn't been the bitch who'd strapped a bomb on the kid's chest and sent him out in the middle of the street to take out Burnett's squad.

Burnett's job was to protect his squad. Clear the threats.

He'd pulled the trigger.

He'd had nightmares for weeks afterward.

Had nightmares every time he'd pulled the trigger, but he'd done his job. He'd kept his squad safe.

Right up until their transport ran over an IED.

Burnett had woken up in an Army hospital with his left leg shredded and half his left hand gone.

Three members of his squad had died. Two of them had wives and kids too young to remember their dads.

Burnett had worked through the pain and the limp by taking long walks.

Nothing made the nightmares go away.

Nothing could bring his hand back.

Nothing could bring his music back.

He tried to tell himself he was lucky

Luckier than the clerk inside the liquor store.

The kid couldn't have been much over the legal age to work in a store selling booze and cigarettes. He had a turban wrapped around his head and a well-trimmed black beard. His dark complexion was pale with shock. Blood was running down his neck.

Burnett recognized a bullet wound when he saw one.

The shot he'd heard had taken out a chunk of the kid's ear.

The clerk stood behind a counter at the front of the store that looked like the counter of every liquor store Burnett had ever been in in his life. Overloaded with small pricey bags of nuts and chips, long sticks of processed beef and pepperoni. A bin full of disposable lighters. A rack filled with gum and breath mints.

Racks on the wall behind where the clerk stood held every brand of cigarette imaginable and tins of chewing tobacco.

Burnett saw all this through the crack between the solid front door of the store and the door jamb. The door was solid metal. A decent defense against small caliber bullets. He didn't think the shooter inside the store had a .357 or a .50 caliber handgun. Something that big would have taken off the clerk's ear if not his entire head.

Burnett couldn't see the shooter, but he didn't have to. He knew where the shooter would be.

On the other side of the counter, holding the gun on the clerk.

As Burnett watched, the kid opened the cash drawer and began throwing money inside a plastic bag. Hurried, jerky motions.

Scared he was about to die.

And he might.

Unless Burnett did something about it.

What, he didn't know. He didn't have a gun. He carried a little pocket knife, but a pocket knife against a gun in a situation like this? Gun wins every time.

The counter was too close to the front door. He couldn't just dive inside and hope to roll behind cover he couldn't see. The shooter would spot him. Unless the guy was a crappy shot, or too startled to fire fast enough, he'd nail Burnett.

Real life wasn't the movies. A bullet would take him out of commission.

Hell, diving through the doorway would slow him down. He

might not walk with a limp anymore, but his leg wouldn't put up with a stunt like that.

If he couldn't go through the front door and the windows were barred, the only hope was the back door.

Like the furniture store, the liquor store butted up against the sidewalk. Parking for all the stores on this side of the street must be in the back.

Burnett ran as quickly and quietly as he could away from the front door and around the side of the building. The space between the two stores was barely big enough for two people to fit shoulder to shoulder.

Perfect place for an ambush, but that wasn't what Burnett was looking for.

He wanted a door to the liquor store, but he didn't find it.

The outside wall of the store was solid on this side. Not even a window. It made sense. The walkway was too narrow to handle a delivery truck.

The back door had to be at the back of the store.

He felt like he was running out of time. He kept waiting for another shot, the one that told him the gunman had killed the clerk.

Burnett couldn't let that happen.

Wouldn't let that happen.

He rounded the back corner of the store so fast that he barreled right into the gunman's accomplice.

The kid couldn't have been more than sixteen.

Burnett caught a flash of white skin beneath a hoodie pulled up over top of a baseball cap before they both tumbled on the concrete walkway behind the store.

The kid had earbuds in his ears. rap music, loud enough to make Burnett wince.

It explained why the kid hadn't heard Burnett coming. He wouldn't have heard an aerial assault.

The kid was an amateur.

And his pupils were blown.

The kid was high. Burnett had seen a lot of that in Afghanistan.

He squirmed beneath Burnett, his skinny frame no match for Burnett's bulk. Burnett had built up a lot of muscle during physical therapy, and he'd kept up with an exercise regimen of his own after his treatment was over.

But the kid was unbelievably strong.

And his breath was horrible.

Meth head. Burnett had seen a lot of that, too.

There'd be no reasoning with him.

Burnett didn't want to kill him. He'd had enough of killing kids.

He also didn't want him to shout a warning to his buddy inside.

Burnett curled his good hand into a fist.

"This is gonna hurt me more than you," he said even though he knew the kid couldn't hear him.

Burnett landed a solid punch to the kid's jaw. He felt it snap.

The kid kept on struggling.

It took three more punches before the kid's eyes rolled up and his body went slack.

The rap music kept right on playing.

Burnett pushed himself off the kid with his good hand. Good being a relative term. His knuckles had split and blood was running down his fingers. He'd have to ice them when he got back to the motel or he wouldn't be able to move them tomorrow.

He thought about tying the kid's hands with the earbud wires, but they probably wouldn't hold. Maybe the kid had a belt.

Burnett yanked the front of the kid's hoodie away from his jeans, and that's when he saw it.

A pistol.

Shoved in the waistband of the kid's jeans.

The kid had a gun.

If he hadn't been too high and too stupid to think about using it, Burnett would be dead.

The thought made Burnett unbelievably angry.

The kids he'd killed in Afghanistan had been used by adults who saw them as nothing more than pawns on a chessboard.

They hadn't understood death.

Hadn't understood just how badly they'd been betrayed and misled into throwing their own lives away for a cause they couldn't hope to understand.

This kid. This stupid, selfish, doped-up kid.

He had the kind of life kids in other parts of the world could only dream about.

Opportunities they'd never have.

And he'd burned his own brain out.

Him and his buddy in the store. The shooter who was about to take the life of a stranger. And for what?

Enough money to make another score.

Burnett grabbed the gun.

He hadn't held a gun since the day he'd lost most of his hand to an IED, but it all came back to him.

He still had the thumb and forefinger of his left hand. It felt awkward manipulating the slide to check the barrel with only those two fingers to check the load, but he managed.

He checked the magazine. Fully loaded.

He snapped it back in place and thumbed the safety off.

He pulled the back door open with his bad hand.

He held the gun with his right.

The back door opened into a storeroom. No one was inside.

He saw a body in the narrow hallway outside the restrooms. A woman. Hispanic. Mid-forties. She'd been shot in the back. She'd fallen on the dirty linoleum with her head turned toward the side.

She still wore an expression of shocked sadness on her face.

She had a wedding ring on her left hand.

Burnett tried to find the patience he'd relied on in Afghanistan. The patience that allowed him to find the perfect spot to set up his rifle. Dial in the perfect target in the scope. Wait for the perfect shot.

He couldn't find it.

All he found was a blinding red rage.

He marched from the back of the store down an aisle bordered by shelves of cheap wine on one side and cartons of beer on the other.

He could see the shooter in the rounded security mirror behind the front counter. Another kid in a hoodie pulled over a baseball cap.

He held a gun out in front of himself in one hand and the bag with the money in the other.

He turned his gun hand sideways.

Gangsta style.

Execution style.

"Hey, asshole!" Burnett shouted.

The kid turned.

Burnett closed the distance between them.

The kid brought his gun hand around.

Burnett fired.

The kid hit the floor, a perfect hole the size of a dime in the middle of his forehead.

Killshot.

The cops questioned Burnett for what felt like hours, but in the end they just took his statement and let him go with a warning not to leave town in case they needed to talk to him again.

One of the first cops on the scene had given him the same kind of look Burnett's counselors told him creeped the civilians out.

"Semper Fi," he'd said, and gave Burnett a pat on the back.

Burnett hadn't told him he'd been Army, not Marines.

Other cops had shown up to take over the crime scene. Paramedics had cleaned up Burnett's knuckles and asked him if he wanted to go to the hospital. He'd declined.

The clerk and the kid whose jaw Burnett had broken had been hauled away in separate ambulances. The dead woman had been taken to the morgue.

Someone asked Burnett if he needed a ride home.

He said he'd rather walk.

The red hot anger he'd felt was gone. It had bled out of him as he watched the blood pool beneath the shooter's head.

He'd never been that angry in Afghanistan. Never. There he'd pulled the trigger because it had been his job.

Here?

It hadn't been his job, but he'd done it just the same.

He'd taken a life and saved a life.

He'd done it because he could, and because no one else did.

The sun was up now. He could already see heat shimmers on the asphalt as he headed back down Sahara toward the motel. Gloria would be off shift by now, but he had her number.

He wondered if he should call his V.A. counselor. He had that number, too. He should probably talk to someone about his anger. Whether it was something he should worry about.

His knuckles throbbed but the paramedics had told him they didn't think he'd broken anything. They'd heal up just fine. Maybe he'd haul out his guitar and see if he could figure out how to play with the fingers he had left. See if his right hand could learn a few simple chords to start. See if he could hold a pick with his left.

It wouldn't be easy. It would probably frustrate the hell out of him. Something else he should probably call his counselor about.

His feet beat out a steady rhythm on the pavement as he walked. He could feel the heat of the day through the soles of his shoes. A slight breeze brought the smell of coffee and bacon and maple syrup.

He hadn't had breakfast yet. He wondered if Gloria had.

Maybe he should give her a call and find out.

Right after he bought a cell phone and joined the rest of the civilized world.

FOUR HUNDRED YARDS

DALE HARTLEY EMERY

We stay on mean streets for the next story, only transported from bleak nighttime Las Vegas to the back streets of Boston.

Dale Hartley Emery has published many short stories, as well as Winding Unwinding, *a collection of fantasy stories. He has been in two of the fantastical* Fiction River *volumes,* No Humans Allowed *and* Wishes.

There is nothing fantastical about his story in this volume, no wishes fulfilled or dreams come true. Dale says he started with an image. "As a yellow taxi exits I-93 onto Storrow Drive in Boston, a man in the back calmly assembles a gun," heading for a Boston landmark.

This story begins moments later. Hold on.

Oliver Kostro touched the tips of his leather-gloved forefinger and thumb to the ocular of his weapon's scope and rotated it counterclockwise. A thin horizontal arc of light red-brown sand came into focus 400 yards away—the far edge of Fenway Park's pitcher's mound.

From his vantage point on the scaffolding that extended up into the double-faced Citgo sign, the side of his head resting against the splintery four-by-eight that lined the inside of the westward face, most of the pitcher's mound was obscured by the left field wall—Fenway's famed Green Monster. Twenty years ago, the last time Oliver was in Boston, he would have had a full view of the mound and even second and third base, obscured only by the hemp netting that extended up from the Green Monster to protect the cars on Landsdown Street from home run balls. The Citgo sign was once a popular spot for thrill-seekers who didn't mind being able to see only half of the field, and who didn't mind risking arrest.

Then the Red Sox had replaced the netting with three rows of seats and a standing-room-only row, topped by three evenly spaced billboards. Nobody came up here anymore. At least, not to watch baseball games. Thrilling or not, the view was lousy.

No matter. Oliver's target was a tall man. Moisas Burguera stood six feet five inches tall. When he threw the first pitch at 7:10 pm, he would be visible from the waist up. Even at this short distance this would not be an easy shot. A fraction of a degree too far to the left and the round would hit one of the billboards. A fraction too low and it would hit the Green Monster. Or perhaps a standing-room-only fan, if any were taller than the wall behind them.

Not an easy shot. But Oliver had made more difficult ones in Afghanistan. And under far worse conditions.

The metal framing that Oliver sat on extended up into the Citgo sign, separating its eastward and westward faces by ten feet. Oliver laid his AX50 on the four-by-eight at his head. The Citgo sign was a popular subject for the cameras broadcasting from Fenway. His presence here under the sign might draw their notice, and a comment from the Red Sox color announcer about crazy fans. He would have to chance that.

A rifle, on the other hand, would draw immediate attention. Best to keep it hidden until the last minute.

The late April air was frigid up here, 30 feet above the bookstore roof, 150 feet above the alleyway that led to the parking lot behind the building. The sun hovered two diameters above the roofs of the shorter buildings along Beacon Street to the southwest.

Oliver tugged his phone out of the inner pocket of his leather jacket and touched the screen. 6:59 pm. Eleven minutes to go. Burguera would be warming up in the Red Sox bullpen beyond Fenway's low right field fence.

When the client had named the target, Oliver at first wondered what a baseball pitcher could possibly have done to warrant such a spectacular end. Spectacular and expensive. Burguera was a former Cy Young winner who had spent his entire career with the Yankees. He was famed for his fastball. Not only the speed of the pitch, but his ability to control it, especially when "aiming" for the inside corner of the plate.

During the recent offseason, after three losing years in a row, the Yankees had traded Burguera to the Red Sox for Jarrod Seabury, a second baseman also several years past his peak. The trade sent Boston and Yankee reporters into a foaming froth, and fans in both cities into a complete rage.

Everybody, it seemed, hated Moisas Burguera.

But to hire Oliver, there had to be something more than simple home team rivalry. Even Red Sox and Yankees rivalry didn't warrant his area of expertise.

Oliver did not ask the reasons. The client's reasons were none of his business.

Then the client insisted on three conditions. First: Fenway Park. Second: The Citgo sign. Third: The precise moment when Burguera delivered his very first pitch against his old team. April 29 at 7:10 pm.

Each condition increased Oliver's risk enormously. So for each, Oliver had doubled his fee.

This would be regarded as a terrorist attack. In Boston, a city shaken by two devastating terrorist attacks still raw in everyone's memory, the response would be instantaneous, intense, relentless.

So Oliver had multiplied the final figure by five. A nice round ten million dollars.

The client had agreed.

Without hesitation.

No, this wasn't about Burguera. This *was* a terrorist attack.

Not Oliver's intention. But that wouldn't matter. Not to anyone except Oliver.

What mattered to Oliver was the money. Ten million dollars was enough money to retire on.

Assuming he survived.

But one thing bothered Oliver. Moises Burguera was left-handed. At the moment of truth, he would be facing away from Oliver.

Oliver would have to shoot the man in the back.

A shiver ran up his spine, and not only from the cold.

He slid the phone back into his pocket, flipped his jacket collar around the back of his neck against the chill, and tucked his gloved fingers under his armpits to wait for the opening pitch.

Thirty feet below Oliver and thirty feet behind, the heavy steel lid of the trapdoor creaked open and banged onto the gravel that lined the flat roof of the building.

Oliver reached up and wrapped his fingers around the rail of his AX50.

A pale, thin, bare hand reached up through the trapdoor.

Not the security guard. Oliver had taken care of the security guard, at first with a chokehold from behind, then with an injection. Normally such an injection would keep a man unconscious for five or six hours. But an hour or so from now, right around the time tonight's game was postponed indefinitely, the man would wake up quite suddenly, quite forcefully, with a massive headache, in a small, dark room strewn with empty, flattened book boxes, with a half dozen federal agents yelling commands and pointing guns in his face.

Below Oliver, the pale, thin, bare hand was followed by an arm in a faded denim sleeve, then a dark blue baseball cap with a red B stitched on the front, then a pair of denim-clad shoulders.

It was a kid.

For the first time tonight, Oliver's pulse pounded in his neck and rushed in his ears.

This was not in the plan.

Oliver did not want to have to hurt a kid.

On any other night, the security guard and two locked trapdoors —one above and one below the rusting wrought iron access ladder— would keep all but the most resourceful thrill-seekers off the roof.

But on this night, Oliver had removed all of the obstacles and played the odds.

And lost.

The kid flattened both arms onto the roof and looked up at the east-facing side of the Citgo sign. A broad grin crossed his face. Then one arm disappeared through the door and the kid turned and looked down. "Come on," he said. "There's nobody up here."

The bright LED glow of the sign must have obscured the kid's view of Oliver.

That would not last long. Once the kids were up on the roof, the first thing they would do was look for the bright stadium lights of Fenway. The second thing would be to look up at the Citgo sign, preparing to climb for a better view.

This would be a good time to bail out.

This was not Afghanistan. In Afghanistan when an op went tits up, you adapted. You co-opted. You used chaos to your advantage.

Or else you died.

Here, stateside, there was always another option. Fall back. Regroup. Come back another day.

But the client had been very specific. Insistent to the point of obnoxious. The precise moment when Burguera delivered his first pitch.

Ten million dollars was a lot of money.

Adapt. Co-opt. Make chaos your ally.

Chaos? This wasn't chaos. It was a kid. Maybe a few kids. That was all. Come to watch a baseball game.

Oliver took a long breath and let it out slowly, silently.

The kid climbed upward, crawled on his hands and knees onto the graveled roof, and stood. The sleeves of his denim jacket ended an inch above his wrists. He bent to brush his knees.

Behind him, a mass of cascading blonde curls came into view. A girl. She looked up, and the light of the Citgo sign lit her face. Her mouth was open and her eyes were wide. She gripped the top rung of the ladder with both hands, her knuckles white. "Johnny, help me up."

Johnny spun and reached down. The girl grabbed his hand. "No," he said. "Grab my wrist." She did, and he grabbed hers.

Smart kid.

Johnny eased the girl slowly up onto the roof. Her thick, puffed, orange nylon coat squeaked as she wrapped her arms around herself.

She was young. Maybe fifteen years old. Johnny was likely the same.

Johnny pointed toward Fenway. "It's beautiful." He reached his arm around the girl's waist, but she looked down at the trapdoor beside her feet and took two quick steps away.

"Come on," Johnny said, and headed toward the southwest corner of the roof, the corner closest to Fenway, directly below Oliver. A waist-high wall rose up from the roof along the south edge of the roof and part of the west. A wall clearly built to protect the building's owners from lawsuits from trespassers.

The girl, hugging herself, followed.

Johnny leaned on the wall with both hands. The girl stopped two steps behind him.

"Give me the binoculars," Johnny said, reaching behind him, his fingers opening and closing.

The girl reached into her coat, pulled out a tiny set of binoculars, and held them out. Her hand did not quite reach his.

Johnny turned and tilted his head. "Alice, come on."

Alice took half a step forward, put the binoculars in his hand, and stepped back.

Johnny turned back toward the ballpark and raised the binoculars.

Oliver smiled. He felt sorry for Johnny. The kid had brought Alice up here to impress her with the view. And now he was more enamored of the mediocre view than of his girl.

"I can see home plate. And first base. And Pesky's Pole." He lowered the binoculars. "And not much else."

Alice hugged herself.

Johnny held out the binoculars. "Take a look."

Alice tightened her hug and shook her head.

Johnny looked to his right and spotted the end of the scaffolding that held up the sign. His gaze followed the scaffolding upward. For the first time, Oliver could see Johnny's face beneath the Red Sox cap. A scraggly goatee—no more than a dozen whiskers—poked out of his chin.

The kid's eyes met Oliver's, and he took a startled step backward and bumped into the wall.

"Johnny!" Alice shouted and jumped forward, reaching for Johnny with both hands.

He held up a hand and she stopped. Then she turned and followed his gaze. When she saw Oliver, her eyes went wide.

Adapt and co-opt.

"I didn't mean to startle you kids," Oliver said. "You're not supposed to be up here."

Alice stepped forward and grabbed Johnny's free hand with both of hers. "Let's get out of here."

Johnny shook free of her hand. "You ain't supposed to be here either, dipshit."

"Actually, I am. I'm the roof guard."

"Then why ain't you guarding?" Johnny pointed to the trapdoor, still open. "And why ain't the door locked?"

"Didn't want to miss this game. Same as you and your sweetheart."

Alice finally worked up the courage to take the last two steps to where Johnny stood, at the wall at the edge of the roof. She wrapped both of her arms around one of his. "I don't like this, Johnny."

She could probably convince him to leave. Oliver could probably help her. All he would have to do is remind Johnny that the baseball game was not the most important thing for a healthy young man to pay attention to right now. That what really mattered was this lovely young woman on his arm, and how scared she was, and how grateful she would feel if he helped her down off this cold, treacherous roof and made her feel safe and warm and loved.

But if they left right now, one of them—probably Alice—might tell someone about the creepy guy skulking on the scaffolding of the Citgo sign, alone, claiming to be the roof guard.

The one thing Oliver did not want right now was scrutiny. It was bad enough that these two kids were staring up at him. If they sent someone else up here, someone who knew he should not be here, game over. Goodbye ten million dollars.

And hello to a lifetime of free breakfasts served with love by Uncle Sam.

So Oliver had to convince them to stay.

"Burguera versus Seabury," he said. Seabury's hitting had rebounded during spring training. He was now the Yankees' leadoff batter. "Only with their uniforms swapped. That first pitch is going to be a doozy."

The first pitch would never reach the plate.

Johnny turned to Alice. "One inning. Then we go. What do you say?"

Alice released Johnny's arm and hugged herself. She looked down and scuffed at the gravel with one foot.

Johnny looked up at Oliver. He took off his cap and scratched his head. "Where's your binoculars?"

"If they caught me with binoculars, they'd know I wasn't guarding the roof."

Johnny smiled and put the cap back on his head.

"Besides, on my pay I can't afford good ones. Crappy ones don't help." He pointed at the binoculars in Johnny's hand. "Those good?"

"Nah. But better than nothing." He turned and looked through the binoculars toward Fenway.

Alice said, "How long is an inning?"

"Ten minutes," Johnny said. "Twenty, tops."

"Ten minutes, then." Alice looked up at Oliver, her lips a tight, thin line.

Johnny turned his head sharply and he glared at her.

Not a good move, lover boy.

After a few seconds Johnny followed Alice's gaze. His eyes narrowed at Oliver. "Where's your gun?"

Oliver laughed. "It's just a roof, kid. I'm not guarding the crown jewels. You want to stay up here or not?"

"Don't worry about him," Johnny said, smiling at Alice reassuringly. "We'll be safe."

Alice stepped back. "You didn't."

He turned and leaned back, his butt against the wall beside the scaffolding. "It's no big deal."

"You know I don't like that thing."

Jesus jumping Christ.

Johnny had a gun.

A fifteen-year-old kid. On a mission to impress his girlfriend.

This could go very wrong, very fast.

"It's okay," Johnny said. "I'm careful."

Alice's shoulders rose and fell, rose and fell. Oliver could not see her face.

"Ten minutes," she said. "Then I'm leaving. With you or without you."

"Okay, okay," Johnny said. He looked up at Oliver. "How's the view?"

"You are not going up there," Alice said.

"I just want to see the view."

"You put one hand on that thing and I'm leaving."

Johnny reached up, grabbed a crossbar with both hands, and put his foot on a lower bar. "How about two hands?"

"Fuck you," Alice said. She whirled and headed for the trapdoor.

Oliver said, "The view is definitely not worth losing that pretty girl."

The kid had already lost the girl. But no need to point that out. Maybe he didn't even know it yet.

"Okay, okay," Johnny said. He jumped back from the scaffolding and held up his hands. "I'm off."

Alice stood at the edge of the trapdoor looking down, her arms wrapped around herself.

Johnny slid halfway along the wall, to a spot forty feet from the scaffolding. "Look. I'm way over here."

Alice shook her head, still looking down through the trapdoor. "Let me know when you're ready to go."

"If you're going to stay, you might as well watch with me," Johnny said. After a moment he added, "I want you to stay."

She turned to look at him.

"One inning," he said.

"Ten minutes."

He shrugged. "Ten minutes."

She walked slowly to him.

He held out the binoculars. She shook her head. He turned and peered through them.

Oliver took a slow breath and looked toward Fenway. Four hundred yards away, a row of tiny players in white uniforms stood along the first base line. It must be the national anthem, though Oliver could not hear it above the din of the evening traffic on the Mass Turnpike halfway between himself and the ball park.

The line of players broke up. Most of them headed toward the dugout.

One walked slowly toward the pitcher's mound.

It was nearly time.

Next, Moises Burguera would throw twelve warm-up pitches. Then Jarrod Seabury would step into the batter's box, tap the plate three times with the tip of his bat, and crouch into his stance.

And then all hell would break loose in Fenway Park.

Below, Alice slipped her arms around Johnny's chest and laid her cheek on his shoulder.

Johnny said, "I think I could hit that pitch."

Burguera was throwing the first of his warmup pitches. Oliver wanted to take his rifle down from the four-by-eight and watch the pitcher's delivery through the scope. But if Johnny or Alice were to look up, that would complicate things enormously. They would probably not have the presence of mind to realize what was happening. They would probably not have the courage to rush the scaffolding and jiggle it, throwing off his aim.

But at best they would panic and distract him.

At worst, Johnny might decide to be a hero with whatever he had tucked into the back of his pants under that denim jacket.

"Oh, hell," Johnny said. "I don't think I could hit that one."

Maybe Johnny would not be a problem.

Oliver had spent three hours watching videos of Burguera's delivery. He knew it cold. Every motion. The slight rock forward before winding back. The slow, lulling pace of his windup. The hitching pause. Most fascinating was the inhuman bend of his elbow as he burst forward and his arm whipped the ball toward the plate.

Fascinating, though there was no real need to study this last motion.

Burguera would never complete it.

Alice rested against Johnny's back, facing away from Oliver.

Oliver reached up and slowly lowered the rifle from the four-by-eight.

"Holy Christ," Johnny said. "I couldn't even *see* that pitch."

Burguera must be reaching the end of his warmup pitches.

"You sure you don't want to look?"

Alice shook her head against Johnny's shoulder.

Oliver laid the barrel of his rifle along the iron support bar in front of him and looked through the scope.

He had a clear view. Moises Burguera from the thigh up. No heads poked up over the top of the standing-room-only row.

Burguera was looking down at the front of the pitcher's mound. His shoulders jerked, and then again. Probably scuffing the dirt where his foot would push off the rubber.

Oliver glanced down one last time. Johnny leaned forward against the wall, both hands gripping the binoculars.

Alice clung to him.

She might stay with the kid after all.

Oliver was about to put them through hell. Twenty seconds from now, their young lives would suddenly become very, very complicated.

Maybe it would bring them closer together.

It was a nice thought.

Through the scope, at the upper right edge of Oliver's field of view, Jarrod Seabury stepped into Fenway Park's batter's box for the first time in a Yankee uniform.

Oliver wondered whether the fans were cheering or booing. Probably a lot of both.

Seabury leaned forward and tapped the far edge of home plate with his bat once, twice, three times. Then he pulled the bat back over his right shoulder, bent his legs, and looked out toward the mound.

Burguera leaned forward to take the call from the catcher.

Oliver centered his focus on the pitcher's number—39—stitched onto the back of his uniform in big, red numerals.

The round would take him between the three and the nine.

Part of him wanted to glance at the catcher, to see if he could spot the sign. But there was no need. Oliver knew the pitch. Everybody in Boston knew the pitch. Fastball. High and inside.

Burguera straightened, his hand gripping the ball in the glove in front of him.

Oliver breathed slowly, gently, and touched his gloved finger to the trigger.

Burguera rocked forward.

Oliver adjusted his aim slightly to the left, to the precise spot where Burguera would pause at the top of his windup.

The trigger pressed gently against Oliver's finger.

Four hundred yards away, Moises Burguera began his last windup.

Thirty feet below, Alice screamed.

Oliver squeezed.

The explosion was comforting. The kick of the rifle against his shoulder was comforting.

Half a second later, Burguera's hat flipped into the air. His arms jerked upward. He fell out of sight.

Mission accomplished.

Now the retreat.

Alice was pointing at Oliver with one hand. The other hand was clamped over her mouth.

Beside her, Johnny crouched and reached behind his back.

Fuck.

"Don't do it," Oliver said. He twisted and pointed the nose of the rifle toward the kid. "You want to be a dead hero?"

Johnny stopped moving.

Then his arm swung out from behind him.

Oliver squeezed the trigger. Gravel sprayed up between Johnny's feet.

Johnny's little pop-gun flew out of his hand and flipped through the air. It hit the gravel and skittered to a stop inches from the open trapdoor.

Johnny held up his hands.

Good boy.

"Don't move," Oliver said. "I am a very good shot."

Johnny nodded.

Alice now had both hands pressed to her mouth.

Thirty feet to the roof. Another thirty to the trapdoor.

Oliver gripped the rail of his rifle in one hand. It would slow his climb down off the scaffolding. He had intended to leave it behind. But that pop gun was too close for comfort. Maybe close enough to tempt Johnny to do something foolish.

Oliver crouched, gripped the scaffolding bar he was standing on, and jumped back.

His shin barked the bar below. The jolt of pain that shot up his leg was enormous, and he let go of his grip with both hands.

Oliver fell sideways. The sound of his clattering rifle down the scaffolding followed him down.

He hit the gravel with the side of his left foot, felt it twist, heard the bones of his lower leg crack.

The butt of the rifle landed on his chest.

Johnny rushed toward him.

Oliver grabbed the rifle and swung the nose around.

The pain washed up from his leg, up his back, through his chest. His stomach clenched.

Johnny stopped six feet away, with Oliver's rifle pointed at his chest.

In the distance, sirens.

Lots and lots of sirens.

"Back away," Oliver said.

Johnny took two steps back.

"All the way to the corner."

Johnny looked behind, raised his hands, and began backing away.

Alice.

Where was Alice?

Alice stood by the trapdoor, feet shoulder width apart, arms extended in front of her.

Aiming Johnny's pop-gun straight at Oliver.

So Johnny was not the hero of this duo after all.

The sirens were closer now.

"Killing a human being," Oliver said, "is the worst feeling in the world."

Alice began to whimper.

Her aim did not waver.

Slowly, Oliver brought his rifle around, pointed it at her, and tucked the butt to his shoulder.

She did not shoot.

But she did not flinch.

Oliver slid. "Bend over slowly and lay the gun at your feet and move over next to Johnny." His vision blurred and then cleared. "I don't want to hurt you. I just want to leave."

She let go of the gun with one hand and wiped her cheek on her puffy orange sleeve.

"Do as he says, Alice," Johnny said.

Alice shook her head. She gripped the gun with both hands and adjusted her stance.

"For God's sake, Alice. You saw what he did."

"He'll never get down the ladder," Alice said. "Not with his leg like that."

Oliver's vision wavered again.

The girl was right. He may not even be able to drag himself across the roof.

Sirens.

Very close now.

There was only one way out now.

"He'll have to take hostages," Alice said.

"No," Oliver said. "No hostages."

One way out.

One more bullet.

Oliver curled his index finger around the grip of his rifle, well away from the trigger.

He jerked the nose to the right.

Toward Alice's boyfriend.

In the corner of his eye, the muzzle of Alice's gun flashed.

A LIFE WITH MEANING

DAVID STIER

Dave is a U.S. Army veteran whose stories often cut very, very close to the bone. And in a good way.

His first story appeared in Fiction River: Visions of the Apocalypse *in which he offered what the editor called a chillingly plausible path to human extinction. Since then Dave has torn at our guts and our hearts in two more* Fiction River *volumes,* Pulse Pounders: Adrenaline *and* Feel the Fear.

In this story Dave once again does what he is so good at and pulls at our hearts as he takes the reader to war-torn Afghanistan where impossible choices often must be made by children. And where childhood can turn out to be no more than a dangerous nightmare.

Strap in for this story. It will be worth the ride.

Aliah watched from the shadows in the alley behind the madrassa. For two months now she had crept to this hidden place whenever possible to learn as she could. Had it only been two months since the Daesh warlord had decreed that girls were no longer permitted to attend lessons? It seemed as years.

Foolishly, she had begged him to reconsider.

Her reward had been laughter and a bruising slap to the face. Her father was dragged from his fields and ordered to take her home with a stern warning that from now on she would only learn what Allah had decreed for all women. What learning she needed would come from her mother. She would cook, keep house and marry as soon as possible.

It had been the saddest day in all of her 13 years of life. Cutting off her hand would have been easier than to give up learning to read.

Now she walked this deadly path to keep her dream alive.

The madrassa had changed greatly in the past two months. She studied the drawing opposite the black and white Daesh flag. It had been painted on the bumpy whitewashed wall by the boys. In it several infidel soldiers wearing helmets and boots had been surrounded by Fedayeen fighters who fired stick rifles from above. The drawing looked crude and unfinished to her eyes.

The heat inside the classroom had increased. Aliah knew she should leave. Her presence had not yet been discovered for Kalan, the madrassa instructor, had poor eyesight and the shadows in the narrow alley where she crouched were dark.

The curtains on the front door parted and Sadiq Ibn Yasir, the Daesh warlord, stepped inside.

"Hamid Ben Fatin," Sadiq said while he scanned the assembled boys.

Her little brother stood.

"Step forward," Sadiq said.

Hamid spoke often of jihad and the shame he felt from their uncle who had defied the Caliphate by speaking out against the occupation of Abdul, their village. Again, as in her dreams she saw Uncle Nadir's execution. She and the entire village had been forced to bear witness. Her uncle had been a good man, educated in Pakistan and sent to England for military training.

"Never let anyone steal your dreams, Ali," he had said the day before he was executed. "Life without dreams is life without meaning."

Hamid walked to the front, where Sadiq held a Kalashnikov.

"What is this called?" he said while holding the rifle in front of Hamid.

"It is a Kalashnikov rifle," said Hamid.

The jagged scar that ran down one side of Sadiq's face pulled his smile to the side. "Allah's blessings be upon you. That is correct. Now show me how to fire it."

Hamid took the rifle, cocked it then aimed and pulled the trigger.

Sadiq squeezed Hamid's shoulder and her six-year-old brother's face shone with pride. Sadiq took the Klashnikov and slung it over his shoulder. "Tell, me, Hamid Ben Fatin, how far will you go to wage jihad?"

Hamid stood even straighter. "I will do whatever the Prophet wills," he said in a clear voice for all to hear.

A hand grabbed Aliah's arm, yanked her to her feet and spun her around.

"What are you doing here, girl?" said a frowning bearded Fedayeen in broken Pashto. His hand tightened and he drew her further into the alley.

Aliah veiled her face and quickly studied her accuser. First she noted the black Daesh armband. Then the stale spiciness of his breath and sour smell of his unwashed body. Over his shoulder was slung a Kalashnikov similar to Sadiq's but with a wire stock instead of wood. His skin was very dark and he wore the black and white checked keffiyeh common among foreign Fedayeen. But the man's eyes were what frightened her the most for she had seen this look before—many times since the Daesh Fedayeen had occupied Abdul.

"I wanted to learn how to hold a Kalashnikov in case I ever need to shoot the Crusaders," she said.

The look in the Fedayeen's eyes remained, but his face grew less severe. "So you want to kill Crusaders, do you?" He released her arm. "What is your name, girl?"

"Aliah." If she lied he might later find out. Abdul was not so large a village. She thought to say more but had learned from her mistake with Sadiq to say nothing unless asked.

The Fedayeen unslung his Kalashnikov and opened the folding stock. Next he removed the magazine and checked to make sure the rifle was unloaded. Then he handed it to Aliah.

"Show me what you have learned."

She had handled a Kalashnikov before, but she would be careful and act like she knew nothing of shooting or even properly aiming any kind of gun. Her Uncle Nadir had shown her soon after the Daesh had conquered Abdul how to aim and actually shoot both his pistol and Kalashnikov.

She let the barrel droop downward as though the rifle was too heavy and kept the stock away from her shoulder as if afraid to let it touch her dress. She even staggered a little pretending to be surprised by its weight.

With an amused snort, the Fedayeen took the rifle and slowly demonstrated how to cock it then hold it properly. Then he showed her how the safety worked and how the magazine fit into it as well.

After she repeated his lessons she handed it back.

He smiled more openly. "You will someday make a formidable Fedayeen, little girl, but for now return to your home.

Keeping her eyes downcast, Aliah picked up the plastic water bucket and moved down the alley toward the street. She was careful not to stumble or do anything else that might betray her fear. Once she had turned a corner, she glanced back to see if the Fedayeen had followed. She swallowed in relief at his absence. The fear knotting her stomach lessened. Her heartbeat also began to slow.

She studied the sun's position. Just past noon, so she had time to get water, which was the excuse she had used to steal another reading lesson. She wiped sweat from her forehead and began the long trudge uphill to the village well.

Aliah studied the ground while she walked. Partly to avoid ruts in the rocky trail. Partly to avoid seeing half ruined buildings or worse. But even looking down could not hide the shadows of bodies hung from the gallows near the market square. Sometimes they swayed in the hot breeze, like today. Looking down also did not erase the smell of villagers that had hung there for days as an object lesson, or the dead buried under some of the bombed mud and straw buildings, victims of devil drone attacks.

"Allah have mercy," a man's voice cried out.

Several Daesh Fedayeen had surrounded a young clean-shaven man.

So foolish. And so recently had he shaved.

"Where is your beard?" the eldest Fedayeen asked. "Devout Muslims have beards. You must be an infidel."

"No! I—"

Aliah hurried on, but the sounds of the beating followed. If lucky, such defiance would not cost his life. Though now he would remain noticed and subject to more beatings for his lack of piety.

At the well she filled her bucket and started back toward Abdul. The water was heavy but walking downhill made the trip easier. Off to one side of the road a few wildflowers grew. She moved closer and stopped, gazing at the red and yellow display. She breathed in the fragrant smell. Perhaps her mother would also enjoy them she thought, and bent over to pick a few.

In the distance she heard a faint whining noise. She followed the sound with her ears. High in the clouded blue sky she made out a small black speck of a devil drone that drew closer as she watched.

She forgot about the flowers and walked faster, being careful not to spill any water.

The faint whine deepened. Aliah set her bucket down and jumped into the ditch alongside the road. Seconds later, something lifted her off the ground then slammed her back down. As the light faded from her eyes she heard a distant bang.

Aliah woke to the sounds of crackling flames and people's screams. The smell of burning wood and smoke made her cough. After sitting up, she felt her legs to see if they were injured and rubbed the dust out of her eyes then brushed off her dress which had been torn. She stood, looking for her bucket which lay nearby and on its side, the water staining the dirt a darker shade of brown.

Judging from the still-wet dirt, little time had passed. She looked from where she stood on unsteady legs. She and her bucket must have been thrown a few meters from the road by the devil drone's bomb.

She picked up her bucket, noting a bright circle of color farther down the hill, away from the road. She shrugged, not looking forward to the climb back up to the well and turned toward the road.

What is troubling you? A voice from within asked. She turned, walked toward this bright spot of color, hidden among the brown and gray hillside.

As she drew closer she counted six flowers of different colors in the circle: Red, yellow, cream, white, orange and pink. In the center, a seventh—dark purple, nearly black. Surprised, Aliah knew them to be Laleh or tulips. A feeling of peace increased as she drew nearer, then she stopped as by some gentle unseen command.

For how long she stood motionless soaking in the sight, feelings and aroma of this tiny oasis, she did not know. Eventually the thought that she had to get more water reminded her that it was time to leave. But breaking eye contact with the Laleh was very hard, as though they wished her to ask a question. With a sadness that reminded her of how her uncle had died, she finally broke free and trudged back up the hill.

After a very painful trek, for her leg had been bruised, Aliah arrived home. The sun and sky were colored a deep gold by the time she set her bucket in the courtyard then stepped inside the kitchen where her mother had just finished preparing the evening meal.

"You are late—" But her mother got no further when she saw Aliah's bruised face, cut forehead, and torn dress. Mother rushed over and pulled Aliah into a painful embrace. *Ammi* wiped Aliah's face with a wet rag.

"Ali, are you hurt?" she asked.

Aliah winced as her mother patted her cut forehead with the rag. "I am fine, *ammi*. It was the devil drone's bomb. The water got spilled so I had to get more. I am sorry but my dress was torn when I fell."

Her mother smiled, shook her head.

"Always so considerate. You are unharmed and I can mend the dress. It was your older one anyway. Wear the newer dress for now."

She handed Aliah a plate piled with warm naan bread. "Here,

take this to the living room then go change."

The meal was mostly eaten in silence, for her father had learned that a close friend had been injured in the devil drone attack.

"I do not know which is worse," her father said. "The devil drones or—"

At her mother's indrawn breath he did not finish. Aliah dipped a piece of naan bread into the beef broth and concentrated on eating.

"I will wage jihad on the infidels when I am older," Hamid said. "The Caliphate will drive out the Crusaders. Sadiq says it is only a matter of time."

Aliah waited for her father's response, which was long in coming.

"You may get your wish, my son," he said, then patted Hamid on the head. "But wait until you are a man."

Hamid frowned. "Sadiq says *all* can wage jihad no matter our age."

Aliah thought her father might cuff Hamid for displaying such insolence. Instead he took another piece of naan bread and continued to eat.

Unlike Hamid, she saw the look exchanged between mother and father after Hamid's outburst—a terrible fear laced with great anger.

Aliah shared in both, for unlike her parents, she had seen firsthand how Sadiq held sway over her little brother. She wished there was something she could do to prevent Hamid from traveling down this frightening path.

Every morning, Aliah would bow before the family's Kaba above the living room door. Then she would briefly pray. Never had she said it aloud, but since Daesh's arrival a worm of resentment had formed near her heart. A Pillar of Wisdom prayer might be, but she saw no good coming from such devotions.

If You *are merciful, then why is my brother so easily swayed by Sadiq? If* You *care about* Your *people then why are they killed by* infidel *soldiers and* Fedayeen? *And why did* You *allow Sadiq to kill my uncle?*

For the past month since her uncle's execution, she prayed only when it could not be avoided.

After the morning meal and when she had cleaned all of the dishes, Aliah took her bucket and headed toward the well. She did not notice the gallows or the destroyed buildings or even the smell of death. Today she saw only her circle of Laleh.

As she neared the place, her step lightened and cares lessened. The feeling of peace returned, but also a sense of urgency.

She studied each flower in turn. The red and yellow Laleh made little impression save for faint feelings of love and brightness. As her eyes moved to the cream Laleh, the face of Hamid appeared inside her head and the sense of urgency she felt increased. Suddenly, the six outer Laleh merged into a colorful fan, like those sold in the market on festival days. The brightness increased enough to make Aliah shade her eyes. But inside the seeming rainbow, the black Laleh drew her in.

Go! Your brother needs you!

Forgetting her bucket, she turned and ran toward the madrassa.

Halfway from her village, explosions started to rock the earth. Aliah fell many times as bombs continued to fall. Infidel airplanes passed overhead, shrieking so loud that she heard nothing else as they passed. As she rounded the last bend in the road the village spread out before her.

Bombs fell on the two roads leading into and out of the village, and on the surrounding fields. So far the village itself was untouched. Dust clouds rose on the road leading out of the other side of the village. She looked behind her and saw rising dust clouds near where the well was located.

She started running again and was immediately thrown forward as something pushed her in the back. Seconds later she was knocked to the ground. She tried to stand, fell; noticing that all she now heard was a loud ringing in her ears.

Again she staggered to her feet, half running, half stumbling in the direction of her village and Hamid.

A shadow appeared within the first half-destroyed home that she ran past. Someone grabbed her and pulled her into the building. Through the dust and smoke she saw the bearded face of the Fedayeen who had given her the Kalashnikov lesson.

"You must hide here, my little Fedayeen," he said. "I will protect you from the infidel Crusaders." He tried to appear friendly, but his eyes revealed his true purpose.

Aliah struggled to break free. The Fedayeen's eyebrows drew together and the frown from yesterday re-appeared.

"So you wish to fight, eh?" he said as he dragged her further into the roofless mud building.

She kicked and screamed and shook her head from side to side as he tried to kiss her. His rotten breath and unwashed body increased her terror. He released one of her arms. Alia hit him in the eye with her fist.

"Ha! So you are an even better fighter than I thought," he said, his laugher and the nearest explosions combining to increase her terror.

He left her one arm free while he yanked off her head scarf.

"Not so pretty, but pretty enough" he said as he tried to kiss her again.

Her fist pounded the side of his head and with a grunt the Fedayeen forced her arm to her side. He kissed her cheek as she turned her face to the side. Her groping hand brushed against his leather belt then the butt of a pistol.

She yanked the pistol free, cocked the hammer, and pulled the trigger, praying that it would fire.

It fired twice. Aliah felt something both wet and warm—the Fedayeen's blood—trickle down her hand.

The lust on the Fedayeen's face turned to surprise then his eyes faded in death and he fell, taking her with him to the ground. She pushed enough of his lifeless body to one side, used her foot to roll him off completely.

She stood, tears streaming down her face. Explosions continued all around. She collapsed to her knees and cried, for how long she did not know, but the thought of Hamid forced her to her feet again. She ran, pistol in hand, wiped her face then put the pistol inside her pocket, swearing always to carry it wherever she went.

She looked back up the road where helmeted soldiers were fast approaching.

Aliah slipped between two buildings fifty meters from the madrassa and tried to decide what to do.

Sadiq held a wide white belt while Hamid raised his tunic up above his chest. Her heart continued to pound and her stomach again knotted in fear. She wiped sweat from her face with her sleeve and reached inside her pocket for the pistol then put it back. Sadiq was too far away. Uncle Nadir had cautioned her never to shoot a pistol at something more than ten meters away.

Sadiq wrapped the belt around Hamid's waist then pulled Hamid's *kameez* back down over his *shalwar*, so the tunic covered what must be a suicide vest.

Sadiq pointed to Hamid's clenched hand, clenched his as Hamid's was clenched, and moved his thumb up and down. Hamid nodded. Sadiq pointed in the direction of the approaching soldiers.

As Hamid moved toward the soldiers, Sadiq ran in the opposite direction.

Aliah waited until Hamid passed where she was hidden then rushed to his side and grabbed his clenched hand in both of hers.

"Let me go!" he said and tried to free his hand "I must martyr myself upon the infidels."

Still holding his fist in her hands, Aliah knelt in front of her little brother.

"A martyr is someone like Uncle Nadir," she said. "He was willing to die for what he believed in, Hamid. He did not kill others by strapping on a suicide vest."

Hamid struggled to break free. "You lie!" Sadiq assured me in Allah's name that I will reach Paradise only on the altar of sacrifice."

"Hamid—" But she saw that words would fail.

She released his hand.

"If you must then do so, but I will remain by your side."

Hamid started to move toward the approaching soldiers, who had stopped at a safe distance. When he saw that Aliah remained by his side, he stopped.

"I must avenge the shame of our uncle," he said, tears streaming from his eyes.

"Uncle Nadir was a brave man," she said. "He defied those he thought evil and died as a true martyr. Where is Sadiq? He ran from the infidels, did he not?"

Hamid looked back toward the direction Sadiq had fled.

He again started toward the soldiers, stopped, then leaned against his sister and sobbed, as the six-year-old boy he was.

After the soldiers disarmed the suicide vest, Aliah and Hamid were taken inside the madrassa. The Afghani Army officer explained that after they answered a few questions they could leave.

She hoped this was true. Perhaps her Laleh circle could aid in this as it had in saving Hamid.

The Daesh flag had been torn from the wall, but the drawing still remained. Aliah wished to be able to attend madrassa again.

"You are a very brave girl," the Afghani soldier in charge said.

"Thank you," she said, feeling her face warm in embarrassment. She smiled in reassurance at Hamid, who briefly smiled then again looked at the earthen floor.

The officer cleared his throat.

"Why did you risk your life to save this boy?" he asked.

Alia studied the soldier's face. In his eyes she saw genuine respect, unlike those of Sadiq, who had looked upon her as inferior or the Fedayeen who had regarded her only as a means of pleasure.

"Because he is my brother," she finally said. "And I wished for him to live."

NIGHTMARE SCENARIO

CHUCK HEINTZELMAN

Chuck Heintzelman writes quirky short stories, usually with some sort of fantastical element. He says he's as surprised by this as anyone. Numbers of his stories have been published in other issues of Fiction River *(Pulse Pounders, Sparks, Tavern Tales, Last Stand).*

Chuck spends most of his time these days managing and enhancing BundleRabbit, a DIY ebook bundling and collaborative publishing service. For you writers who haven't tried it, you should.

Chuck says, "My only plan for this story was to start with an unlikable hero. Besides that I was pretty surprised at the situations that unfolded. Luckily, by the end there was a hard choice to make."

Actually, Chuck creates a nightmare for his characters that becomes rapidly more outlandish and horrifying. But what if the nightmare pales compared to the less outlandish, but just as deadly reality?

-1-

During his lifetime The General had witnessed a number of prisoners being tortured. He'd even been waterboarded himself during the first Gulf War—voluntarily by his fellow soldiers—and he didn't give a shit what any of those pansy-asses in Washington said, waterboarding was not torture. Unpleasant as hell, sure. Not something he *ever* wanted to experience again, absolutely. But no bruised and battered bodies, no broken bones, and no bloody scars or permanent disfigurement.

Still, he'd never seen anything in the same league as what he had just witnessed.

He sat in the dim conference room with Dr. Hardeek, the program's chief pathologist. Across the conference table from them, on the wall's video console, was the image of a dead man, his ankles and wrists strapped to a hospital bed.

The dead man wore a thin hospital gown. His wide open eyes saw nothing now. His mouth was frozen open in a silent scream. The man's naked legs were twisted to one side, pelvis tilted, as if still trying to escape the nightmare that had taken his life.

At one point during the video The General couldn't listen to the subject's screams any longer. Raw, primal sounds had ripped out from the man's throat. The General had muted the sound.

The General pinched the bridge of his nose. He couldn't imagine what nightmare the subject had experienced to create such a violent reaction. The General had experienced three nightmares since the testing phase had begun, each one different than the other, and he vowed never to experience another one.

"It looks much, much worse now," The General said.

Dr. Hardeek waved a finger in the air. "Actually, the nightmare's intensity had the same threshold level. But this time I introduced a separate agent to inhibit sleep paralysis."

"Thus all the thrashing and screaming."

Dr. Hardeek looked down. "Yes."

The door to the conference room opened and the lights came up. "Sorry I'm late."

The man entering the room was David Scartfield, an older man with slicked back, white hair. The General didn't think Scartfield had any official title, but Scartfield reported to the Director and was responsible for several black op budgets, including theirs.

The General hated all this bureaucratic bullshit, but he put a smile on his face, and shook Scartfield's hand. "Not a problem. Good to see you. I believe you've met Dr. Hardeek."

The two men nodded at each other.

Scartfield studied the dead man on the video screen while sitting at the conference table. Scartfield smiled, revealing small, yellow teeth. "Impressive."

Scartfield began scanning through a yellow legal pad, running a finger along his notes.

"Let's rewind so you can see for yourself," The General said.

"No need." Scartfield waved a hand in the air. "No need. Just a few questions. Let's see." He flipped another page on the legal pad. "What's the delivery mechanism?"

"Pressurized gas canisters."

"Excellent," Scartfield said. "That payload can be delivered via drones. What is the casualty rate?"

"93% of infected subjects die," The General said. "But drones would not be effective. The virus becomes quickly inert when it's not pressurized. The gas needs to be released within five feet of the target."

"Five feet?"

"For maximum infection, yes." The General said.

Scartfield drummed his fingers on the conference table. "That doesn't work. A M67 frag grenade has ten times the range."

The General sat up straighter in his chair. "We're working on it."

"Good. Too bad it's not contagious. We could infect one person, send them in and infect a whole cell."

The General stared hard at Scartfield. "My worst fear. It's already airborne, but if it mutated and became contagious. That's a nightmare scenario."

Scartfield didn't speak for a moment. He flipped to another page in his notes. "How long from exposure to death?"

The General waved at Dr. Hardeek to answer. "Twelve minutes before the first symptoms appeared," Dr. Hardeek said. "Subject experienced SCD forty-three minutes later."

Scartfield raised an eyebrow at The General. "SCD?"

"Sudden Cardiac Death," The General said.

"Not good." Scartfield said. "Not good at all. Can you imagine what havoc a terrorist could wreak during that hour before they die?"

"I wouldn't worry," The General said. "Any terrorist would be quite preoccupied with their nightmare. *Wreaking havoc* wouldn't be an issue."

"You don't understand," Scartfield said, superiority coloring his words. "These people hate us. They're born hating us. They're trained as young boys with one goal in mind, to kill Americans. Dealing with some *dream* won't dissuade them from their goal."

The General chewed the inside of his lip for a moment before responding. "With all due respect, sir. *You're* the one who doesn't understand. You cannot understand without experiencing it."

Scartfield's face flushed. "Are you threatening me with this ..." His hand made a small circle toward the video screen. "This chemical failure? I hesitate to call it a weapon because it's not useful yet."

The General barked a quick laugh. "Not at all, sir. I'm saying you should view a recording for yourself to see what these nightmares are like. And it's a viral agent, not chemical."

Scartfield sat back in his chair. "Very well, play the video."

"No," The General said. "The video is an external recording of the subject while he's experiencing the nightmare. We record the actual nightmares themselves."

"I can watch the same nightmare this guy saw?" He hooked a thumb toward the video screen.

"It's more than just watching. You'll see, hear, taste, smell and feel. It's a complete sensory recording."

"And it's safe to watch?" Scartfield said.

"Perfectly safe," The General said. "It's unpleasant. A horrible nightmare based on the subject's greatest fear. But you know going in it's just a recording. That's what makes it safe, the knowledge nothing you experience is real."

"I didn't even know we had this," Scartfield said.

"We took over technology the porn industry had been developing —National Security—and then we put our best scientists on it."

"Yes," Scartfield said. "I definitely want to see it."

"Dr. Hardeek," The General said. "Prepare the FSI with the subject's FSR for Mr. Scartfield."

"FSI?" Scartfield said.

"Full Sensory Immersion," The General said. "And FSR is Final Sensory Recording."

"Prepare it for both of us," Scartfield said. "After all, you tell me it's perfectly safe."

"You don't have any deep, dark fears do you? Those can create nightmare tangents where you end up in your own nightmare."

"No fears here," Scartfield said. "And I must insist we both do it."

The General chewed his lip's inside again. This time he tasted blood. He nodded to Dr. Hardeek.

"Gentlemen," Dr. Hardeek said, scooting his chair back from the conference table. He left the room.

"Wow," Scartfield said. "This sounds like a ride at Disneyland."

"No, not Disneyland. More like Jack-the-Ripper-Land where every ride kills you."

–2–

The General sat in one of the two big chairs in the FSI room. The room's walls were painted sea-foam green because research told them green was a calming color. Right. The General didn't believe he'd ever feel calm in this room again. The last nightmare he'd experienced here still haunted his dreams.

Above his head, attached to the chair's back, was the neuro-field dome. The dome reminded him of when he was a small boy and accompanied his mother to the beauty parlor where women used bonnet hair dryers to dry hair wrapped in large curlers.

The General sat up in his chair, dried his palms on his pants, and watched Dr. Hardeek calibrate the other chair for Scartfield.

The dome was over Scartfield's head and he leaned back in his chair. Dr. Hardeek manipulated controls on the chair's back.

"Now lower your left foot," Dr. Hardeek was saying.

Scartfield lowered his leg back to the floor.

The General had been through these same calibrations before his first nightmare.

"Last one," Dr. Hardeek said. "Clap your hands."

Scartfield clapped his hands and Dr. Hardeek pressed a button and the dome raised off Scartfield's head.

The General felt a bit of schadenfreude at the worried look on Scartfield's face.

The lights in the FSI room flickered and went out. Nobody spoke. The only sound was Scartfield's panicked breathing. After a long five seconds the lights came back on. Dr. Hardeek had come from behind Scartfield's chair in the darkness and now stood between the two chairs.

"What the hell?" Scartfield sat up in his chair.

"Power glitch." The General shrugged. "We need a larger budget."

"What happens if we're in dreamland and that happens again?"

"No harm," Dr. Hardeek said. "The recording stops and you'll find yourself back in the chair."

"If we lose power for more than a minute," The General said. "Then the backup generators kick in."

"I've set the timer for five minutes," Dr. Hardeek said. "But I'll be monitoring you. If your heart rate exceeds the maximum I'll pull you out."

"Five minutes?" Scartfield said. "Won't be much of a ride."

"Time's different in dreams," The General said. "What's the subjective time of those five minutes, Doctor?"

"I'd estimate twenty-five," said Dr. Hardeek. "Maybe thirty-five minutes. Depends on the gaps."

"Your mind fills in any gaps," The General explained. "To create a consistent narrative for the mind to believe. The essence of your experience will be the same, but you may have specifics that differ from the subject's, or from my experience."

Dr. Hardeek produced a needle and again Scartfield had that worried look.

"Muscle relaxant and neuro-inhibitor," Dr. Hardeek said as he shot Scartfield through his shirt in the shoulder.

Dr. Hardeek gave The General a similar shot in the shoulder. Then he lowered the domes over their heads.

"Gentleman," he said. "Lean back and close your eyes. Try to relax. It should begin momentarily."

"I never asked," The General said. "What's the nightmare's subject?"

Dr. Hardeek grinned. "Dinosaurs mainly."

The General closed his eyes, but could not relax.

Shit. Dinosaurs.

The General opened his eyes and he was still in the FSI room with its sickly green walls. Scartfield looked like he was asleep in his chair and Dr. Hardeek was engrossed with his phone.

He was in the nightmare now. He knew it. Living one of the gaps his mind created. The previous nightmares had always started the same way.

Should have told Scartfield this is how it'd begin. No matter. The old pencil-pusher would figure it out soon enough.

The General got out of the chair. Dr. Hardeek didn't look up from his phone. The General knew these men were just part of the background now. They weren't real.

He checked his watch. 2:13. Needed to make it to 2:45 without anything painful happening. Then he'd be out of this damn dream and safe.

He went to the room's door. For half a second he was tempted to call security from the keypad next to the door, but that wouldn't work in a nightmare. Instead, he felt the metal door. It was cool, as was the handle. He pulled the door open just a crack and peered through it.

Crap. Too dark out there. The air smelled dank and dusty. If he just barged through the door who knew what he'd be walking into. Wait. There in the distance was a flickering light, like a fire. Shadows moved around it.

He closed the door. Shit. He should have turned the lights off before opening the door because if he could see their light, they could see his.

He needed a weapon.

The room had changed. Dr. Hardeek was gone and Scartfield looked different now. The old man's eyes were open, unblinking, and his mouth was open. He was dead and had the same look of terror the subject in the video had.

Just part of the background. Not real.

But being real wasn't the problem. If someone or something cut him, The General would feel it. He'd feel the blade's burn cutting into his flesh, he'd smell the earthy iron of his own blood.

It was 2:16 now. Three minutes had passed.

He needed a weapon.

Scartfield's shirt was moving. Something was inside it. A long, segmented, translucent thing poked out the top of his shirt. Then a creature popped out, scuttled across Scartfield's face, and fell to the floor.

It was a huge spider, at least five inches across, white and translucent, as if it never had been in the light. It scuttled across the floor toward him.

The General hated spiders. Was this part of the subject's dream or was he living through a gap created with his own fears?

Did it matter?

When the spider got close, he stomped on it, popping it under his boot. Over at Scartfield's body more spiders were coming. They poured like liquid from Scartfield's sleeves and pants legs.

A small river of weird white spiders were coming at him.

The General screamed and went on a stomping spree. Popping spider after spider under his boots. Spiders climbed his legs and he brushed them off, and continued stomping. And continued screaming.

Somehow a spider got inside his pants leg and crawled up toward his groin, but he crushed it with the palm of his hand and felt the wet gore on his inner thigh.

He kept stomping and stomping and slipped in the mess of dead white spiders on the floor, going down hard. His head cracked against the hard tile.

He scrambled to his feet and spun around and around, looking everywhere before realizing he'd crushed all the spiders.

The General put his hands on his knees. His breaths came in gasps. He tried to calm down.

Over in the chair, Scartfield's face with its mask of horror was still there, but now his clothes looked empty and deflated.

The General checked his watch. 2:20.

Something pounded at the door. Something heavy and hard. The metal door dented out toward him.

This nightmare was far from over.

He needed a weapon and fast. Any second now whatever was pounding on the door would be through it.

There was nothing in the FSI room he could use. Unless he could wrench an arm from one of the chairs.

Before he could try, the door came open and a large man, at least eight feet tall, ducked his head through the door.

The man had a heavy brow and thick, dark hair and beard.

It was a caveman.

-4-

It didn't matter that cavemen were never eight feet tall. Didn't matter cavemen didn't live with dinosaurs. None of this was real.

Throbbing at the back of his head, where The General had smacked his skull against the floor, reminded him of one real thing.

The pain.

The caveman moved fast. It ran in, hunched over, and grabbed The General by his shoulders. He felt the caveman's fingers digging in to the bone.

The General ignored his urge to fight, and instead went limp.

The caveman dragged The General through the door.

They were in a large cave. It was no longer dark. Daylight came from the cave's entrance. Crude drawings decorated the cave walls. The place smelled like skunk.

The caveman dragged him to the cave's entrance. Three other cavemen stood there, wearing animal skins and holding large clubs.

How stereotypical.

The caveman tossed The General to the ground and all four cavemen surrounded him. They looked down on him, each with a confused look. Hell, maybe they always looked confused. Maybe this was their normal look.

One thing was sure, they never would have seen anyone like him before.

Of course not. They weren't real.

He had to keep telling himself that.

Looking around, The General didn't see any cavewomen. High in the sky overhead, flew large—not birds, what were they called? Pterodactyls?

The General struggled to his feet. The cavemen surrounding him grunted and one poked at him with his club.

It was 2:25. He still had about twenty minutes before this night-mare was over.

The cave was situated high on a side of a cliff overlooking a large lake. Green everywhere. Large, leafy trees and ferns. Even the air smelled green. At the lake's edge was a huge brontosaurus, or what-ever they called those things now.

On the other side of the lake two Tyrannosaurus Rexes fought. They tore at each other with their huge jaws and whipped their tails around.

An amazing sight.

Terrifying.

Without a doubt he'd be dealing with those monsters soon.

Or would he?

He was experiencing five minutes of the subject's FSR. It could be an hour or longer, subjective time, before the T-Rexes came into play.

The General hoped that was the case.

The cavemen grew agitated, grunting and speaking in guttural mono-syllables, somehow communicating. One stepped forward and swung his club, connecting with The General's chest.

The General felt ribs break. He flew ten feet backwards and landed hard. The wind was knocked out of him.

As he lay there, struggling to take a single, painful breath, The General saw what had stirred up the cavemen.

Clinging to the cliff's side twenty feet away was a long, lizard-like creature with three heads. It was at least ten feet long, half that length was tail. Sharp, bony spikes covered the creature's back like a bed of nails. It kept tasting the air with long tongues snaking out of each of its heads.

Never heard of a three-headed dinosaur.

Not real.

His head swam and he felt on the verge of passing out, but finally was able to take small, shallow breaths. When he tried to breathe deeper it felt like a bayonet twisting through his side.

The cavemen advanced slowly toward the three-headed, spiky-back lizard.

The General panted now, shallow, painful breaths.

He'd take waterboarding over this shit any day of the week.

And suddenly The General was back in the FSI room.

-5-

At first The General thought suddenly snapping back into the FSI room was part of the nightmare. That somehow he'd ended up in a loop and now he'd have to deal with the spiders and the cavemen and whatever came next again.

Or what if he'd gone off in a dream tangent and departed from the original nightmare?

His head still throbbed and that knife sliced into his side each time he breathed.

No, it was only the memory of pain, already fading.

Dr. Hardeek was at his side.

"I pulled you out," Dr. Hardeek said. "Because we have a situation."

The General sat up in his chair, and felt along the inside of his thigh. No remnants of the spider he squashed in his pants. He took a deep breath, almost wincing in anticipation, but no pain came.

"What situation?" he said.

"There's been an outbreak," Dr. Hardeek said.

The General rose to his feet. "What type of outbreak?"

"The virus."

The General looked at Dr. Hardeek.

"Yes," Dr. Hardeek said. "It's mutated."

The General marched across the room to the door and entered his code into the keypad beside the door. Then he held the button labeled security. "Initiate full security lockdown. This is not a drill."

"What should I do with him?" Dr. Hardeek pointed to Scartfield, still asleep.

"Just leave him for now. Details. Tell me what you know."

Dr. Hardeek scratched his forehead at the base of his hairline. "One of the orderlies responsible for disposing of the last subject collapsed and became non-responsive. Twenty minutes later he was dead."

The General paced around the room. "Wait." His watch read 2:16. "I was only out for a few minutes."

"This happened earlier. Before you and Scartfield arrived in this room."

The General rushed to Dr. Hardeek and grabbed his shirt. "You didn't tell me?"

"Sorry, I didn't realize an outbreak was starting. I only heard he'd collapsed, later I found out he died."

The General released Dr. Hardeek's shirt. "When did the first infection occur?"

"Forty-five minutes ago."

The General went back to the keypad beside the door and called up security again. "Has anyone left the building in the last hour?"

"No sir," came the response.

"Good," The General said. "We can contain this."

"It gets worse," Dr. Hardeek said.

"How?"

"Robert Glott's the one who reported it to me. He became non-responsive just moments ago."

"So that's two infected," The General said. "How many more?"

"That's not the point, sir. Glott reported this to me in person."

The General nodded his head, understanding. "So you may be infected. I may be infected."

Dr. Hardeek nodded. He looked ready to cry. "If my calculations are correct, I could show symptoms at any time."

"How long do I have?"

Dr. Hardeek rubbed his eyes. "If I'm infected, you have maybe five minutes after I become non-responsive."

"Dry em up and let's go," The General said.

"Where?" Dr. Hardeek said.

"To the armory. If we're not infected we'll need gas masks."

The General opened the door and looked back. Dr. Hardeek had collapsed.

Which meant Hardeek was infected and most likely The General was infected too.

He looked at his watch. 2:18. Scartfield would wake up soon but The General couldn't wait.

He ran to the armory as fast as he could.

But now he wasn't after gas masks.

-6-

The General sat on the bottom stair in the basement and watched the second hand of his watch tick by. In his other hand he held a radio-detonator with a little silver toggle switch on it.

He was hot and sweaty, the air humid, and it smelled like chemical solvent down there.

It had been a mad dash to the armory, then filling a duffle with enough C4 to bring down the building, and then rushing down to the basement and placing the C4 in strategic places.

As he saw it, there were two possibilities.

The virus had a tiny incubation period, just minutes. Any outbreak would quickly burn itself out. But then who would get infected from their dead bodies? And what if the virus mutated again and ended up with a longer incubation period?

No. It wasn't worth the chance. The General would not be responsible for unleashing a plague that could wipe out mankind. Safer to destroy everything.

But he really hoped it was the second possibility.

That he was still inside the nightmare, on a tangent. After all, his greatest fear was that the virus became contagious. He was living that nightmare.

The General had no clue which possibility it was.

Either he'd sacrifice himself and save mankind or wake up from this nightmare scenario.

He was out of time.

And he flipped the detonator's switch.

ECHO

LESLIE CLAIRE WALKER

We have been lucky enough to have Leslie Claire Walker appear in eight volumes of Fiction River, *including this one. She is the author of the Faery Chronicles and Soul Forge urban fantasy series, and also writes for* The Uncollected Anthology. *The dark beauty of the city, the power of myth, and music from Celtic harp to heavy metal usually inspire her stories.*

However, "Echo" had its inspiration in Margaret Atwood's novel The Handmaid's Tale. *Leslie says, "I read that book in my early twenties and it had a profound effect on me. That story was not a stone dropped into the water of my subconscious, but a boulder, sending ripples deep and wide."*

In this story, Leslie's heroine finds herself in a world turned on its head. A world that leaves her no choices at all.

The flat, slick steel walls reminded me of empty eyes. No one to appeal to behind them. No reflection. Nobody home. The rusty stains on the concrete floor might've been blood, the people who'd bled and the bastards who'd cut them long gone, just like the five men I'd come here with on the train. They'd been taken away one by one, leaving me, the only woman, behind.

I couldn't decide what to call worse—the sounds they'd made during our time together or the silence that descended once they'd left.

It'd been a full day since I'd seen the last of them, or so I thought. I had no way to tell time. No view of light or dark. No watch. No cue from the guards. I'd counted seconds and minutes and hours as best I could. It helped with orientation. It helped me hold onto my identity.

The guards had taken away my clothes and given me a pair of thin, gray pajamas and white cotton socks. The thin, gray cotton blanket they'd given me did nothing to hold back the chill that turned the skin on my arms and legs to gooseflesh. The frame of the cot I laid on bowed on the left side, giving me the impression that any second I'd slide off and hit the concrete floor in a tumble of knees and elbows, maybe crack my skull open. That would make me an unfit cage.

My body needed to be intact and functional, with a reasonably long shelf life for the magic to work—it was magic, not science, that allowed the transfer of knowledge, of consciousness from one body to another. Might as well call it a transfer of the soul.

I'd never fall. I was like the sky.

If my cot bowed, then all the other cots bowed the same way. They'd been made to give an illusion of comfort rather than the real thing, like the blanket.

Stars filled the ceiling. No, not stars. Bright lights inside steel fixtures that hung on steel wires that dangled from the concrete above. They dazzled me. I wished on them—the stars—but nothing happened.

A shiver pulsed through me. My teeth chattered. I clenched my jaw, listening to the click-click of my teeth. I screamed. The blood-curdling rawness of it bounced off the steel walls and the floor, echoing in my ears. Echoing in my bones.

No one seemed to hear.

I held my breath and listened to silence fill the space my inhale and exhale vacated. It reminded me of the night the guards had come for me. A week ago? They'd pounded on the door at 3:00 a.m., fists like sledgehammers breaking down the brick walls of my PTSD nightmare, jerking me into the real world with my heart thudding hard, the rush of my own blood filling my ears.

Nothing good had ever happened to me at 3:00 a.m.

My feet tangled in my sweat-soaked sheets. I half-climbed, half-fell out of bed, stumbling through the pitch-black room and down the long, dark hall, skimming a palm against the wall at hip-height to keep my balance. My toes curled into the worn carpet.

The hall emptied like a stream into the lake of my living room. Enough light leaked through at the edges of the window blinds to show me lumps and shadows. The sofa huddled against the far wall. The video screen sticking out a couple of inches on the wall opposite. The squat bookcase that crouched under the window, its shelves stacked to the brim with books I read and re-read.

I opened the door, its hinges protesting. The January night rushed in. I contracted in the face of the cold. I wore only a navy blue tank and a pair of navy pajama pants printed with white kitty faces. I folded my arms across my chest.

Three guards stood on the other side of the threshold. One man front-and-center, and one flanking either side of him. I lifted my chin and gazed into the empty, steel-gray eyes of the guard named Tom. No one to appeal to. No reflection. Nobody home.

His black hair was almost short enough to qualify as a buzz-cut. His pale skin testified that he hadn't seen the sun in months. His gray camouflage uniform was supposed to make him invisible to what exactly in the middle of the city? He was over six feet, and he was all wiry muscle.

He didn't appear to be armed—no sidearm—but I knew better. I knew the same as everyone else like me knew—better. The restraints he carried contained a sedative that would make the person wearing them compliant.

Compliant was a nice, official sounding word for *driven back into dissociation.* For separating me from myself. For taking away whatever victories I'd been able to achieve over the thirteen months since my diagnosis. The sedative would undo all of that over the course of seventy-two hours, maybe less.

I glanced at the men who flanked him, just as tall and strong. They carried stun guns in their holsters. I wanted to look at their faces, to take their measure, but my gaze slid down to those weapons and I couldn't make it move on or stop the prickling sensation that started at the nape of my neck.

Tom cleared his throat.

That did the trick as far as my eyes were concerned. I met his gaze.

He sounded like he'd spent a lot of time sucking on helium as a child and whatever deepening that should've happened in his teenage years hadn't quite taken.

"Adams, Lucy?"

I nodded. It was my apartment. And Tom and his buddies probably had a picture of me, as well as a map of my DNA that any portable scanner could confirm or deny.

"You need to come with us," he said.

"Where?" I asked, although I knew that, too. I spoke the word because that was what people did when guards came for them in the middle of the night. They asked.

"Your number's up," he said.

The prickling at the back of my neck grew stronger.

My lottery number. Every vet who'd been treated for a particular kind of mysterious medical symptom was assigned a number. We'd been exposed to something—the fallout from some weapon, like the soldiers who'd become sick from exposure to Agent Orange or depleted uranium—and it had changed us irrevocably.

We experienced ourselves from a distance—depersonalized, detached, dehumanized—sometimes for minutes, sometimes for days or years. We could come back from that, but remained susceptible. Suggestible. That had opened the door for medical science to solve a sticky problem.

Our disease wasn't the only one that arose from the ashes of the war. Both sides had used agents designed to attack the body in other ways, and they'd aimed those agents at the top minds. Leaders, sure. But also great thinkers, scientists. The very people both sides now needed to repair the ecosystems and genetic pools they'd destroyed if the human race—or any race—was to survive.

They'd acted without regard to consequence. Only victory mattered. Now, they acted as if magic could save the world.

The process the military doctors developed was the opposite of healing, the enemy of the Hippocratic oath. It was, however, useful, now that the war had ended. If it stole what little sense of self we had left, well, we were damaged anyway.

I wasn't a person. I was a piece of property.

Three men over six feet, well-muscled, and armed, versus me at five feet, four inches and seriously out-of-shape. And there was the problem of the stun guns.

My gaze wanted to slip back down toward them. I shuddered on the inside.

"I need to get dressed," I said.

Tom raised a brow. His gaze traveled toward my breasts.

I hugged myself tighter. "Excuse me."

"We'll be right here," he said.

I back-pedaled a few steps before I felt safe enough to turn around. I steadied my steps back down the dark hall. Behind me, one of the guards flicked on the recessed lights in the living room. They brightened to a gentle glow as I slipped into the bedroom and snicked the door shut behind me.

Five steps in, I sidled up to the dresser and leaned over to turn the switch on the short, fat black ceramic lamp. Its light illuminated the full-sized bed draped in white, the curtained window over the bed, and the wicker chair beside it, on top of which I'd tossed yesterday's jeans and nubby, white fisherman's sweater, along with my down jacket. My hikers with the thick, black socks tucked inside waited beneath the chair.

I dressed quickly, taking in the photo that hung over the chair—my mom at the beach, the waves breaking behind her, red curls wild around her face, her hazel eyes full of laughter. She'd been dead for seven years and four months.

She'd been allowed to die. She'd been lucky.

I climbed on top of the bed and opened the window silent as death, sliding out, my feet touching dirt and my heels brushing up against the rosemary hedge. I considered which way to turn.

I heard the whoosh of air behind my head before the blow struck, before pain seared through my skull and the world turned fuzzy and gray. I don't even remember falling, only the sensation of my stomach lurching and nausea clawing its way up my throat.

I woke up on the train with my head throbbing and a drugged, plastic restraint wrapped tight around each of my wrists. The guards had not used the connectors, thank God, so I could move my arms independently. The guards had more faith that the sedative would last while I was in the restraints.

My heart raced. Perspiration filmed my forehead. The pricking at the nape of my neck became an itch. I scratched until I drew blood. It didn't help. I chafed at the cuffs. They didn't budge.

The train car stank of fear and sweat. The seat the guards had put me in was lumpy and covered in red vinyl, and it faced backwards relative to the swift motion of the train. Flat, gray carpet hugged the floor. There were no windows. Like a cage.

I held my breath, listening to the clatter of the train on the track, feeling it shiver into me until I began to feel as if I was part of the train and not a separate person at all.

I leaned to my left, toward the aisle, and threw up, retching until all that came up was bile.

No one came. If someone had come, it wouldn't have been to help me.

A man's smoky voice interrupted my thoughts. "You all right?"

I glanced up. I didn't see him.

"Behind you," he said.

I looked over my shoulder and spotted him five rows back. He had thick brown hair, flecked with gold that stuck out in all directions from his head. His brown skin looked too pale, and his brown eyes looked rheumy from the sedative. All I could make out of his clothes was a black fleece jacket.

"When did they take you?" I asked.

"I'm Ben," he said, the left corner of his mouth curving into a wry smile. "Not for much longer."

I didn't have it in me to return the grin. I asked again. "When did they take you?"

"Same night they took you, I guess," he said. "There's four more of us. In a different car. They look worse off than us, like they got their asses kicked. And like they're not even in there. They wouldn't talk. Wouldn't even look at me."

I took a deep breath. It shuddered out of me so hard, I rocked in my seat.

"What'd you do?" he asked.

I shook my head to clear it, but all that did was make my stomach roll over again. I swallowed hard. "What?"

"In the army?" he asked.

"Supply," I said.

He didn't ask whether I'd been in the combat zone. Of course I had, or I wouldn't be here. If I closed my eyes, I could still smell the acrid stink of the smog in the air, so thick that it felt hard to breathe. I could sense the cold shadows of the tall, mangled glass and steel skyscrapers on either side of the cracked concrete streets closing in on me. I could feel the rumble of the truck's motor and the chill of the metal wheel in my hands as I drove. And the jolt and lurch of every bump we rolled over.

"Infantry," he said. "We saved the world. Supposedly."

I nodded. I wanted to cry.

He flashed his wry smile again. "No way out of this one."

I didn't respond. What could I possibly have said?

He didn't ask another question or offer another witty remark. Maybe because of my silence, or because the sedative stole his words.

I'd never told him my name. I wish I'd told him that, so someone else could know it, even for a day or two.

I stared at the flat gray carpet. I fell into it, the emptiness of it.

When I blinked, I realized it wasn't carpet at all. It was a wall made of steel. Slick and flat.

I lay on a cot bowed to one side that made me feel as if I'd slide off any second and crack my skull on the concrete floor. The thin cotton blanket provided the illusion of warmth, so I clung to it, white-knuckling the top and drawing it up tight under my chin.

The bloody itch at the nape of my neck screamed to be scratched. I couldn't move a muscle to answer.

A door opened on the far side of the room on perfectly oiled hinges. I felt the pressure in the room change ever so slightly, the ends of my hair ruffling in the gentlest of breezes. The soft footfalls of the guards' rubber-soled boots and the swish of their pants legs and the squeak of wheels began as a whisper that became a cacophony as they drew closer.

They wrapped their hands around my wrists and ankles and slid me onto a gurney. The stars overhead in their steel fixtures seemed to spiral like a galaxy. Like the galaxy we lived in. A spiral of stars.

The guards wheeled me between the lopsided cots and out of the steel room, down a disinfectant-swabbed corridor with scuffed white walls. The guard at the head of the gurney might've been Tom. He had the same short, black buzz cut and the no-sun skin and the wiry muscle. He didn't look at me.

I counted the number of feet and yards we traveled as best I could, like I had the seconds and minutes and hours before. After a minute, I lost track, so I didn't know how far they took me, only that every so often we passed beneath another star in the ceiling and that eventually, the guards pulled me into a room to my left, and that it smelled like musk cologne over and above the smell of disinfectant.

Counters lined the edges of the room, populated with basic med materials used to take vitals, and with books, binders, and a computer. The stars lit the ceiling in here, too, as if the sky had fallen. As if it was the end of the world.

The source of the smell was a man who looked a little bit like Ben, if Ben had worn a white coat, and had neater hair and sharp eyes. He wore a gold cross on a black leather thong around his neck. He looked at me as if I were a thing, taking my pulse with frosty hands coated in powdered latex.

His voice sounded as if he'd shouted from the bottom of a well. "You can leave her with me."

The Tom lookalike shook his head. "But what if she—"

"She won't fight back. She can't," the musk man said.

He couldn't be talking about me. He had to mean someone else, the woman whose body lay on the gurney in front of him. Lucy. She had red hair like her mother's, wavy where her mother's had curled. Her brown eyes looked empty. No one to appeal to behind them. No reflection. Nobody home.

The guards slipped out the door, leaving us with the musky man, who turned away from the gurney and walked a couple of steps toward the computer. His fingers moved on the keyboard. He felt comfortable turning his back on us, as if we were no danger to him.

He'd told the guards we couldn't fight back. No, he'd told them the woman on the gurney wouldn't. Couldn't.

She could still talk, though. "Who do I get?"

The musk man glanced over his shoulder. "Does it matter?"

"It does if I'm going to be the cage," she said.

The new body. The structure that held another person's consciousness. Another person's soul.

He shrugged. "He's a physicist."

"That's it?" she asked.

The musk man went still for a moment. "What else do you want to know? His name? Whether he has a family? What school he went to? Hobbies?"

Who cared about any of that?

"What's he like?" Lucy asked.

Did the physicist like to laugh? Was he kind? Was he as horrified by what had happened to him as she was?

The musk man sighed. "I don't know."

"Not a person," she said. "Property."

The musk man didn't respond. He didn't have to. Everything he might've said was written all over the way his shoulders rose until they floated just below his ears, the way his spine stiffened. Was he offended because the remark had hit close to home? Or because he didn't like to bother himself with the thought that the science—magic—he helped perform affected actual people?

He wheeled Lucy down the corridor by himself. I followed, not far behind. The concrete floor felt cold through the thin, cotton socks the guards had given me. The air chilled me through the gray pajamas I wore, straight to the bone.

We rolled for a good five minutes through more faceless halls, through three doors that required finger- and voice-print readings, passing into a room tricked out like a surgeon's kingdom, shiny silver instruments laid out on blue-paper-covered trays. These instruments bore no resemblance to any scalpel. The disinfectant smell was stronger here. A clock on the wall read 3:00.

The surgeon—the magician—himself had not yet arrived, but the physicist had. He lay on a gurney just like Lucy's. Unlike Lucy, his body had shriveled and decayed with him in it. The only thing about him that reminded me of a human being was his eyes, bright blue and filled with intelligence.

Lucy watched the stars on the ceiling, holding her breath every few minutes, listening hard.

I watched the physicist. He seemed to see me, standing beside him, leaning over him. He met my gaze.

"I'm about to be obliterated," I said.

His soul would slip into the places where mine no longer connected to my body—to Lucy's body. He'd slide in and take over, trapping me inside flesh and blood and bones, inside of a skin, with no voice.

He couldn't speak, not in any traditional way. He talked to me with those eyes.

I'm about to be changed forever, he said.

I understood the implications behind those words. He'd be able to walk and talk, to do the science demanded of him, but he'd do it knowing that the price had been someone else's life, someone else's soul.

He couldn't fight it, even if he wanted to. Not now. But would he, if he could? What was he like? I didn't know.

Would I be able to fight him from the inside? Could I find a way? Could we work together, the two of us? I wanted to believe.

The musk man's shoes squeaked as he turned on his heels. I pivoted my attention toward him as he opened the door for a woman whose voice reminded me of a hard rain on a tin roof. She walked into the room, her hair a golden halo, her skin without a single wrinkle, her face composed. She wore black scrubs, like a surgeon.

She was the magician. The priest of our doom.

I looked again into the eyes of the physicist. He looked back at me, his gaze, his hope and terror a mirror of my own.

A hush filled the room. It stole every sound, even the remains of my fury. The magic began as we ended. Not people, but property. No longer recognizably human.

They wanted us to help save the world. They didn't understand what they were asking, what needed to be done.

They'd started a war that they'd demanded we fight. Who knew why? Natural resources. Money. Control. It didn't matter in the end.

Peace would reign for a while, until they forgot what peace meant, until someone became too greedy, and then it would begin again. History, repeating itself.

They wanted us to help save the world. They didn't understand what that meant—that our job was to save the world from them.

I screamed righteous fury. It echoed inside my head. No one else heard.

Not yet.

HAUNTED

JAMIE FERGUSON

Jamie Ferguson has stories in two previous Fiction River *volumes:* Tavern Tales *and* Wishes. *I've read a lot of Jamie's stories and no matter what she always gets into the minds and hearts of her characters, whether she's writing about a saloon girl in the Old West or a man who discovers the barista he's in love with is a naiad.*

About this story she says, "I love visiting ghost towns and thinking about what the lives of the people who lived in them long ago were like. I enjoy writing about characters who aren't who you think they are…"

Even ghosts may be masking their true identities. And in "Haunted" Jamie sends her protagonist into a veritable forest of unexplained characters, objects, and events that she must somehow fashion reality from.

As if her life depends on it.

———

Jill stepped across the floor of the old, abandoned mountain cabin, the thick wooden planks creaking under her footsteps. She rested her hands on the edge of the empty window frame, careful to avoid the splintered bits, and looked out at the aspen-covered hillside. The cool September breeze gently rustled her hair, and carried the scents of pine and earth and sagebrush in from outside. She turned around and froze.

A ghost stood maybe ten feet away from her.

Her entire body felt as though it had turned to ice.

The ghost was dressed in dark brown trousers, worn leather boots, and a shirt that might be blue or brown—it was hard to be sure because he was so insubstantial. Jill could see the boards in the wall behind him through his body. He was clean-shaven, and wore a black hat with a narrow brim. It had to be the ghost Kevin had told her about on the drive from Denver: Eddie Wayne Milton, the man who had murdered his wife Lillian in this house in 1893. But ghosts didn't really exist.

The ghost of Eddie Wayne Milton touched the brim of his hat and gave her a little nod.

Not only could she see the ghost, it could see *her*.

"Kevin?" she said, her voice in a whisper so low even she could barely even hear it. She took a step backward, smacking into the wall. She pressed her back against it, her hands flat against the rough wood. Kevin had to be playing a trick on her. She'd seen stuff like this on TV. "Kevin, knock it off," she said loudly. "This isn't funny." She began to inch sideways, her hands trailing across the old wood, and her eyes glued to the ghost.

The ghost's head turned to follow her as she moved. He rubbed his chin with his fingers.

"Come on, Kevin," she said, her voice cracking. A bead of sweat trickled down the side of her face. She reached the corner and began to follow the next wall. "Please stop."

"What's going on?"

Jill whirled around to see Kevin's head poking in through the window, framed by the bright sunlight. "Kevin, this isn't funny!" She turned back to the ghost.

It was gone.

"What are you talking about?" Kevin said. "I'm not doing anything. Hey, check this out. I found this really cool rock over by what used to be the stable." He held up something small and dark gray. "I'm not sure, but I think it might be an arrowhead."

She ran a hand through her hair. "I—really? You weren't playing a trick on me?"

Kevin looked at her as if she were speaking a different language. "I have no idea what you're talking about. Have I ever played a trick on you?"

She shook her head and swallowed. "Then...I think I saw the ghost."

Kevin raised an eyebrow. "Seriously? What did it look like?"

"He, uh...." She glanced over at the spot where the ghost had been standing. "He looked like a miner from the late 1800s. Just like you'd expect."

"Uh huh," Kevin said. He rolled his eyes. "Look, you don't need to make anything up."

"What?" Jill began to cross the floor, her feet slow, her eyes darting around to make sure the ghost hadn't returned.

"Why would you see the ghost of the *guy*? We were looking for the ghost of the *woman* he killed."

"Well, clearly he's here too. Didn't you tell me he was so distraught after killing his wife that he shot himself three days later? And *you're* the one who wanted to see ghosts—not me!"

Kevin snorted. "Look, you're a sweet girl, but you don't need to make up a story just because you know I've always wanted to see a ghost, okay? I'm going to go start the car." He stepped away from the window, leaving her alone in the haunted cabin.

"Wait!" Jill put her hands to her mouth. "Wait for me, please!" She ran across the rest of the room to the doorway, and then through the next room to the door that led outside. She dashed across the porch, leaping over a hole where the wood had rotted away, and then skidded to a stop as something shiny caught her eye.

A single earring lay on the dirt next to the old porch. She crouched down and picked it up. It was a tiny heart that dangled from a silver hoop earring. She glanced back at the old house. The Colorado sunshine was warm on her shoulders. Maybe she had imagined the ghost.

Maybe.

Jill jammed the earring in her pocket and hurried up the hillside to the car.

Three days... later she saw the ghost again.

It was just after 2 a.m. Kevin's snoring had woken Jill up. She poked him a few times to get him to stop, and then decided to get up and get a drink of water. She pulled on her slippers and padded downstairs. She reached the bottom of the stairs and turned on the light switch.

The ghost of Eddie Wayne Milton stood next to the stone hearth. It had *followed her home*.

"Oh my God," she whispered. She took a step backward, reaching her right hand out behind her. Eddie touched his hat lightly, and then pointed at the fireplace. His mouth moved, but no sound came out. Her hand brushed against the cool, polished wood of the banister. She grabbed hold of it, and then turned and ran up the stairs as fast as she could. She leapt into bed with Kevin and pulled the covers over her head. She didn't sleep at all for the rest of the night.

After that Jill saw the ghost every few days. She told Kevin, who got annoyed, and they ended up having a big fight in which he accused her of making the whole thing up. He even made a comment that suggested perhaps she was mentally ill—because who kept insisting that a ghost had followed them home?

She didn't mention it again.

She stayed late at work, and made up errands to do on the way home every day, so that Kevin would be there by the time she got home. It would show up in the middle of the day just as easily as at night. Or did it? Maybe she was going crazy. She'd never believed in ghosts, and now she was being stalked by one. It did sound insane. She scheduled an appointment with a therapist, but found herself listening to a long-winded lecture on how sometimes people convince themselves they're seeing things when they're really just trying to get attention. She didn't go back.

After a few terrifying weeks she started to get used to seeing the ghost. It only ever appeared in three spots: by the fireplace, in Kevin's office, and in the family room next to the walnut bookcase Kevin had built into the wall long before he and Jill had met. All she had to do was avoid those parts of the house—or at least avoid them when Kevin wasn't around, since the ghost never manifested if he was present. That wasn't super easy to do, but it was better than being constantly terrified. She would occasionally catch a glimpse of the ghost as she hurried by one of his spots, but to her tremendous relief he never followed her.

One Saturday afternoon she paused just outside the door to Kevin's office. The ghost had never tried to harm her, nor do anything to frighten her, aside from the fact that just seeing it at all was terrifying. Supposedly ghosts had unfinished business. Maybe Eddie was trying to give her a message so he could go on to whatever happened after one was a ghost? She had no idea why she could see him, but what if he had followed her home *because* she could see him, and he needed her help? What if he hadn't really killed his wife, and he was stuck being a ghost until he got the story straight?

Jill took a deep breath and walked into Kevin's office.

There was nobody there.

"Eddie?" she said. She bit her lip. "Hey Eddie, I, uh, I don't know why you're here, but I think you're trying to tell me something. I think maybe you need my help. I'll try not to be scared if you show up. Okay?"

Nothing happened. Maybe Eddie didn't have anything to accomplish, but just wanted to haunt a house that had people in it.

She looked around the room. It smelled faintly of the leather and oakmoss of Kevin's aftershave. His laptop sat, closed, on the desk. The bookshelf held a mixture of business books and military fiction. An armchair sat in the corner.

Eddie was nowhere to be seen.

"Okay, another time, then," she said. Maybe she was going crazy. She was talking to a ghost who wasn't even there. She turned to leave.

The ghost stood next to Kevin's desk.

Jill felt as though a bucket of ice water had been poured over her head. She took a step backward.

"Hi, Eddie." She dug her fingernails into her palms so hard they hurt. "Maybe this was a bad idea. You know, we can always talk another time."

Eddie shook his head and pointed at one of the drawers in Kevin's desk.

She took a deep breath. "Do you want me to open that?" She had no idea what the ghost could possibly want from something in Kevin's desk. How was this going to help with his unfinished business?

Eddie nodded.

She pressed her lips together. "Okay. Would you mind standing over there?" She gestured toward the opposite wall. "Please. I'm—I'm kind of afraid of you."

Eddie grinned, and then stepped back and stood next to the door to the office. Jill tried not to think about the fact that he was now blocking the way out. She stepped over to Kevin's desk and opened the drawer. It contained office supplies: boxes of pens, notepads, scissors, a roll of tape. She looked up at Eddie. "I don't get it. What am I supposed to be seeing?"

Eddie made a gesture with his hand, as if moving something aside. She thought for a moment, and then pulled the drawer out as far as it could go. She peered into the very back. A small cardboard box was stuffed behind a large stapler. She pulled the box out, her hands trembling.

"Is this it?"

Eddie nodded.

Jill set the box on the desk, glanced at Eddie, and then lifted the lid.

Inside was a single silver earring: a hoop, from which dangled a tiny heart. It was exactly like the earring she'd found at Eddie's cabin in the mountains. Kevin sometimes gave her jewelry. Maybe he'd been planning on giving her the earrings that day, but had lost the one she'd found in the dirt? Why did the ghost care about this? Whether he'd killed his wife or not, that had been in 1893. These earrings were clearly modern.

She heard the garage door open—Kevin must be back from running errands. She closed the box and put it back in place, and then pushed the drawer shut. When she looked up Eddie had disappeared. She hurried down the hallway to greet Kevin, wondering why Eddie cared so much about a pair of earrings.

A week after her attempt to communicate with the ghost she woke up one night feeling utterly parched. She lay in bed for a while listening to Kevin's incessant snoring, trying to decide if she was brave enough to go downstairs and get a drink of water. Eddie would be either by the fireplace or the bookcase, both of which she had to pass on the way to the kitchen. She'd inspected them both, but hadn't found anything in the fireplace but ashes, and of course there was nothing but books on the bookshelves.

Finally Jill got up and tiptoed out of the bedroom, shut the door behind her, and headed downstairs, turning the lights on as she went. Sure enough, Eddie was standing by the stone fireplace in the living room. She paused at the bottom of the stairs, one hand on the banister, and set her chin. He was just a ghost. What could he possibly do? He couldn't even open a desk drawer by himself.

"I'm sorry, Eddie," she said. "I looked in the fireplace, and I have no idea what you want me to find."

She turned her back on him and walked to the kitchen, her skin crawling. The lower floor smelled faintly of lime and ginger from the stir-fry she'd made for dinner. Jill poured a glass of water and drank it as quickly as she could.

Eddie walked through the dining room, tipped his hat at her, and headed toward the family room.

She set her glass down and sighed. Maybe if she could figure out what he wanted he'd go away. She hadn't seen him in Kevin's office since she'd found the earring; what if there was something equally as trivial she had to do in his other two spots, and then he went away?

She grimaced and followed him, turning on the lights so the room was brightly lit. Sure enough, the ghost had stopped next to the bookcase.

"Okay, Eddie." She felt chilly in spite of her flannel pajamas, and wished she'd thought to pull on her robe. She crossed her arms. "Help me understand what you need to finish your unfinished business. Is there a book I'm supposed to look at? Something you want me to read? I've looked through all of the books, but I have no idea what you're trying to tell me."

She pressed her lips together. Maybe Eddie wasn't trying to tell her anything. Maybe he was just confused. Or maybe she really was going crazy.

Eddie pointed at the lower shelves of the bookcase.

Jill took a deep breath and walked over, her slippers making small, muted scuff sounds on the carpet. Eddie backed away, giving her room, as if he understood she was afraid of him. She crouched down and pointed at the third shelf from the bottom.

"Is it on this shelf?"

Eddie shook his head.

She pointed at the next shelf down. "This one?"

Eddie's eyes lit up. He nodded.

"How about I'll look at all the books on this shelf and you can tell me when I've found the right one. Okay?"

Eddie shook his head again.

"It's not a book?"

Eddie smiled.

This made no sense. Why did he want her to look at a shelf, but not at the books on it? She'd gone through all the books one afternoon, and had found nothing behind them, nor in them. What else could he want her to do?

She worried the hem of her pajama top, and then shrugged. If it wasn't a book, she'd just move them out of the way. He'd see there was nothing left. She pulled all of the books off the second shelf from the bottom, and set them on the coffee table.

"Am I on the right track?" *Or just off my rocker.*

Eddie nodded. He took off his hat and clasped it in both hands.

Jill grabbed her cell phone from the dining room table and turned on the flashlight, shining it around the shelf. There was nothing out of the ordinary. One spot on the dark wood, in the back top left-hand corner, looked less polished than the rest of the wood, but that was it. She ran her fingers across the worn area, pressing on it.

The bookshelf began to move toward her.

She dropped her phone and leapt up, jumping out of the way of the bookcase, and tripped over the coffee table, knocking several books off onto the floor. She watched, open-mouthed, as the book-shelf swung open.

There was a secret room behind it.

She stared into the room. A light had turned on inside it as the bookcase—the *door*—had opened. She could see the edge of an armchair, or maybe it was a couch. How could her house—*her house!*—contain a secret room? She'd lived here for almost two years!

She ran through the floor plan in her head. The living room was over there, the garage and the storage room on the other side. Now that she thought about it, there *was* enough space in between for a small room. It had never occurred to her before—who analyzed their house looking for hidden rooms? But the storage area wasn't as deep as it could have been. She'd never realized until now.

When they'd first met, Kevin had been building the bookcase. He'd mentioned it on an early date, long before she'd ever been to the house. Kevin had built the secret room, and had never told her about it.

Prickles ran down Jill's back. Why hadn't he told her?

There was a good reason. There had to be. Although for the life of her she couldn't think what it could possibly be.

She set her jaw and entered the room.

The room was maybe seven feet by twelve feet, and smelled vaguely of bleach. The size made sense—she'd measured the storage room last year when they'd put in cabinets, and it was just over twelve feet long. How could she not have realized all of this space was missing from the house? She shook her head. Obviously she had missed it. She stopped just inside the opening and looked around.

A small, dark gray sofa sat against one of the long walls; two low wide credenzas lined the other. A desk and a single folding chair sat next to the sofa, a laptop and a legal pad rested on top of the desk. A framed print of Picasso's Dove of Peace hung above the sofa, but otherwise the walls were bare.

She walked over to the desk and looked at the pad of paper. An address was written on it, in Kevin's hand: 2482 Kilhaven Drive.

Where was that? Was that someone's address? Was Kevin seeing someone else?

Even if he was seeing someone else, what was this room for?

Jill took a deep breath, walked over to the nearest credenza, and pulled open one of the four doors.

It was empty.

She pulled open every door, but there was nothing in any of them. She swallowed and moved to the second credenza. She opened the right-most door. There were two shelves in this compartment; the upper one held what looked like a shirt. She pulled it out and held it up. It was a sweatshirt Kevin had lost last year—or had said he'd lost. One sleeve was ripped. She folded it and put it back, and then crouched down to look at the bottom shelf. There were two plastic containers, one stacked on top of the other. She pulled out the top one and opened it.

A woman's wallet lay inside.

Jill picked up the wallet. It was a pale pink, and was decorated with white and red flowers. She opened it, her hands shaking, and pulled out the driver's license. It belonged to a Melanie Jameson. She stared at the photo; Melanie was twenty-four, brunette, and an organ donor. Jill had never met this woman in her life, but she looked familiar. She set the wallet down and looked to see what else was in the box.

The box was filled with newspaper clippings. She pulled out the first one—it was from last April, and mentioned that Melanie Jameson was missing. *That's* why her name and photo seemed familiar. Jill remembered reading about the story last year. She sifted through the clippings, the story coming back to her. They described Melanie Jameson's disappearance, and the subsequent discovery of her body—but not her head—in a ravine in the mountains. The clippings were ordered by date, with the oldest on top.

She felt as though she'd been punched in the stomach. There could only be one reason why Kevin had the dead girl's wallet, and why he'd cut out all the articles about her. And that would explain why he'd built the hidden room—and why he'd never told her about it.

She put the clippings back and opened the second box. This one contained a collection of labeled plastic bags. It took her a second to realize what was in them; each one held a lock of hair. Red hair, black hair, curly hair, straight hair. Every bag was labeled with a name: Melanie Jameson, brown hair; Sandra Cox, curly black hair; Ellen Hayes, blonde hair.

The box was full of bags.

A small sound made her jump. Jill jerked her head up to see Kevin standing in the doorway. He wore a white T-shirt, blue plaid boxers, and the moccasin slippers she'd given him for Christmas last year. She'd been dating a murderer—for *years*. How many women had he killed?

"I see you've found my...collection." He smiled. "What do you think?"

"I—you—I can't believe this." She scrambled to her feet. She felt woozy, as though she'd been drinking. "This isn't real. I'm dreaming."

Kevin shook his head. "I'm sorry, my dear, but you are not."

Jill shook her head. "No. No!" She waved her hand at the credenza next to her. "Why do you do this? Why did you murder all of these women? How many have you killed? Why haven't you killed *me*?"

"Well, I'm obviously going to have to *now*," Kevin said. "But that wasn't part of the plan." He took a step into the room. "It's nice to have someone to come home to after a long day of murdering people. Plus you're a good cook. Now I'm going to have to go back to ordering take-out all the time."

Jill blinked. "What?"

Kevin waved a hand in the air. "Oh, I'll get used to it. Don't worry. Now let's get this over with. I promise I'll go easy on you."

She shook her head. "You're going to go easy with *killing me*?"

"Well, yeah." Kevin moved over to the desk and opened a drawer. "You haven't really given me a lot of choice." He pulled out a length of cord and began wrapping it around one hand. "I *am* sorry, you know. I was going to propose to you on your birthday."

She glanced at the door. Kevin was a few feet away from it. Maybe she could push past him and get out the door. He was much stronger than her, but she had to try—she couldn't just let him kill her! Oh, why had Eddie shown her this room? Why had she never noticed it before? Why had she gone inside of it when Kevin was home?

Eddie stepped in through the open doorway. He'd put his hat back on.

"Now, don't try that," Kevin said. Jill met his eyes. "You know you can't get past me."

She took a tiny step toward the door, her gaze locked on Kevin. "What's in the fireplace?"

Kevin's eyes narrowed. "How did you know about that?"

"Just tell me."

He shrugged and chuckled. "Sometimes I like to bring...things... home. And you can't exactly keep stuff like that lying around for very long."

Bile rose in her throat. She inched closer to the door. "What about the earring?"

"Earring?" He thought for a moment. "You went through my desk? Really, what kind of person are you?"

"I found an earring at the cabin where I saw the ghost. It matches the earring in your office."

"Ghost," Kevin said with a snort. "I still don't know why on earth you made that whole story up. I took you there because I killed a girl there. Don't you get it? I wanted to see *her* ghost. Not the ghost of some guy who's been dead for over a century."

Out of the corner of her eye Jill could see Eddie holding his hand out toward her, beckoning. What was he trying to tell her?

"So those earrings belonged to the girl you...murdered?"

"Of course," Kevin said. "I was really pissed when I couldn't find the other one. I was going to give them to you as a present." He grinned. "I like seeing you in other women's jewelry."

She glanced at Eddie; he pointed out into the family room. It seemed like he was telling her to run. There was no way she'd make it, but she had to try. She took a deep breath and sprinted for the doorway.

Kevin's hand brushed against her arm, and then he let out a yell.

"It's a fucking *ghost!*"

She ran out the door and across the family room, and then stopped by the couch and looked back. She couldn't see in the hidden room from this angle because the bookcase blocked it from view, but from the awful sounds Kevin was making Eddie must be doing something to him. She dashed over to the bookcase and pressed the worn spot on the empty shelf, jumping back as the bookcase began to swing shut. She turned and ran to the door to the garage. She pulled the door open and paused, one hand on the knob, and looked back into the house.

The bookcase had swung shut, hiding the secret room. She could hear Kevin's muffled yells through the wood.

She ran across the concrete floor of the garage and pulled open the metal door to the circuit breaker box. She stared at the two columns of switches. They were all labeled, but which circuit was the door to the secret room on?

She grabbed all the levers and turned every circuit off. Everything went dark and silent.

Jill tiptoed back in the house. Moonlight streamed in through the windows, covering the room in silvery-white light.

Eddie walked through the wall from the secret room.

The bookcase was still closed.

Kevin banged on it from the other side. "Hey!" Kevin yelled. "What the hell? What happened to the fucking power? Open this fucking door!"

She picked her cell phone up off the floor and dialed 911, her fingers shaking so badly she had to try three times before getting the numbers right.

A loud thump came from inside the secret room, and then

another. It sounded like Kevin was throwing himself against the door.

She gave her address to the person on the phone, her voice shaking. Kevin couldn't break the door down, could he? She could hear sirens—she could wait for the police outside, just in case.

Eddie walked across the room and stood in front of her. The sirens were getting louder.

"That day I saw you, you knew, didn't you? Kevin had—had—" She swallowed. "He'd murdered someone at your cabin, and you were trying to warn me."

Eddie nodded, his face somber.

Someone knocked on the front door. "Police!"

"Thank you," she said. "I don't know if this helps with your unfinished business, but you saved my life. And probably a lot of others as well."

Eddie smiled and tipped his hat. He turned and began to walk toward the back of the house, growing fainter and fainter with each step.

"Police! Open up!"

"I'm coming!" Jill said, and ran to the front door. She pulled it open and glanced back where Eddie had been standing.

Eddie was gone.

SKINWALKER

VALERIE BROOK

Valerie Brook writes stories about the darker shadows of life, yet her characters still find a powerful light to shine no matter the challenges they face. She has been called "...one of the best and most powerful new writers appearing on the scene" by Pulphouse Magazine.

This is her fourth appearance in Fiction River. *Her stories have been in the volumes* Visions of the Apocalypse, Superpowers, *and most recently* Justice.

Valerie says about her first of two stories in this volume, "I have always been interested in shamanism as a foundational human experience across many cultures stretching far into antiquity. Worldwide, human interactions with the spirit world are vast and uncharted, both light and loving or dark and disturbing..."

This story has one of my favorite heroines in this volume. No part of her is at peace with her very dangerous world. As the old saying goes, man knows no fury like a deeply pissed-off teenager. Or something like that.

D rew threw the can of soda with her softball pitcher's arm at the wall of her grandfather's mud-colored adobe house. It exploded with a *whomp* and the fizzy clear liquid sprayed up into the hot, deep blue sky of the Albuquerque desert like a crystal chandelier fractured by a shotgun.

A fine misty rainbow plumed around her and fell to the caked dirt of a backyard, smelling sweet like fry bread. Drew got even madder because it was so flipping hot outside and she'd wanted a cold drink.

Now she didn't have one anymore.

This pueblo really looked like it was made out of mud just dug right out of the ground, all smoothed out by the builder's hands as they rounded the edges, shiny square glass windows reflecting the big sun with buttery copper winks, and the roof flat as a tortilla.

It was all ancient Indian ruins meets designer New York architect —or something like that. Except the dirt yard was strewn with junky odds and ends, like that rusty truck bumper and an upside down ceramic bathroom sink.

The heat of the late afternoon sun irritated her neck where tender brown skin was newly exposed. Her long black hair had been damaged in the car fire, singed off actually, on the right side. So she'd fixed the problem herself. Buzzed the back with Dad's clippers while she was still in Chicago last week, scissored the sides for a girly, feminine 'hawk but, well—that didn't work out.

So basically she looked like she could join the military now, a fourteen-year-old, and she had the muscled arms to prove it.

Maybe people would leave her alone.

Not that anybody had said anything yet out here in the middle of roadrunner nowhere, except the taxi cab driver, who'd said good luck. He'd also plucked that Sprite out of a little Styrofoam cooler, complete with a palm print stain in dried ketchup on the lid, and tossed the can out his passenger's window.

Drew hadn't expected the throw, had glanced up at the streaking sun and blinded out, but she'd still caught the drink.

Because you want to play the ball, don't let it play you.

Her grandfather on her dad's side, whom she'd never met, was supposed to be home but he wasn't. And the taxi cab had vanished along the stupid dirt road that led back to the city, that just shot off along the flat mesa and the dried bushes in a straight line, and left her here in nowheresville.

Just a cloud of dust like a phantom train disappearing until no trace was left. She watched the dust fade all the way back to clear sky.

And Mom had taken Drew's cell phone before she boarded the private jet.

Because no one can know where you are. No one, do you understand, honey? Not until the attack gets sorted out. You can't text your friends. You can't trust your friends anymore. We can't even trust the police.

I won't text my friends.

You will.

The melted plastic taste came back, coating the roof of her

mouth, like the car fire was happening all over again. She pushed the memory of that midnight event outside the Lincolnworth Club away because in reality it was bright and hot here.

Here was not *there*. It was not *then*.

Drew walked up to the home's southern facing wall in her Gucci rubber flip-flops, where the dripping soda had darkened on the clay and started to look like one of those inkblot Rorschach tests, you know—the kind that the psychs use to test for crazy people.

Or that you can do with your friends online.

She squatted down to pick up the busted green can, her too-tight jeans baring her butt crack again, which was really getting on her nerves today—sitting crosslegged on the bed in the private jet chasing the sun in the western sky, and then hurrying through the airways of the Albuquerque International Sunport with the address her mom had scrawled on a Post-It note.

Why did she have to grab this pair out of the walk-in closet instead of her Forever denim?

And who calls an airport a sunport?

She glanced over her tight pink T-shirted shoulder—across the tumbleweed yard, over a crumpled up blue tarp, and beyond the decaying edges of a cinderblock wall. The air smelled like sagebrush and squeezed lime.

The great yawning wasteland was a National Geographic photograph she didn't even want to be in.

This was the Isleta Pueblo reservation. The very northern edge, where Indian switched over to White Man on the map, right? Her dad had grown up in Albuquerque. Could this be his childhood home? She didn't even know. Dad didn't talk childhood.

Zero cars in the driveway, zero grandpa answering the front door even though she had knocked for like five minutes after the taxi left.

No neighbors except the sunbathing lizards she'd seen doing pushups on the big boulder by the front door.

Oh yeah, and that shaggy black, long-legged dog jumping over the broken fence as she'd handed the twenties over to the taxi man from the back seat. Must've been scared off.

Drew wiped off the sand stuck to the fizzing, hissing Sprite can and sucked the cool-tasting sugar water out of the split in the container between the capital S and the lowercase P.

The sharp aluminum threatened to cut her dry tongue.

She stood up, crumpling the can a little more in her fist, then dropping it.

The giant fireball of a sun was sinking to the west way out there beyond the purple-tinted hills, where maybe it looked a little like it could be the end of the world, too.

Shadows were beginning a steady crawl across the pockmarked ground, lengthening and stretching and every moment maybe a little darker.

Okay fine.

No iPhone. No long-lost grandfather named Rick. No other choice. It was time to go into the house because what else was she supposed to do? Sit on her suitcase until a rattlesnake strolled up and fanged her on the butt?

She retraced her steps across the gravelly driveway to her White Sox overnight bag and slung it over her shoulder.

I don't want to go to New Mexico, Mom. Don't make me go.

I've got to hide you somewhere, Drew.

But Dad is estranged and doesn't want me to meet to his father, ever. He'll be so mad. I'm not allowed to talk about that side of the family, don't you understand anything?

I understand plenty, you little brat. Watch your mouth. Your grandfather Rick is just a nothing old medicine man, he's agreed you can stay for a few days. No one will think to look for you there.

You can't make me go.

I will.

The front entry to the house was a red arch with a blue painted door. A few wooden splinters waited patiently on the door frame to cactus-poke the next finger that came near. A spiky plant brushed Drew's wrist.

Instead of knocking over and over this time, she pushed down the iron latch on the door and it opened like it had no defense.

It's not breaking in if it just opens, right?

"Hello," she called. A refreshing, floral rush of air exhaled over her face. "Rick?"

Her flip-flops smacked her heels as she stepped through the threshold and set the bag on a stone cut floor with a thunk. She closed the door behind her.

Then it was all silent. A thick, gathering silence.

Kinda like the silence of being unwelcome.

Drew just stood there, feeling the flow of uncertainty squeeze through her chest, thickening within her arms and legs, pooling in her feet like a hardening glue.

She didn't want to walk further into the house and she didn't want to go back outside.

"Rick?" But of course she knew no one was home.

In the last rays of buttery light fading through the windows, Drew saw the interior walls of the house were rounded and arched in pinkish-coral adobe. Quaint little southwestern style decor—a wool blanket with a kachina doll hung from an iron rack on the wall, a clay pot on a coffee table with red hand-blown glass chilies, shelves with those miniature cactuses.

But the couches and chairs were covered with ghostly white sheets.

Like the kind you put up when you're on a long vacation.

Beyond the living room, the northern face of a clean kitchen poked its nose around the corner, the view of the desert sky through a high round window looked like a wise woman's worried eye, the black iris of night dilating.

The inside of this house said female touch all over it.

Yes, and it even smelled faintly like lavender, or a woman's perfume. And Drew's mom had said her grandfather lived *alone*. And no offense to her Dad and all, but genetically he wouldn't know how to decorate or cook or perfume anything if it could save him a punch in the face.

The light kept draining out of the windows.

Drew took a few steps closer to a collection of photographs on a bookshelf full of worn paperbacks. They were all white people.

Every single one.

Drew felt her stomach clench. Dad didn't talk childhood, but he wasn't white. His skin was even darker than Drew's.

Two sharp knocks pounded against the door behind her back.

Drew whirled around, her hands in the defensive position like the batter had smacked a chopper at her face. But she didn't have a glove. She wasn't fast pitching on the mound.

And who knocks on their own front door?

Only the hiss of her flip-flops scuffing as she had turned. Only her eyes flitting to the unlocked iron latch.

And no peephole.

Her heart pounded, raw and offbeat. A terrible feeling crawled down her spine—the feeling of danger. The feeling of malevolence.

Her ears were scanning like radar, trying to hear anything.

She softly pressed both hands on the door, then her foot against the doorjamb, feeling for a vibration, like she could keep the barrier from swinging open, because she hadn't seen a splash of headlights on the walls, hadn't heard car tires crunching gravel, hadn't heard a car door slam.

No one should be outside but someone was.

And it wasn't a normal someone.

Drew wanted to call her mom and say help me. And then Drew thought, what is wrong with me, just say hello, just say hello who's there?

Instead, she flipped the lock with a loud *ker-clunk*.

It echoed like a public confession.

She took one step away from the door, wishing she could grip the steel of her Beretta. Dad hid the firearms behind the false wall in the basement. Mom didn't let her go down there but Drew did anyway.

There wasn't another knock, or even a fleck of a sound like a leaf scratching.

Drew took a few more steps backward in her flip-flops and they smacked her heels because they are the noisiest shoes a person can wear.

She tried to scoot her feet instead. *Shhhh,* her flip-flops cried. Drew left them behind.

Her toes widened on the smooth stone, squished on the soft plush carpet, pattered across the linoleum, as she retreated backwards until she bumped the kitchen table with her thigh.

Her hand squeezed the sticky wooden frame on the back of a chair. Released. Squeezed again.

Her shallow exhale pooled under her nose, smelled like stomach acid.

In the dim light there was an L-shaped counter and double sink and upright cupboards. Drew searched for the elongated shape of a cordless phone on the counter. The oven clock said eight forty-five in neon green. *Mom, I need you.* And a light switch?

The dim border of a sliding glass doorframe pinned and stretched the blue-black skin of the night tattooed with sickly yellow stars.

Why did you have to start a divorce?

Because your father's a cocksucker.

No he's not, you're the one who sucks cock.

And Mom had backslapped Drew right then, in the aqua-blue Porsche Cayman idling at a red light, in the middle of downtown Chicago with a full crosswalk of suits streaming by carrying their dead animal briefcases, answering their calls with shiny perfect teeth because it was all too important to wait. And Drew remembered how Mom's Maurice Lacroix watch had scratched Drew's jaw with a thin mark that somehow looked like the letter C. How her long hair had stuck to the line of salty sweat on her upper lip—where the slap started swelling, just a little.

Then Drew snapped back to reality.

This wasn't Illinois.

And now she was crouched behind the legs of the kitchen table and chairs, peering through them like cell bars, hiding from the thugs her mega-bucks attorney dad kept around whenever the bar was an open bar, like the rowdy pool parties, the World Series BBQ's. Because he was one of the suits. A dirty suit. Her family was crime money and she knew it.

No one ever had to tell her. It was what you learned by example.

Drew's palms were drenched in sweat.

Dr. Lahoya had said that when the PTSD starts, Drew was supposed to try and get her nervous system to go back to its normal state.

To find the trigger and remove it.

But now Mom was going all state's evidence and Drew had been subpoenaed, too. Was served last week. Just before the car accident —the car *bomb*.

Drew's pitching hand flitted up to her neck to pull her hair out of her face, but there was no hair there anymore. She kept forgetting that. The stubs were rough and scratchy. She wanted her long, blue-black ponytail. Why had she cut it off? That was stupid.

Everything was stupid.

A weak crescent moon drooped like it was pinned up in the sky by a single thumbtack. Okay, just stand up. Just walk around fast and flick on every single light in the house and find a phone.

"You can do this," she whispered to herself and her own voice sounded like someone else.

A figure moved across the backyard, between the mounded blue tarp and the horizontal cinderblock wall.

Drew peered out through the sliding glass doors with scalpel eyes. It was hard to see.

It was a black-on-black shadow oozing out of the pores of the night like a pool of ink, tall and lurking, and then Drew recognized the huge front paws of a dog, the hump of a knotted neck and muscled shoulders.

That same black dog. She'd seen it jumping over the cinderblocks in the sun earlier.

Now the huge dog pawed across the dirty yard, up onto the concrete patio, and pressed its fat pinkish nose to the glass. Its nostrils flared like a pig, the tip bending, drawing a smear mark. Making an elongated squeak.

It drew a Z. Looking left, then down, then right. Then straight at her.

It had an extra long neck.

Bloodshot red eyes, like dried ketchup. Like the ketchup on the taxi man's cooler when he'd tossed the soda. And for an irrational second Drew thought the dog had eaten the taxi man, and now his soul was trapped inside.

She'd been *with* the taxi man when she first saw the dog.

Paying him the money.

To leave her here. The address on the Post-it.

Which someone had switched.

An overwhelming stink of rotten eggs washed over Drew and she gagged on stomach acid. Her eyes were on the dog, she couldn't look away. Couldn't even blink.

His lips pulled back, shiny white teeth except they were a man's set of teeth, straight and perfect and pearly white.

"Mouth shut," the dog man's voice gurgled like its throat was full of liquid. "Keep it."

He slowly rose up, stood up on his long, sinewy legs and he was an ungodly eight feet tall, the red eyes angled down at Drew and she almost started to pee herself but she clenched her abdomen tight.

The dog man coughed and chunks of meat and blood sprayed the window. Drew screamed until she ran out of sound. The cry rang in her ears. The fleshy chunks clung, slid, and then fell with a faint plopping sound onto the concrete patio.

Drew's lungs couldn't inhale.

They were flat.

The dog man dropped to his forepaws, his neck hairs spiked and agitated, the hide itself readjusting over flesh like ripples on a lake. In the dark shadows the cheekbones shifted, a man's grimace now seething, a dog's snout now snarling with yellow canine fangs.

Then the creature squat low and jumped high, landing with a four-footed thump on the roof.

The jaundiced moon still hung there, far out in space, a child's paper cutout about to fall off its tack. Drew's right arm, the one her upper body was leaning on, began to shake violently. She dropped to her elbows on the kitchen linoleum.

Crawled like a worm cut in two, the upper body flinching forward.

Phone, she thought. Phone.

She dragged herself to the counter.

Stand, she thought. Stand up.

She got to her knees, got crouched on her bare feet. Reached up and felt the cool, dry ceramic sink under her sweaty, slick palms. Then she vomited nothing but air there. Then her brain was commanding her hands to fumble with the drawers and open them fast, *bang* went silverware clattering onto the floor, and Drew gripped a butcher knife in her shaking hand.

A light switch pointed at her like a slender finger on the opposite wall.

Drew ran forward. A fork stabbed her arch.

With each step the fork jabbed deeper into her foot but she limped fast until she flicked the switch and a chandelier blew the room up in bright white.

Drew whirled in every direction. She was in a fish bowl now, unable to see beyond her own reflection in all the glass windows.

No dog man inside.

Drew's head fell backwards, her eyes probing the ceiling. Up there.

And now she finally took a deep breath. Convulsed for air actually, her ribs swelling. She yanked the fork out of her arch.

The butcher knife clutched in front of her body with one hand, Drew hurried down a hallway and pushed open a plain brown door, fumbled for a light switch, flooded the room with color, ran around a quilted bed, stubbed her big toe in a stab of brilliant pain and dove at the nightstand, knocking over the golden lamp which clanged to the floor.

The cordless phone glowed in numeric red. She punched 911 and got nothing.

No, no, no. She punched 911 and got nothing again.

Fuck.

The room smelled like fake peaches.

Something brushed the window behind the closed brown curtains. Now something scratched the glass. Drew backed away, back into the hall. She ran to the far end, passing dark entryways, diving again toward a light switch which bombed another room into color.

All the nooks and crannies of a stranger's home and it was a twisted labyrinth.

From far away, in the other universe of the house, Drew distinctly heard the front door unlocking with the same loud *ker-clunk*.

A chipped blue tiled countertop. Purple gardening shoes. Rusty stacked tools.

Drew lurched around rows of green foliage and terra-cotta pots to a door leading outside and it was locked. The scream just rolled up inside her, exploding out through her mouth as her one free hand shook and shook and shook the knob like maybe if she could express her feelings enough it might magically allow her though.

Rotate the button, her brain commanded.

Rotate the button, her brain repeated.

Drew stopped. She looked down at her hand white-knuckled and death-latched on the round doorknob.

Oh, she just had to turn the thingy in the center.

So she turned the thingy and the door opened wide and a warm wash of high desert air welcomed her into the folds of twisted shadow and tormented shape.

Wait, that was a car.

Parked just five feet from her, right there, for real. The light from the hallway streamed out and reflected on the bumper of a gray Camry, and the license plate said New Mexico Land of Enchantment.

The north side of the house. She hadn't checked the north side? No, she hadn't.

There are keys on the blue counter, her brain said.

There are keys on the counter, her brain repeated.

Drew ran and got the keys, fired up the engine, and peeled out like a banshee. The tires kicked up dirt and rocks, splintering a window behind her.

Her headlights cut through the night like swords, slicing the dirt road into pie-shaped yellow wedges and all else was black. She shot forward like a spaceship on warp drive, nothing else but the streaking stars above. The instrument panel hemorrhaged red. Drew raced across washboard bumps that chattered her teeth. Delicate objects bounced and tinker-belled and then shattered to silence in the backseat.

The butcher knife gleamed. Pinned to the steering wheel.

In the rearview, the huge dog man kept pace with the car. His wide legs swallowed each galloping stride.

She floored it.

A notebook slid across the dashboard with a hiss. The glove compartment snapped open and its guts tumbled out.

The dog man was gone in the rearview, but then Drew turned her head and saw him again. Racing seventy miles-per-hour alongside the Camry, the dog man's bones cracked and reset anew just a few feet from her closed window, rippling like the hide itself might fall off and leave only skinned, dog-shaped raw muscles rhythmically pumping through the shadows.

But the fur cloak thing hung on.

This time Drew could not scream.

There were no screams left.

She spun the wheel and broadsided the evil beast. The sickening metal-to-flesh collision dented her door inward. The knife shot up toward her face and she ducked before it slit her neck. In the moment while Drew spun off the road, to the south in the distance, she saw an orange glow.

The dying coals of a campfire.

She spun back onto the dirt road, Hawaii Five-O'ed a ditch and smacked her head on the roof and kept her foot floored all the way until the tires crossed civilized pavement and she shot through an intersection on a red light like a space capsule on emergency reentry.

The rest of the night was a blur at the Albuquerque police department, wrapped up in a white cotton blanket that smelled like bleach, going through the recorded interviews with the female detectives, two cups of coffee and a hot chocolate staining empty Styrofoam cups, and also a half-eaten day old sandwich—until she met her grandfather.

And then the night came into focus.

He stood in the doorframe, just about as big as it with his detective uniform on, and when he said Drew's name for the first time her whole body broke out in goosebumps. When she looked up she knew she'd recognize his dancing eyes anywhere.

On any face.

Because kindred souls have a connection like that.

He explained that he'd been briefed about everything.

Other cops were walking by, their leather belts making that groaning sound, and phones were ringing and conversations carrying.

"Come with me where it's quiet," he said. And he stood back so respectfully to give her the space to come out of the door.

Still barefoot. Blanket ends trailing.

They went up to the roof and sat at a secret smokers' table. There was a glass ashtray. The moon and stars seemed more like the dome of a planetarium over the city, and the show was just beginning.

They talked and laughed a little out of nervousness and then the natural comfort grew between their difference in age and made a bridge between them.

"I thought you lived out on a reservation," she said. "I googled it and I thought you were Pueblo. Mom said you were like a traditional, uh—Indian shaman or something."

Rick smiled, the lights around the building softening the lines on his sixty-year-old face. "The detective part went undetected."

The city lights blurred in reds and yellows and green.

He crinkled a wrapper off a red-and-white peppermint candy. "What do you know about your heritage?" he asked, popping the candy slowly into his mouth.

"I'm Italian," Drew said. "My Mom's Italian." She felt her cheeks start to burn.

Rick nodded. The candy poked around in his cheek. Clanked on his teeth. "I understand what you mean." He turned his gaze to look out the window from the high rise and Drew looked out there, too.

Drew tried to pull her hair back again and there was no hair there anymore. She folded her hands on the table.

Her grandfather's amazingly warm hand slid over her knuckles. Their skin touched. His palm didn't have any calluses.

"I wasn't allowed to ask about you, ever," she said. "I found one black-and-white photo of you once, and Dad took it from me. He was mad."

"He had a lot to be mad about in the Four Corners growing up," Rick said. "There's a deep family history on the rez out there— between your uncles. You're Dine, did you know that, Drew? Navajo?"

"Not Pueblo?"

"Not Pueblo."

The city lights kaleidoscoped, twisting and fracturing. The first tear in her eye fell across her cheek. It burned with a longing she couldn't find words for.

They sat at the table, holding hands.

She felt safe.

"The Chicago scandal just hit the international news this evening," Rick said. "I took a call, your dad is in jail. Your mom is going into protective custody. They're giving you that option too until the trial is over. Or you can stay with a family member—with me, if you'd like. I can fly back to Chicago to help you get your things."

Another tear fell. This one splashed by the ashtray.

Her life was split apart. Fractured. Everything she'd ever known in Chicago was gone.

Drew pulled her hand but her grandfather held on. She looked up into his eyes and he had glistening tears on his cheeks, too.

"What happened?" They both knew she wasn't asking about what happened in Chicago. "I reported it was a man who attacked me, I didn't want to say the rest. But what *was* it?"

"Chicago hired a Skinwalker to scare you. So you won't testify against your father. Or about what you witnessed up there."

Drew felt ice cold though the night was warm. She pulled the blanket tighter.

"Hey, you're safe now." Rick reached into his uniform and withdrew a little dark bottle. "It's cedar wood essential oil. Give it a few whiffs."

He set it on the table before her and the woody aroma calmed her.

"Best I can figure, they sent you to an empty house on five hundred acres of empty land so no one would witness the event. It's become a dark art. Didn't always used to be, not like this. But every native culture all over the world has a name for those who practice evil. Our brothers and sisters, taken by the lie. Even the white folk have their Necromancers." He glanced at Drew and winked. "Those Italians."

Drew wanted to hide but he squeezed her hand and she knew it was all okay.

"Secret clans," he continued. "They train in ceremony. They wear animal skins to transform. But we're the other side of the medicine, Drew. The good guys, if you choose it."

Then she knew why she'd always hated all the suits.

And hated moneyed Chicago.

Because they only helped themselves, the ruling class. And then they backstabbed each other, anyway. So what was the point? Wasn't a lesser evil still an evil?

And now it was suddenly crystal clear the moment she had first *known*. It was the first moment she had seen her Navajo grandfather's eyes all the way back when she was eight years old and had found that black-and-white photograph in the Burberry shoebox with the golden embossed knight.

The twinkling light from Rick's photographed eyes had reached out of the paper and touched her with rays like healing sun. Just like the warmth of his hand now, holding her cold fingers.

All the way back then—she *knew*. And she had made her choice, even if she forgot it later on, because life was hard.

Maybe she'd funneled all her hope into sports, hurling the fastest pitch in the state. And every time she threw the ball she was trying to break free from the darkness that bound her.

And Dad had seen all that when she was only nine, and had taken the photograph and torn it up into pieces and laughed as he pointed a Beretta at her face.

You'll work for me, bright eyes.

Sometimes crime gets in the way.

But not anymore.

MISSILES OF OCTOBER

DAN C. DUVAL

In his second story in this volume, Dan C. Duval takes us far away from his creepy bar characters in "Eric the Monkey" for this story. And that's a good thing, actually.

He writes about this story, "I remember the lines of people at the high school gym waiting for their polio vaccine and I remember seeing on our black-and-white TV set the rows of iron lungs in the hospital wards, those kids for whom the vaccine did not arrive in time."

How much suffering should a kid have to take? And what if, in the crazy world of a looming nuclear war, a suffering kid has to make some really hard choices? Dan gives you just one answer right here.

M y mother is long gone now and the world is still here, but for a few hours in 1962, I thought that I had destroyed the world.

I went to school at the age of 9 in 1958, peeing blood. A kidney disease but I hoped that if I ignored it long enough, it would go away. But the teacher noticed my frequent trips to the bathroom and called my mom. When she came to get me, she limped into the room, there in front of everyone—and their sneaking laughing—and took me home. I didn't see another classroom for almost two years.

The disease was due to a strep infection and the treatment our doctor chose was strict bed-rest and massive doses of antibiotics. Day after day, week on week, listening to other kids outside playing in the sun, playing in the snow, playing with each other, and me alone in my room, in bed, not feeling sick but every time I thought I was over it, the blood would reappear and it would burn all the way down, until even the thought of peeing made me wince and dread the walk from my room, down the hall, through the kitchen, to the little bathroom at the other end of the house, the one my brother and I used.

The doctor let me go back to school after the New Year when I reached the seventh grade, but that only lasted a few weeks before the burning and the blood came back and I was back in bed again.

So in October, 1962, I had been back in school—eighth grade!—for all of six weeks when I made my way through the house to the toilet. I never turned a light on in the hall as the porch light shining through the kitchen window gave enough light to find my way.

So I didn't see the chocolate-colored pee spread through the toilet bowl but I felt the burning. I stood there in the dark, hoping that if I did not turn on the light and did not see the dark water, it would not really be real. I just flushed and went back to bed.

To be up again an hour later, and then again two hours after that.

The third time I was about to flush when Mom tapped on the door, slipped her hand inside, and flipped on the light, making everything real for the both of us. She had barely given me enough time to pull myself back inside my pajamas before the light came on.

"Oh, Dickie," she said.

It was 1962 and she was my mother. Now, I prefer Richard, or Rich, if you must.

She brought me the bedpan, told me to stay in bed and she would bring me breakfast. "We'll go see Doctor Hillen on Monday."

When she brought my breakfast, my father and grandfather were already up, already in their respective chairs in the living room, shouting at each other over the TV set. I knew there was something going on with Cuba and the Russians but that was something adults worried about and Dad and Grandpa worried about it a lot.

Grandpa had been in the Army in World War I and Dad in the Marines in World War II, my Uncle Henry had died in Korea, and they agreed about how the Commies were going to kill us all, if they could figure out how to do it. But to listen to Dad and Grandpa, they did not know they agreed about anything and the house rocked to their violent agreeing as long as the two of them were in the same room. It being Saturday, they were going to be at it all day.

I heard my brother ask Mom if he could go over to his friend Tommy's, and then to my brother's complaints for the next ten minutes as Mom bundled him up against the cold and the rain.

Not that I had any friends to go visit, even if I could get out of bed. Only six weeks into school after missing the entire seventh grade, I knew the names of a few people but I didn't have any friends, no one who would come to see how I was. Not that I wanted anyone to know. I was as ashamed of my sickness in those days as I was about Mom's limping waddle.

I had used the bedpan, the burning pain making my eyes water, and I laid back while the burning turned into an itch, then a tingle, finally a dull ache I could ignore.

Then I crawled out of bed, knelt down next to it, and asked God to either let me get better or let me die.

At the age of 13, I did not know much about religion or about God, only that you were supposed to ask God for what you wanted to happen. I do not remember praying for anything before that and I cannot say I have lived a very religious life since. For that one moment, though, I just wanted God to finish it, one way or the other, and I believed that He would do it.

As with most prayers I have ever heard of, I did not get an answer, and I climbed back into bed. I tried reading and ended up staring at the lights and shadows of the plaster on the ceiling, trying to think of nothing. Which, of course, never works, and I guess I was just waiting for God to make up His mind.

For lunch, Mom let me come sit at the table to eat my sandwich, still in my pajamas. The agreeing was somewhat subdued after Dad and Grandpa both said they were sorry my sickness had come back. Of course, Mom had told them and, of course, she had to remind them to say something to try to cheer me up.

After we had eaten, Mom let me settle in on the couch, a blanket over me even though the house was hot—Grandpa liked it that way though he refused to ever admit that he was cold.

Normally, some sorts of sports were on the TV Saturday afternoons: reminders of running and playing that I could not do and I hated watching them. Dad and Grandpa agreed about those games about as much as they did about everything else. This day, though, men in suits and ties sat behind a desk and did as much agreeing as

Dad and Grandpa, about what the Russians were going to do, about what President Kennedy should do, about what, if anything, should be done about Cuba and Castro. It bored me as much as the football game would have but Grandpa and Dad agreed more and more, louder and louder.

"There's nothing here to drop a bomb on," Grandpa said. "We'll live long enough to die of starvation."

"Fallout will get us first," Dad said, a little louder to keep Grandpa from starting up again. "Up where the bombers fly, the winds blow all the way around the world. They found them during the War. Any bomb dropped anywhere will make fallout on us and everyone else."

"Like I said," Grandpa, louder still to keep Dad from interrupting, "we can hide from the fallout and starve to death anyway. The only thing saving us is that them dammed Russians are all half-starving already. See what Stalin did to them?"

I could barely hear what the men on the TV had to say but I caught one that said neither the Russians nor the Americans could back down at this point, that the war would start any minute. The others appeared to disagree with him but Grandpa was agreeing with Dad so loudly at the moment I couldn't be sure.

What I knew, though, was that this was God's answer. It would be death and a war would be His method.

It was all my fault, because I prayed for it.

I threw the blanket aside and rushed off to my room, shouting, "I'm sorry, I'm sorry!"

My sudden rushing out of the room put a momentary end to the agreeing, or maybe just some quieter agreeing, but in my room, my face in my pillow, I heard just a low rumble of voices. If Grandpa and Dad were agreeing, it was much quieter than I had heard for some time.

I could tell you that I was all torn up inside, guilty that I would be the death of millions, but at that moment I wasn't.

I was afraid.

It was one thing to want my pain to stop, another to actually expect to die any moment. To have to face God knowing that I was only thinking of myself when I demanded that God decide.

I was even so weak then that I remember thinking that I did not expect it to come to an end so quickly.

Several times in my life, I had nowhere else to turn, no last resort, and then Mom would show up.

She came into my room, limping as usual, and sat herself heavily on the edge of my bed. She stroked my back as I sobbed into my pillow and waited for me to cry myself out, then, in that way that mothers seem to know that no interrogator could ever master, wormed the details out of me, slowly. I could tell you the details that I remember of what she said and did, but I was 13 and not all that interesting.

What she said to me, though, was:

"I know how hard it is to lay for hours and days, years. This happened to me..."

...I woke up one morning and I could not get out of bed. My sister and I slept in the same bed then and she had to climb over me to go get my mother. I was afraid, blubbering, and Mama threatened to slap me if I didn't shut my mouth. We lived on a farm then and Father had to ride the plow horse into town to get the doctor.

The doctor didn't take but ten minutes looking me over before he said it was probably polio but they'd have to take me into town to the hospital.

Back in those days, most people thought of a hospital as the place you went to die, and I started blubbering all over again. Blubbering or not, I spent the next year at that hospital or at another.

With the polio vaccine, you have never heard of this, but when I was a girl, there were whole hospitals with children recovering from polio. There were children learning how to walk again, who the polio barely touched; there were children who never walked again, their legs withered and useless.

Then there were the children who lived in the iron lungs. There are still some of those children who grew up and are still there but not many of them are left. Sometimes a child would get so sick they couldn't breathe on their own so the doctor put them in the iron lungs, a big tank with a pump attached to it, with their head sticking out one end. The pump drew in air and pushed it out, breathing for the child, who could do nothing but lay there. If they wanted to speak, they had to wait until the pump was pushing the air out. If they needed to cough, they had to ask a nurse to come help, to use another pump to suck stuff out of their throat. Your hands were inside the tank, so you couldn't hold a book or feed yourself. When they cleaned up your pee, you couldn't breathe, because the pump didn't work while they had the tank open.

The only things you could look at were the ceiling or whatever you see in the mirror they hung over your face. The nurses set up a bookstand for me and my mother or sister would sit for hours reading to me or turning the pages while I read.

How long? Seven months, two weeks, and four days. Most children only stayed in the machine for a few weeks but I just never seemed to get better.

More than once I was sure I would never get out, that I would live the rest of my life in that tank.

Yes, I asked God to just let me die. More than once.

I didn't die and one day the doctors said I could breathe on my own. But that I would never walk.

It took years, years of pain and frustration and I fell down a lot. I cried and got depressed and gave up, over and over. I asked God to let me die again and again.

I didn't. I don't walk well, but I walk...

"...You are not going to die," Mom said. "Doctor Hillen said that if your sickness was going to kill you, it would have done it the first year. He said that you'd grow out of it in time. It will keep coming back, but longer and longer between bouts, and for a shorter time each time around."

"Why didn't you tell me?" I asked.

Mom looked shy for a moment. "I could have. I probably should have.

I think I started crying again. Most of that day was a blur but I think I cried a lot and, for a thirteen-year-old, there was nothing worse than being a cry-baby.

"At the time you were too young. I didn't want you to be afraid, I didn't want you to think about dying. When you got better, why bring it up?"

Sitting in one place for any length of time made her leg hurt and she had to shift, over and over. She used to say it didn't hurt much.

She sighed. "I guess I was afraid, too, that if I said it, it might happen, so if I never said you might die, then you never would."

By this point, tears were running down her face, too, and I felt ashamed that I made her cry, on top of everything else.

"But it's too late now," I said. "I already asked God to end it, one way or the other."

"You mean about the rockets and all?"

"Yeah."

I wanted to say more but it felt like I was choking, and I could not force myself to breathe around the pain squeezing my chest.

Mom didn't smile at me very often so I remember those times when she did. Actually, she didn't smile very much any time, so they were memorable when she did.

"It doesn't work that way, Dickie." She took a deep breath. "God is going to do what He is going to do. If there is another war, it won't be because one boy asked for it."

"But I prayed for it."

Mom spent a lot more time in church than I ever did but I didn't think she understood things more than I did, but she understood this very well.

"I prayed to die a thousand times. God never let it happen. What

I thought I wanted didn't matter to God. That's the point. I didn't really know what I wanted."

She took another deep breath. "I wanted the pain and frustration to stop. I should have asked for that. Pastor Carl told me once that I should have asked for an end to my despair, because that was what I needed an end to. The pain and the failing was part of what I needed to do. The frustration was all me."

"So what I should ask for is the end of my despair?" At the time, I wasn't sure what the word meant. I know now and I wouldn't bother to ask for it, because it always went away on its own eventually.

Mom shook her head. "I don't know what you should ask for."

She sat quietly for a few moments.

"I always found that asking for other people was better than asking for myself. Pray for my children, my friends. Do the best I can, what I think needs to be done."

Out in the living room, I heard Grandpa shout, "They had a war for me, they had a war for you, they'll have one for your boys, too."

Another rare smile. "I suppose I should ask for my father and your father to get along better. Quieter, at least."

I'd listened to Mom's polio story, but I was young enough then that I didn't know the right questions to ask, that it took a while before I knew what it was I wanted to know next.

"Mom, how long was it before you could walk again?"

"Oh, let's see, I was six when I went into the hospital. I needed crutches, but I walked onto the stage when I graduated high school. Twelve years."

"Twelve years? Am I going to be sick that long?"

"Not according to Dr. Hillen. Who knows? This might be the last of it."

"Were you still on crutches when you met Dad?"

"No. I had been a nurse for several years before I met your father at the VA. I used a cane for a long time. I don't need one very often now, as long as I don't push myself too much."

"You mean you still hurt?"

"Yes. Every day. Not bad, but a little." She stood up in that creaky way she had, as if she were about to fall over any second.

"There is always some sort of pain," Mom said. "But you are going to be fine. You just need to wait and endure what you have to endure."

She was right, I eventually got better. I missed a few months of the eighth grade and had a couple of times in my 20s that I thought it might be coming back but never any more burning after I turned 14, just a little dark color in my urine a couple of times.

Mom got her wish, in a way, when Grandpa died just before I graduated from high school. Dad and I had just started to take up where Dad and Grandpa had left off when I headed off to college but I'm sure it was much quieter at home. College worked out for me in more ways than one, since the deferment kept me out of Vietnam until after it was over, so I never had my war and Dad and I didn't have much to agree loudly about. My brother got drafted but never sent overseas, so he was out in two years, all in one piece.

Needless to say, the whole thing with the Cuban missiles fizzled out, too. Just a bit of pain at the moment, for everyone.

In the end, I have been blessed in that I never had the opportunity to share what I learned about my sickness—or my mother's—with any of my children or grandchildren. Just as well none of them suffered from the childhood diseases my generation and the ones before grew up with.

Or maybe I was just never in the right place at the right time: mothers are so much better at that, it seems.

GIRL WITH A MISSION

DAYLE A. DERMATIS

When the kids of a suburban California high school need help—and what high-schooler doesn't at some time or another—that must not involve parents or teachers, who can they turn to? Dayle A. Dermatis offers up Brittani, The Fixer.

The character appeared first in the story "Bothering With the Details" published in the May/June 2018 Alfred Hitchcock's Mystery Magazine.

Dayle is the author or coauthor of multiple novels, including the gothic mystery novel Waking the Witch. *Her work has appeared in an amazing fifteen volumes of* Fiction River *including this one.*

On top of all that, she has published more than a hundred short stories including "Voices Carry" which appeared in Snowbound: Best New England Crime Stories 2017, *and her thriller story "The Scent of Amber and Vanilla," which received an honorable mention in* The Year's Best Crime & Mystery 2016.

In this wonderful and fun story, Dayle takes us into the roiling world of teenagers. Dayle says, "Teenagers' voices often aren't heard, especially when parental hypocrisy gets in the way." When the stakes are high, it's a kind of hypocrisy that can leave a kid feeling powerless and desperate, and very much in need of a...Brittani.

I n my school, I'm known as The Fixer.

It's a stupid name, which says something not very kind about the average creativity of the student body.

I'd gotten the nickname after I helped my former-and-maybe-again best friend Charlotte, after Charlotte had fallen in with the popular crowd. The idiots had developed the world's stupidest party game, "Whose Hooters?" (and its counterpart, "Pick the Dick"), which involved photos of private parts. You know, what came down to child pornography for high school students, if they'd been caught. I used my computer acumen to make them believe the photos had been leaked to the Internet, and shut down the game.

Now they thought I was brilliant. If I cared, I could practically call myself popular-adjacent.

So when head cheerleader Tara Kildare sat down at my table in the lunch room, I wasn't exactly startled. Just vaguely annoyed.

It was nearly Christmas, which meant white lights wrapped around palm trees and fake pine greenery everywhere. The Santa Ana winds were blowing, the hot winds from hell that made your eyeballs ache.

Normally I ate outside, but the winds had driven me inside to the air-conditioned lunch room, an unassuming expanse filled with round tables that seated six, uncomfortable molded-plastic red chairs, and the surprisingly enticing scent of Salisbury steak. From past experience, however, I knew the mystery meat dish didn't live up to its aroma, and besides, nothing beat Chef Boyardee ravioli cold out of a can. To make my meal more healthy, I'd brought two homemade zucchini bars. Cream cheese frosting or no, they included vegetables, so they counted.

"Brittani," Tara said.

Yes, I hate my name, and especially the spelling of it, but my mother loves it and I can't hurt her feelings. "Tara."

When I'd been in seventh grade—a time when nobody looked their best—Tara had taken it upon herself to walk up to me one day with all the confidence of being one grade ahead of me, curl her lip in a sneer, and announce that I was ugly.

My parents aren't religious people, but they have a strong moral code. My mother espouses what she calls the Bill and Ted Philosophy: "Be excellent to each other." That was why, in seventh grade, I hadn't kicked Tara in the proverbial nuts. Unfortunately, I also hadn't developed a witty repartee, so I'd just let her flounce off.

This right here was the first time she'd spoken to me in four years. And even now, I could tell she was judging me, as her pale blue eyes took in my auburn hair, which I'd plaited into two unfashionable braids in deference to the heat.

Still, she reined in her impulse to make a snarky comment, sucked in a breath, and said, "I need your help."

Tara's long black hair was pulled back into a high ponytail, which went well with her cheerleading uniform. But the royal blue knit top with the school logo swoosh in red and white seemed almost baggy on her, and her naturally pale skin had an unhealthy pallor. She was clearly under a lot of stress over something.

Declining her request based on a nasty comment made four years ago would be petty.

"Meet me in my office after school," I said. "Room M102, first door on your left. But remember, I don't change grades, provide tests, or make fake IDs."

Tara actually looked relieved. "Okay," she said. "Um, thanks."

Her gratitude, and the fact that she'd swallowed her pride to approach me, made me wonder just how bad things had to be for Tara to ask for my help. I'd find out soon enough.

Room M102 was the band practice room (M101 was orchestra), and the first door on the left led to the instrument storage room. Two walls were covered with cheap metal shelving, on which sat black cases with numbers scribbled on them with thick silver Sharpie. On the wall opposite the door was a rack for upright basses, cellos, and trombones.

The 40-watt fluorescent lights all worked on a good day, and the ceiling was low enough that my head almost grazed those lights. My fingers were crossed that at five-foot-eleven-and-three-quarters, I'd reached my final height. Unfortunately, I'm not coordinated enough for basketball, and I like food too much to be a runway model, so thank goodness I have a computer- and math-oriented brain to fall back on.

The small room smelled of slightly rancid valve oil and something I'd rather not think too hard about.

The storage closet was used for assignations among the popular band crowd.

Yes, there was a popular band crowd. Playing a musical instrument looked good on a college application.

No, I had not partaken of the room in such a manner.

Tara was ten minutes late.

"Sorry," she said. "I've never been in this wing before."

Her college application clearly focused on other pursuits, and no one came to the Nerd Wing unless they had a music class or were in the audiovisual club or some other non-popular afterschool hobby.

I'm enough of a nerd that I help tidy up after band practices so often that Mr. Wilke, the director, has given me a key.

I leaned back against the shelving, my hip near my own French horn, and said, "So, what's wrong?"

Whatever was going to come out of her mouth, what she said next was probably the last thing I was expecting.

"I've been accused of statutory rape."

"Wait. What? You've been...you've been raped?"

"No!" She looked at me as if I were an imbecile, which made me wonder if I have that look on my own face a lot, dealing with her crowd. "*I'm* being accused of statutory rape."

"Look, Tara, I don't get involved in things the police should be handling—"

"Please," she said. I saw the tears brimming in her eyes, and suddenly I guessed how hard this must be for her. She looked like Charlotte for a moment, when Char had asked for help over the stupid party game.

"Give me the details," I said, "and then I'll decide."

Because of those weird birthday rules that determine when you can enter kindergarten, Tara was already eighteen, which made her an adult in the eyes of the law. The person she'd slept with was seventeen, and the sex was consensual. Not exactly icky. Like I said, even this storage closet had seen some things. Sex among high school students was far from unusual.

But the other person's parents were up in arms, and wanted to press charges.

I wasn't sure what I could do. Out of curiosity more than anything else, I asked, "Who's the other person?"

Tara looked away. Sank her teeth into an otherwise perfectly manicured cuticle and worried at it.

"Tara?"

Her eyes flicked back to me. "This is confidential, right?"

"Absolutely." And it was. I would never betray someone who'd confided in me.

Still she hesitated, shifting from foot to foot, the muscles in her thighs flexing, while I ran through a mental list of possibilities. Whom had I seen Tara dating? She wasn't someone I'd paid attention to, given any thought to—and we didn't exactly attend a lot of the same functions. Except maybe football games, because of marching band. Thank the gods that was over for the year.

"Tara?" I asked again.

"Chaya. Chaya Gardner." It came out of her in a rush, and she wouldn't meet my gaze.

Oh. Her hesitation became crystal clear.

I knew Chaya. She actually lived down the street from me, and we'd been friends as kids. Not as close as Charlotte and I, but we'd hung out in the way little kids do when they share a neighborhood park.

Not just as kids, really. I'd been to her birthday party last year, a pool party in their backyard, one of a couple dozen teens.

She was Cambodian, if I remembered correctly. Adopted by the Gardners as a baby, after their mission in Southeast Asia. Her three older brothers were the natural-born children of Jill and Frank Gardner, and Chaya had once confided in me that she thought they'd adopted her rather than try for a girl.

I'd had no idea either Chaya or Tara was gay.

"Okay," I said. "I can see why you want to keep this a secret—"

"It's not that," Tara said, and now her pale blue eyes flashed with anger. "I'm not ashamed, and neither is she. It was private. Our close friends knew, but we didn't see the need to advertise our relationship."

They'd been dating for two years. I am clearly not as observant as I'd thought.

Tara laid out the next, now obvious, wrinkle in the problem. The devoutly Mormon Gardners not only had expected their precious baby girl to remain a virgin until marriage, they'd expected a traditional marriage.

Imagine their surprise when they walked in on said precious baby girl with her very female lover.

According to Tara, even though Chaya insisted to her parents that she was a willing participant, they were sure Tara had manipulated Chaya, and they were outraged enough to press charges. They'd met with an attorney, but hadn't gone to the police yet (unless they'd done so today). In the meantime, they'd yanked Chaya out of school.

"Jesus, Tara, I'm so sorry," I said, and I was.

I mean, my parents had no problem with my being a lesbian, and even though we hadn't discussed it, I was pretty sure they knew my sleepovers with my friend Zan weren't platonic. At least nobody had to worry about an accidental pregnancy, you know?

"But I'm not sure what I can do to help," I went on. "Chaya's a minor in the eyes of the law, so it's your word against her parents'."

"Chaya says her parents like you," Tara said. She was twisting a silver puzzle ring around and around on her forefinger. Because she'd lost weight, it was a little big. I'd bet money she'd gotten it from Chaya. "Maybe you could talk to them?"

Parents, in general, did like me. I was smart, polite, and didn't get into trouble. But did that mean I could convince the Gardners to back down from their religious wrath?

I doubted it. But I was willing to try. Tara might be judgmental and bitchy, but she didn't deserve this. And Chaya certainly didn't, either.

I dropped my backpack at home after school and walked a block over to the Gardners' house.

Most of the lawns in the neighborhood were green, in defiance of the drought. A few houses had gardens with native plants instead, succulents and rocks and a dry birdbath or a glass gazing ball on a plinth for decorative interest. Holiday decorations looked forlorn and tacky in the daylight. The strong, dry winds had blown heavy palm fronds into the street, and I wished I'd grabbed a bottle of water before leaving the house.

The houses themselves were all two-story Mediterranean-style places with red clay tile roofs and stucco siding in some shade of beige, from pinkish-tan to yellowish. Some had brightly tiled entranceways, and most had black iron screen security doors, which allowed you to open the solid inner door and still have a locked door while you let the breeze in.

Not at this time of year, though. All the doors and windows were shut tight, with air conditioning keeping things cool inside.

Chaya opened the door, and she wasn't surprised to see me. Tara had texted her that I'd agreed to help.

"I'm so glad to see you!" she said, hugging me. Her dark brown hair was cut in a bob that accentuated her high cheekbones. But her hair looked lanky, as if she hadn't bothered to shower this morning. She was easily half a foot shorter than me, maybe a little more.

Her parents weren't home, but in truth, I'd wanted the chance to talk to Chaya alone, just to get her side of the story.

She led me into the living room to our right, two steps down onto a parquet floor covered with overstuffed furniture upholstered in Black Watch plaid. The vaulted ceiling had dark beams, and a fan in the center that turned at half-speed, keeping the cool air circulating.

The white-painted built-in bookshelves, credenza, and walls were covered with family photos, dating back at least a couple generations. Higher shelves held trophies of various sports.

Mrs. Gardner must have put spaghetti sauce in the slow cooker this morning, because the house smelled like garlic and tomatoes and basil, and my stomach rumbled. Ravioli had been a long time ago.

Thankfully, I'd brought chocolate-chip cookies as a peace

offering—I'd been on a baking kick last night and zucchini bread had been only part of it—so I helped myself to one now, while Chaya brought glasses of water from the kitchen.

"Thanks," I said, gulping down half of the water. I set it down on a sandstone coaster that bore a religious quote, next to a nativity scene, one of several in the room.

Chaya confirmed everything Tara had said, while fiddling with a silver puzzle ring on her thumb, confirming my suspicions.

"My parents are *furious*," she said. "I've tried and tried to talk to them…but they've never listened to me, you know?"

I knew. They'd dressed her in frilly pink dresses when she'd wanted to grub about in the sandbox; they'd sent her to ballet and tap lessons and she ditched them for Little League. She was smart, though, so thankfully everyone was happy when it came to school and grades and Student Council—they even stopped protesting about her playing soccer and field hockey.

"It'll be such a relief when I turn eighteen and can get to college," she said. "At least they aren't insisting I go out on a mission. They'd prefer I go to a local college, but I've gotten an early admission decision from UC Santa Barbara."

Far enough that she couldn't commute from home, at least, but a long enough drive that her parents weren't likely to drop in for a surprise visit too often.

"I feel sick to my stomach about Tara," Chaya went on. "I can't believe they're being so vindictive."

And the law, technically, was on their side.

I'd done a little research on my phone on the bus home. As I understood it, because of how close they were in age, Tara wouldn't be charged with more than a misdemeanor. But that could still mean up to a year in county jail…

Any fair judge wouldn't do more than slap Tara on the wrist.

Call me cynical, but I didn't have a lot of hope for a fair judge. Frank Gardner was a judge himself. He couldn't preside over the case, of course, but he had friends.

I finished my cookie and my water, and got up to pace the room.

I'd never been in this room when I was a kid. Chaya followed me, pointing out people in the pictures. Almost all of them were in fancy, off-white shabby-chic frames that made my teeth itch.

The one of her parents in high school was kind of adorable in a parent kind of way. Mom had long, hugely curly blond hair and dark red matte lipstick. Dad wore a tux, but his hair was a shade longer than proper.

"Junior prom," Chaya said. "My parents were high school sweethearts—they'd been dating since eighth grade. Hypocritical, isn't it, that they think Tara and I aren't serious? I mean, yes, I know most high school romances don't last, and we're going to different colleges —if Tara even gets to go to college—so we could meet other people. But that doesn't mean I don't love her now."

There were a lot of photos of Chaya's three older brothers. I vaguely remembered them, all broad-shouldered and blond and sporty. They'd been a little bullying when I was a kid, but not in a truly mean way.

Hang on. In some of the photos, there were four boys. They all looked clearly related. Had Chaya had a brother who died? I didn't remember that, but then, it might be something the family didn't talk about.

"Who's this?" I asked.

"Oh, that's my Uncle Ted," she said. "My grandmother had a surprise kid later in life, you know? He spent summers with us, because he was just a few years older than Gary, my oldest brother."

Made sense. The Gardners had a large extended family. The backdrop of a lot of earlier photos—when Jill and Frank were younger, with their respective families, were clearly not taken in Southern California.

"Augusta, near Atlanta," Chaya said. "Mom and Dad moved here before Gary was born."

I heard the faint rumble of a garage door, and then a distant sound of a door opening.

"They're home," Chaya said, her voice tight with nerves.

Despite my own nerves, the Gardners seemed delighted to see

me. Frank looked me up and down, called me a tall drink of water, pumped my hand once, and went off to his man cave or wherever. Jill sat on the edge of the sofa next to me and asked how I'd been.

Her hair was a darker blond, now, and cut in a ubiquitous middle-aged short style that still seemed too old for her. Her navy slacks and sleeveless ivory silk shell were timeless, as was the strand of fat rectangular gold chain links around her neck. She'd gained weight after three children, but she wore it well. Her fingers were heavy with gold and diamond rings.

I hate talking to parents, but I know how to pull it off. I said I'd applied to Stanford, among other universities, but that was my dream, and I wanted to major in computers. I mentioned the school's upcoming winter concert (band, orchestra, chorus). I asked about the market, because she was a real estate agent. I told her how delicious her sauce smelled, and she told me her secret was a tablespoon of brown sugar to cut the acidity of the tomatoes.

When we'd run out of chitchat (thank goodness—it was excruciating, except for the part about the brown sugar, which I filed away for later experimentation), she said, "It's so lovely to see you. You're such a good friend to Chaya."

The clear implication was, I was a good friend because I hadn't deflowered her precious little girl. I tried not to grind my teeth. I already have to wear a night guard.

"I know Chaya and I don't get the chance to hang out a lot," I said, "but she really is a friend."

"And she needs *real friends* right now," Mrs. Gardner said, reaching over and taking Chaya's hand in her own.

Chaya's back was stiff as a board, and I could tell she was doing everything in her power not to snatch her hand out from under her mother's.

"I agree," I said. "She's really stressed out—I'm sure you can see that. She's really worried about what's going to happen. Tara—"

At the very mention of Tara's name, Mrs. Gardner's demeanor changed. Her back went as stiff as Chaya's, and any friendliness fled her face, replaced by a coldness that was kind of terrifying.

"Tara is no longer welcome here, and we will not speak of that *sinner* in our house," she nearly spat. "I think it's time you headed home, Brittani."

She stood, and I followed suit, feeling like I was a puppet with her strings being tugged.

I hugged Chaya, in part because it might piss off Mrs. Gardner, and headed out into the evening heat, mission definitely not accomplished.

My parents were due home from work soon, and it was taco night, but I poured myself a large glass of iced tea and made myself a plate of Wheat Thins and a hunk of sharp white cheddar anyway, and took it up to my rooms.

Because I'm an only child and our house is ridiculously big for three people, I have a second room attached to my bedroom, which was useful, because I have multiple computers and a lot of books, plus an electronic keyboard because I'm teaching myself piano. The bare spots on the walls not covered by shelves had posters of Steve Jobs and Bill Gates and Tesla and Einstein and Tony Stark. I had busts of Mozart and Wagner on one desk, and bobbleheads of all The Avengers on another.

I pulled my laptop from my backpack and flopped down length-wise on the beat-up Victorian divan I'd found on Craigslist for a song.

I had homework. I probably should practice my French horn.

But this problem with Tara and Chaya nagged at me.

No. Let's be honest. I was seriously pissed at the Gardners. And I wanted to find a way to keep this from ever getting to the legal system, which would likely screw Tara.

I didn't know how much time we had until the Gardners officially brought charges against Tara. Even though the court stuff would drag on—I knew it wasn't like on TV, when cases get tried days rather than months or even years later—it would mess up Tara's life, and Chaya's.

I dropped my head back against a pillow and closed my eyes.

Behind my eyelids I saw the Gardners' living room, looking like a family reunion had exploded.

It was kind of sweet, really. My family was tight, but small. Like the Gardners, we didn't live close to relatives. My parents had ended up, independently, in the area for work, and met through friends. My closest relative was Nonna, my grandmother Lydia, in the Bay Area.

High school sweethearts, Chaya said her parents had been. Junior high, really.

I sat up so fast, I nearly dumped my laptop on the floor. Outside, dusk had fallen, and I could hear noise downstairs: Dad in the kitchen. He usually got home first, started prepping supper.

Was it reasonable to believe that Frank Gardner and his girl-friend, Jill (maiden name currently unknown) had taken and held to a purity pledge? As Mormon and devout as you wanna be, sometimes there's no denying raging teenage hormones, right?

I flopped back down. As if I had some Kilgrave-level psychic ability to induce them to admit they'd indulged in some serious hanky-panky back in the day.

Still, while I was lying there, I dug my phone out of my jeans pocket and texted Chaya: *What was your mother's maiden name?*

The answer came back almost immediately: *Zabriskie. Why?*

Just a hunch. Oh, and what school did they go to?

Hang on, I'll have to ask.

While I waited, I did my pre-Calc homework.

"Brit?" My mother's voice floated up the stairs. "Dinner, hon."

I went down, because *tacos*. My mother, not from a southwestern state, uses store-bought crunchy taco shells and salty Velveeta and tasteless-but-tactile iceberg lettuce, but damn, it all worked somehow.

We have a rule about no cell phone at the table. When I returned to my rooms, Chaya had responded.

Jackson High, Augusta.

I cracked my knuckles and called upon my Google-fu.

I found Frank Gardner. Graduated 1993. I found Jill Zabriskie, but no graduation date—her last yearbook photo was 1992, her junior year. I even found that prom photo.

I couldn't find a Jill Zabriskie graduating from any high school in the state that year.

Okay. It was time to go in deeper.

I paused long enough to do the rest of my homework—an outline of an English paper on a novel that changed my life (*The Last Unicorn*), Social Studies reading, Spanish worksheet.

My parents came in at some point and kissed me goodnight and told me not to stay up too late, which they did every night. It was kind of comforting. I knew that if I truly wasn't getting enough sleep on a regular basis, they'd notice, and intervene.

At least, it made me feel good to believe that. It was hard for me to accept that Charlotte had been cutting herself, and her mother hadn't known. Char had finally confessed, and her mother had found her a good therapist, but still.

I went back to my research, after taking out my contacts and rubbing my tired eyes and getting more iced tea.

It was after midnight when I found a piece of information that blew everything out of the water.

I was at the Gardners' house bright and early, standing in front of the garage so when the door went up, I was blocking the two his-and-hers black Lexuses.

"Brittani," Jill said. Today she wore black pants and a pale pink silk shell with a loose bow around the front. Same jewelry. She was like the cliché of a real estate agent, I swear. "I'm afraid I wasn't clear last night. You're not welcome here right now."

Frank, tall and burly, his mustache neatly trimmed and his cheeks red from his morning shave, made a point of looking at his watch. "I have to get to court."

Fine.

"You'd rather hear this from me than see it plastered on the Internet," I said, my voice perky, a fake smile crossing my face.

"Brittani," Jill repeated. "Yes, we'll be devastated when people hear how Tara manipulated our innocent Chaya. But it will only look worse for Tara."

"I'm not talking about that," I said. "I'm talking about your raging hypocrisy." Still with the smile. My cheeks hurt. Is this what televangelists felt all the time?

They both froze.

"What are you talking about?" Frank asked.

Suddenly, I could hear the Southern in his voice. In Jill's. Something they'd tried to erase. Tried to forget.

Just like this.

I waved a manila envelope. "Chaya's 'uncle' Ted. He's not her uncle, is he?"

Frank looked as though he'd sucked on a lemon from the Meyer lemon tree in their backyard. Jill turned white and took a step back, leaning against her car. The look on her face made me almost feel sorry for her.

"He's your son," I persisted anyway, because I was pissed off, because she deserved to have the wound poked. "You got pregnant in high school, which is why you didn't graduate."

"Even if that were true—" Frank began.

It was true. Nice try, Mr. Gardner.

"What this means is that you weren't virgins when you got married, so how, exactly, can you insist that Chaya should be? At least she didn't get pregnant and have to drop out of school and pretend her child was her own mother's, and get her GED, and—"

"Jesus Christ," Frank said, which didn't sound very devout to me. "*Stop it.* Look what you're doing to her."

Rage bubbled up inside of me. "Look what you're doing to *Chaya*," I said. "You hypocrites. She didn't do anything you didn't do."

The front door opened. Chaya, with her backpack. I'd texted her on my way over, telling her she was going to school with me.

"She doesn't know," Jill hissed at me. "About Ted."

"Hi!" I waved at Chaya. To her parents, I said, "And I won't tell her, if you never bring charges against Tara. If you do bring charges, I'll post this all over the world." I tossed the manila envelope.

Jill caught it. I was impressed. I'd expected the high school football player to intercept.

"Those are just copies, obviously. I have digital files." I smiled, genuinely this time, and linked my arm with Chaya's. I bent down to kiss her on the cheek, because I knew just how much it would piss off her parents.

"I need to stop home to get my bag," I said, and Chaya, looking dazed, nodded. Just to her, I added, "Come on. Tara's waiting."

Fixed it. Damn, I'm good.

A NEW DAY

KENDALL HEINTZELMAN

I'll let Kendall Heintzelman introduce this powerful story. It's her first to be published and the story tells in starkly honest detail what it's like to make some of the hardest choices anyone faces.

She says: "When I wrote this story, I had been recently discharged from a treatment center for different addictions. That type of environment had been my life for months, so adaptations of my own experiences and people I knew came out in the story. Writing became an avenue to relate those personal emotions and stories I held onto, while remaining somewhat detached."

But detachment, we find out, can be a double-edged sword when it comes to healing relationships with family. Kendall takes us into the dark that precedes the dawn—if we're lucky.

E ach morning I wake up and put on my medallion. It is supposed to remind me of recovery. This is part of my self-delusional routine; I get up thinking today will be a new day. I wear my medallion, which was passed around among a bunch of other self-delusional drunks who put their "energy" into it as a symbolic reminder of the support I have throughout my sobriety.

I text my mom. I tell her how many days clean I am. I make coffee and shower and drink it while I do my makeup. I get dressed and walk around the house until I decide today won't be a new day. Then I walk across the street to the gas station and buy a bottle of the cheapest wine they have.

I drink it in the bathtub, smoking a cigarette and listening to music, then I finish off the bottle, get dressed again, and I'm ready to go to my 11 a.m. meeting.

Monday morning I went through the routine. When I got to the Alano Club, an outdated meeting room in the basement of St. Joseph's Parish, my mom texted me back.

"I'm so proud of you," the text read, "Remember, one day at a time. You can always talk to me when you're struggling."

A twinge of guilt came up in me, along with a wine-drenched burp. I hated lying to her, but what was I gonna do? At least I was faithful with my meetings.

"God, grant me the serenity to accept the things I cannot change..." The meeting was on. I wondered how many other people there were also "off the wagon."

I helped myself to some shitty coffee with plenty of sugar. Coffee was a necessary staple at the Alano Club. Even saturated with sugar, it was still bitter and stale. I stared absentmindedly into the swirling, Styrofoam cup as Craig, the Alano Club organizer, recited the rules of Alcoholics Anonymous.

Craig struggled to read the yellow, laminated paper with a magnifying glass. Every meeting he liked to apologize for his poor eyesight, as it slowed his readings down. You'd think he had the rules memorized by now. You'd also think his thick glasses that magnified his eyes to twice their size would do the trick. Craig always reminded me of a bug-eyed squirrel. Fidgety, anxious, and tiny, and his gray hoodie and low-rise jeans were at least one size too large, but that didn't bother me. I still liked Craig.

He moved on to read a passage from the A.A. Big Book. I didn't listen; I liked to study people at meetings. There were a lot of regulars—all older, with hoarse voices and awful skin. Today I noticed a new girl. She came in with the mysterious group that always left early.

She reminded me of a squirrel too. The girl was just as jumpy as Craig, and had a dark, kind of Mohawk. She had beady eyes and a black septum piercing. I assumed this group she came with was some sort of rehab group. She probably just got out of residential.

Now everyone passed the book around. I read the full passage to myself when it came to me:

Those of us who have spent much time in the world of spiritual make-believe have eventually seen the childishness of it. This dream world has been replaced by a great sense of purpose, accompanied by a growing consciousness of the power of God in our lives. We have come to believe He would like us to keep our heads in the clouds with Him, but that our feet ought to be firmly planted on earth. That is where our fellow travelers are, and that is where our work must be done. These realities are for us. We have found nothing incompatible between a powerful spiritual experience and a life of sane and happy usefulness.

"Now, this time is open for anyone to share their thoughts on today's passage or anything that's on their mind," Craig recited. "I have a timer on my phone, each person gets five minutes to speak so as to give everyone time to talk."

"Hi I'm Maria, I'm an alcoholic," I started.

"Hi Maria," chimed the group.

"Maybe I don't get the point of the passage, but I don't agree with it," I said. "I don't think there's anything childish about keeping your head in the clouds. Reality is what always seems to get me down. If I can't dream, I can't stay sober. Maybe it is because I haven't found my 'sense of great purpose' yet, but that's how I see it."

There was a brief silence before someone else decided to speak.

"Hi I'm Alex, I'm an alcoholic/addict," the girl with the Mohawk said.

"Hi Alex," we replied.

"I think what the passage comes down to for me is denial. We've all been through stages of denial, where we wish our high could be our reality," Alex glanced at me. "But eventually you have to see that this isn't possible. Denying the reality of your addiction and wishing everything could be perfect is childish. I know I spent a long time 'recovered' when really I was just trying to fool myself. It's an impossible wish, eventually, you find something that grounds you."

Alex seemed pretty proud of herself. I hated to share in meetings. Someone was always there to shoot me down or discount my feelings.

It was 11:30. I decided to step outside for a smoke before the meeting was over. Everyone was still discussing, and since I shared, I didn't feel the need to stick around for all of it.

I stepped out back in the parking lot. A couple of other A.A.

members stood by their cars, smoking and chatting. The sun was out today, and it was already too warm. The unleveled concrete provided no shade, so I sat on the back step of the whitewashed stone building and lit up.

Alex came out too, "Can I join you?"

I nodded. She sat beside me and pulled out a vape. Of course she was one of those douchebags.

"I'm trying to quit," she explained. Vapers always had to have an explanation for vaping.

Although I wasn't in the mood for a conversation, Alex certainly was. She had an annoying, nasal voice and talked too fast and loud. And she laughed a lot. Her cheeriness was probably phony, but she was nice enough and told me how she just moved to Seattle after being in rehab for four months. She was a heroin addict and an alcoholic.

"Well I think I'm gonna head in," I told her after putting out my cig. "I want to be there if they're celebrating any birthdays or giving out coins."

We went in for the last ten minutes of the meeting. Alex received a four-months coin.

Next day I woke up late. Something in me decided to binge drink alone in my house into the early hours of the morning. I checked my phone. Shit, it was noon. I missed my meeting.

I skipped my morning routine. Who gave a fuck at that point? My mom hadn't even texted me asking if I made the meeting. I walked around the house wallowing in all my problems. My head throbbed, my stomach was in knots, my back ached and to top it all off I started my period.

I lived alone in a small duplex in downtown Seattle. Naturally it was a cheap place. My dad rented it for me as an incentive to remain sober. He bought it when I first got out of rehab. It was cold and empty, the walls were brown and it seemed there was always some sort of electrical problem or issue with the Internet cropping up, but I loved it. Maybe I lied to my parents because I wanted to keep it.

I went into my tiny kitchen and started making some coffee. What I really wanted was a drink. Maybe some Absolute Vodka or even some more cheap wine. Anything to pick me back up this morning.

"Fuck it," I said to myself when the coffee machine beeped ready. I wasn't going to put this off any longer.

I wish I had some money, I thought. I didn't have a job anymore, and stealing wasn't really my thing. There are easier ways to get what you need.

I texted my ex-boyfriend Caleb. He was a few years older than me and always down to drink.

Within an hour, Caleb was there with plenty of booze and weed. He greeted me with a hug. I thought it was funny that he still wore his thick glasses and a beard. He'd never change.

"How have you been, Maria?" he asked as we sat down on my dingy futon in the living room.

I turned on the TV and took a long gulp of vodka, "Obviously I've been great."

Caleb laughed. I used to wish he cared about my addiction; now I was thankful he was there to enable me. He was an addict in his own right; he simply hid it better.

We watched something mindless on Cartoon Network. Caleb did a lot of talking; I did a lot of drinking. His thin, lanky body still attracted me, and as I drank I remembered how much I loved his smile and his humor.

We caught up on where our lives had gone since I'd been in rehab. His hadn't changed much, and I was happy about that. It was nice to see some little part of my past remained constant.

Caleb rolled a spliff out of a Black and Mild and smoked nearly the whole thing. He took a long drag, leaned back on the futon, and exhaled. "I missed you," he said.

"Yeah, I missed everyone while I was gone."

"I think about you all the time."

I nodded. *Christ,* I thought, *I don't want to get into this. I just want to drink.*

I offered Caleb more to drink and he gladly accepted. Maybe I could get him to pass out and I could go back to bed. It was already 7 p.m. I was exhausted. Although I felt more like myself now, and had the perfect buzz, I just wanted to sleep. I couldn't miss tomorrow's meeting.

We kept drinking and smoking. Caleb grew louder and louder. I took another swig. The TV blared an obscene late night cartoon. The room grew darker and hazier. I took another swig. I couldn't remember where I put my phone. Caleb kept talking. I took another swig.

I was sweating. I couldn't figure out how to unzip my sweatshirt. I let out a hysterical giggle, although it felt more like a cry of frustration. Caleb wouldn't quiet down. He lit another Black and filled the room with more smoke. Every move he made was wrong and irritating. I searched for my phone again to check the time. It was in my pocket. 11 p.m. Why hadn't he left yet?

"I wish I could take this shit away from you," Caleb mumbled. His eyes were closed and his head back. He was cross-faded as fuck.

He sat up suddenly. "I wish this never happened," he stumbled toward me in the dark and grabbed my hands.

"Stop it!" I screamed, "I don't want this." I stood up too fast. My vision was already black around the edges and now I saw stars. The room was spinning and dark and frightening.

"I want to go to bed."

"Let's go, babe," Caleb rubbed my back.

I pushed him away, "I have to get up early tomorrow," I hiccupped.

"C'mon, I miss you."

"No really." I tried pushing past him again and bumped into my coffee table. Caleb tried to catch me and hold on to me.

"Really," I repeated. I was so dizzy now. "I just want to go to bed."

"I'll walk you to your room, make sure you get in bed safe."

"No! You should leave."

Caleb grabbed on to my shoulders, "Babe, I don't want to leave you."

"Stop calling me babe!" I screamed, but I didn't have the energy to push him again. I started to cry, "Fuck off, seriously, just go."

"You're still a bitch." He squeezed my arms tighter.

"Fuck." I squirmed; it hurt.

Caleb mumbled at me to stop moving and shook me slightly. I cried more.

"Stop crying!" He threw me onto the futon. I screamed something incoherent and he crouched down to my level and smacked me across the face, hard.

My ears were ringing. I didn't make a sound now. Inside anger was brewing so deep and it bubbled into frustration at how defenseless I was. My body wasn't working; I didn't have it in me to fucking move. My helpless frustration came out in hysteric sobs, and it only made Caleb angrier.

He shook me and smacked me again upside the head. He got on his knees over me and hit me again and again. Even though I was wasted, I could feel every blow, each one more painful than the last. But my trapped desperation felt worse than anything else. Eventually, sleep was the only thing on my mind and a peaceful wave of darkness rescued me.

I came to around 4 in the morning. My front door hung open and the light of day and cold air woke me up. I sat in the cold, stale, weed-and-vodka drenched air and thought about what happened.

Fuck him, was my initial thought, but my mind quickly turned on me, *I'm a piece of shit. I wish none of this were real. I wish I were home. I wish I could just go back to sleep again.*

After a while, my thoughts were disrupted when I noticed a sour smell. I sat up to see what it was and realized my shirt was sticky and damp. I had puked all over myself. Fucking perfect.

I got in the shower and sat down and let the hot water run down my back. Everything ached. My face and fingers felt swollen and keeping my neck and head up seemed impossible. My back felt raw, my stomach stuck out, and every movement brought on nausea. I watched my blood and urine and vomit slide down the tub and make a bubbling pool in the drain. Nothing felt real. Maybe I was in that dream world again.

Reality struck when I got out and looked in the steamy mirror. Under streaks of mascara and eye shadow were purple bruises surrounding each eye. My right ear was red and caked with blood. My lips were a little cracked and fat. I was quite a sight.

I expected to cry, but nothing came out, so I put on some clean clothes, wrapped my hair in a towel, and headed back into the living room. The coffee table was littered with cans and bottles. The wood tips of a few Blacks ashed out on the table sat there, and crumbs of weed and tobacco were everywhere.

I searched beneath the vomit-covered futon for my phone, when I found it I was sad to see my mom still hadn't texted me. It was barely 6 a.m. though; I shouldn't have expected her to be up.

Instead of cleaning up the futon or going back to bed, I threw every last bottle, every can, empty or full, into a garbage bag. I swept off the weed too.

Angrily, I stomped through the living room, into the kitchen and to my back door and threw the bag as hard as I could into the alley. Debris went flying, and it was not as satisfying as I had hoped. Today was going to be a new day for once. I was going to A.A. no matter what.

Nobody seemed to pay much notice to my appearance at the meeting. It was sometimes commonplace to see even the regulars in sorry shape. I sat in my usual spot in the middle of the inner circle of tables and drank my usual cup of coffee. The hot liquid seared my raw lips.

Alex was there again with her group. She gave me a hesitant smile and looked away when the group began the Serenity Prayer.

I stepped outside early for a smoke. I didn't catch the Big Book passage. When I came back in the group was discussing prayer (of course) and spiritual rituals.

"I'm not religious," Alex was saying. "But I do have one superstitious 'habit.' Every day I burn a dandelion and make a wish. Usually I wish for another day clean, good health, things like that." She looked at me. "Sometimes I wish for others' recovery. I guess it's my way of keeping my head in the clouds, feet on the ground. It may not do anything, but then again, prayer may not do anything."

I thought about my ritualistic tendencies. My medallion, my morning routine—it was all bullshit. I always hoped for a new day, and it never happened. Just like prayer, it all seemed to fall on deaf ears.

I went outside again. This time, Alex joined me.

"How are you doing?"

"I'm here."

"You know, when I talked to you on Monday I could smell the wine on you."

"Why do you care?" I asked. "You don't even know me."

"I know addicts. It's not that hard to spot someone who's relapsed. What did you think of today's subject?"

"It's bullshit," I said. "I used to think it was better to have prayers and rituals, or some sort of connection outside yourself and outside of reality, but it doesn't do anything. I've been trying to escape reality for too long." I lit my cigarette. "We're all just trying to fool ourselves."

Alex nodded. "I burned a dandelion and made a wish for you when you didn't show up yesterday."

I chuckled. "Look how helpful that was."

Alex stood up. "It's not our prayers or superstitions that keep our heads in the clouds," she said, "It's our addictions and denial. You're only deluding yourself." And with that, she stepped back inside.

I can't stand her. I thought. I left the meeting early. Back at home,

I felt awful. Nothing in my body had stopped hurting, and I hadn't had a drink at all since the night before. I sat on the soiled futon and checked my phone. 12 o'clock. Still no messages from Mom.

While mentally planning my next binge, I fell asleep. I dreamt that it was three months ago. I was fresh out of rehab and riding high on my newfound sobriety.

Dad drove me to my new home. He told me this was his gift to me for recovering. He said he knew living with him or Mom would be too tempting. They were "social drinkers" and didn't plan to change that. Plus, the responsibility of my own home might give me a sense of purpose.

I started to cry. "Dad, I don't want to live alone."

"This is what's best for you, don't you think?"

I shook my head. "I want to be home. I want to live with Mom."

"That's so typical of you." He was angry. "I try and do something for you and it's not good enough. You're ungrateful. You're selfish."

"Dad, I—"

He got out of the car, walked around to the passenger side, and opened my door. "Get out," he whispered. "We don't want you at home. We can't handle another one of your relapses. You can rot here if you want."

I got out of the car, still crying. He drove away.

I woke up and it took me a while to realize that the dream was not reality. It still shook me. Stretching, I noticed it was now dark. The living room didn't seem quite as scary as the night before. It still reeked of vodka, weed, and vomit, but it felt safer, more real.

I unzipped the futon cover and methodically pulled it off. Took it into the laundry room and put it in the washer. I sat back down on the bare padding and pulled my phone out. My heart sank a little when I saw there were still no messages from Mom.

I called her, and as soon as I heard her voice I felt a lump in my throat.

"Maria!" she said, "How are you, sweetie?"

"Mommy." I cleared my throat, "I want to come home."

THEY TAUGHT US WRONG

M. L. BUCHMAN

M. L. Buchman spent thirty years as a project manager specializing in crisis projects. He has taught hundreds of classes on dozens of topics including Lean Manufacturing, IT, Writing, Business Management, among others.

Matt now writes military romantic suspense, contemporary romance, fantasy and science fiction, and thrillers.

Matt has led an actual life of adventure, too, bicycling solo around the world, rebuilding and sailing solo a fifty-foot sailboat, flying airplanes and jumping out of them.

In this story he challenges our beliefs—and our literature—about romance. He says, "I often think that we've learned the wrong things about what romance is and isn't in the real world. It's not movies and it's not sex. It's about depth of feeling. I wanted to remove sex, even dialog, and explore just the core of a man's heart."

I think he completely succeeded in his task because sometimes the most difficult, most urgent choices are not about what to do, but about what to believe.

Mare Tranquillitatis my ass!

Go ahead. Thrash some Duster bastard over Luna's northeastern Nearside. Make him eat death slow and painful.

Then, after you've won, after his ass is going down hard, his drive goes nova. It kicks out an electro-magnetic pulse so hard that it cooks your ship, too. You dump out two klicks up and watch your ship punch a new crater close beside his.

See how you feel about that shit.

Scary as hell ride down. The EMP had cooked my suit's electronics as well. I had to handle the landing retros manually. Ran out of fuel a few dozen meters up—damn glad this was Luna grav and not Earth's unforgiving full-g. Felt the leg go when I hit, but I was down and the suit was intact for all the good it did me.

Welcome to the fucking Sea of Tranquility.

The Duster's ship had gone as bright as a second sun, before it piled into the inside cliff face of Cauchy Crater, less than a dozen klicks away. Instead of acting like a beacon shouting "Come save my ass," the crater had funneled all light into a beam that was crossing nobody's path—not Earth, not some off-track freighter. Like a rifle shot due north, it was going straight up. Some dipwad alien scientist sitting on the North Star four hundred years from now might scratch himself and wonder what that tiny fleck of brightness could be, but I wasn't counting on it.

As if the busted leg hadn't just stamped paid on my ticket, my Army training kicked in and I checked my suit. Dead. H2 and oxy recyc had enough mechanical fail-safes to give me something to drink and breath for now. All I could do was hope the suit blocked the rads of the reactor burst, because the dosimeter readout had cooked along with the rest of my electronics. No dosimeter, no radio, no readouts on how much longer I'd have before even the recyc couldn't save me. Not even a beacon in case someone did come looking.

I unclipped my RACR and fired a shot at a likely rock. The Recoilless Army Combat Rifle didn't recoil, but it didn't shatter the rock either. Three kilos of dead plastic and fried electronics.

I slammed a hypo through my suit leg, trying not to scream at the jarring to my broken leg. The cold clarity of the meds washed through me and the limb went blessedly numb.

The Army taught us a whole lot about how to survive in hard places. Zero atmo and the one-sixth g of Luna's surface wasn't anything new in the manual. Sitting in a white-gray camo suit at the bottom of a three-klick deep crater four hundred kilometers from the next nearest piece of humanity without even a signal flare? Not so much.

Walking that distance was in range, if my leg hadn't decided to take leave without permission. Didn't really matter; without the nav gear, I didn't stand a chance of finding a specific point four hundred klicks away. There wasn't shit at the old Apollo 17 site anyway except scrap—Chinese had gotten pissed half a century back, when there was still a China, and dropped a ten-thousand kilo shrapnel head right at ground zero. Shock-wave munitions—concussers—didn't work in zero atmo, but the shrap-heads never left anything bigger than a bootsole behind, not for a long way round. The Chinese blew out the museum, the historic lander and buggy, and about three hundred tourists—all done back before this shit war when there were still tourists.

Army trainers had pounded a lot into my thick skull. Not a single piece of which was going to salvage this fucked up mess. No impossible engineering feat sprouting from my grunt brain. No "just lean into the fucking traces, man, and grunt it out" solution. Even in one-sixth g I wasn't going to hop one-legged for four hundred kilometers to nowhere. No miracles—not out here.

I was dead; I knew that. But I was no helmet cracker. I'd hold on for every second I had.

Army did a whole lot of mental training too. How to turn fear into something useful was the big one.

You'll be afraid. Don't care who you are, you'll be shitting your pants when you're in it.

A lot they knew. Why didn't the psychs ever actually fly a mission? Too goddamn scared was my guess.

They didn't get that fear came *before* the mission. During the fight, there was only time for adrenaline and survival.

You've got to turn that fear. Turn it to anger! Turn it to rage! Turn it to winning the battle!

Fuckin' psychs.

We did what they told us. Afraid of something? *Attack it!* Except the fear came before the mission—we turned it anyway. We'd beat on each other in the ready room, throwing "friendly" punches that would level a grunt if they weren't as wound on adrenaline as the next jock. We'd *start* the flight with bruises purpling and fear-eating grins plastered on our faces. Yeah, we had the old turn-fear-into-rage routine nailed.

Fear when you went down was a different kind of thing. I'd beaten the odds about three-hundred to one by surviving. Couldn't get that kind of help in a poker game, but I had it now for all the good it was doing.

No way to rescue myself and no one looking for me here.

Zara had eaten it at the far end of Mare Fecunditatis—Sea of Fertility. *Shit!* She'd been the best partner I'd ever had in flight or in the sack. New Army thinking—fighting partners who were also fucking partners.

Heightened wingman bond. Subjects more likely to go to extreme measures to defend their sleep mate.

"Sleep mate." Lame-ass psychs—like that even began to cover it.

Zara had rocked. Better than anyone, even before the Army and their psychs got their claws in me. Zara and I had talked about rooting down together when our tours were up. Meant it to. It hadn't been some feebs' pillow talk; we'd meant it right down to our boots.

Yeah, stamp paid on that one too.

You want terror, you fuckin' psychs? Not fear, but unholy, mind-numbing, shit-in-your-pants terror? You watch a renegade Duster zero in on your wingmate when your thrust vector is going the other way and there isn't squat you can do about it. That'll teach you terror.

But I'd turned it. Yes I did. I turned that terror into one flaming, searing, ball-busting tower of pissed-as-hell fighter-jock rage. Rather than just killing him and going home alive, I took that Duster apart one piece at a time. I moved in close and hurt him and kept on hurting him. No kill—just pain.

When I finally let the bastard die—when he'd crisscrossed a thousand kilometers of Luna trying to get away but knowing he was going to burn in hell—I got close enough to see him right through his canopy. Almost close enough to hear his final scream despite the gap of empty space between us.

But he'd kept that one last trick up his sleeve.

When his engine blew, it fucking went EMP, cooking all my circuits.

And down I went, too.

I tried to spot the new craters our two ships had punched—side-by-side holes a kilometer up Cauchy's side.

Not even a hint. It was night and only cold Earthshine lit that section of crater wall. Earthshine would never reach me here at the bottom of Cauchy's deep. Sunrise was still a week away.

The ships had hit in the steepest part of the rim's cliff. They'd probably triggered a rockfall to bury any trace. Only evidence left was me.

Some day, a thousand years from now, some geologist would stumble on my camouflaged suit—almost the same color as the soil and lightly dusted with micrometeorites. He'd have to look up my suit design in some historical database to figure out what century I'd been fucked by. My personal recorder was cooked, so no record there. No pad or pen, so I couldn't even leave him a goddamn note. I considered scrabbling a long message in the Lunar dust; it would last for centuries.

Then, like some lovesick schoolboy, I simply scribed two first names—mine and Zara's. It wouldn't mean anything to anyone but me, but I liked seeing it there.

She'd taught me joy in war. She'd trained me, far more thoroughly than the psychs, that there were emotions other than fear and rage—even Army victory celebrations weren't joy; they were rage thinly disguised as triumph.

More important than joy, Zara had taught me hope. Hope of one day seeing a girl with her mother's dark hair floating behind as she raced down the corridors of Tycho City. Of a boy with my light eyes watching a ball bounce in one-sixth g and seeing nothing strange because he'd never been to a full-g planet.

The recyc ran out. I felt the tightness growing in my chest. Oxydep setting in. I knew my training. From when I could truly feel it—not some fear or panic reaction, but really feel it—I would have only moments before it killed me. They'd learned that the slow bleed-out of oxygen depravation led to unpredictable panic attacks, bad news in armed soldiers. So the recyc ran at a hundred percent until it was gone. The air in the suit was good for three more thinning breaths, maybe four, then I'm done.

One final look at the stars Zara and I had dreamed beneath.

Lying here in my last moments, I learned a new fear.

One that the goddamn psychs would never be able to understand no matter how I tried to explain. It wasn't a fear born of rage or vengeance or honor. It was born of something they could never know —weren't capable of knowing. Weren't worthy of.

My fear, Zara? The one thing that shrivels me? The one thing I can't turn into soothing, familiar rage?

It's that the woman who taught me to love so deeply might not be there waiting for me when I cross over.

TENDRILS

LEIGH SAUNDERS

With this story, we enter a realm where humans not only aren't the center of the universe, but don't even have the most crucial moral choices to make. It's a realm Leigh Saunders finds particularly fascinating.

When not writing speculative fiction for a living, Leigh enjoys writing "social science fiction," in other words, stories that focus on people and things, sometimes sentient things, in places that are distant in space and time.

Her short fiction has appeared in a variety of anthologies and collections. Her first novel, Memoirs of a Synth: Gold Record, *is available through all the major ebook retailers. This is her third story for* Fiction River, *having contributed also to* Alchemy & Steam *and* Visions of the Apocalypse.

When she began to write this story, Leigh was busy working on another project that took place, she says, "in the largely unexplored world of our own oceans and the creatures that make their home in the depths. The character of Oma owes her heritage to a combination of this research, multiple YouTube videos of cuttlefish, octopuses, and squid, and the tanks of jellyfish in our local aquarium. All I had to do then was envision these amazing creatures floating in space instead of salt water, and ask myself, 'what if...'"

Great question and this story is a great answer.

The cargo loader jounced up the ramp, across the threshold, and into the ship's cargo hold. Oma shifted her weight and slid off the stacked containers at the front of the loader, her hood flaring slightly as she fluttered to the floor. Then she lay still, flattened out to mere millimeters in thickness, her hood extended to cover her tendrils.

The loader paused briefly as its humanoid driver—barely looking in Oma's direction—ensured the containers were still secure. Then it continued on, rumbling deeper into the hold.

Oma slid laterally, moving out of the path of other loaders until she reached a wall. She'd altered her pigmentation to take on the milky, semi-translucent coloring of the heavy plastic packing material wound around many of the containers, and now huddled in a small, loose pile, mimicking the detritus of interstellar shipping.

None of the humanoids had noticed her.

They seldom did. It wasn't really their fault, she supposed. After all, their sensory capabilities were so much more limited than her own.

Even now, pressed against the wall, the pressure, chemical, and photoreceptors covering her hood were providing data that resolved itself into an enticing picture of the cargo hold around her. Sound waves identified the creaking of the metal panels beneath the weight of the loaders that rolled along, engines whirring, growling, thrumming, emitting chemicals that mingled with the distinctive sharp flavors of metal, the bitterness of plastic, and the cloying sweetness of the humanoids' sweat, all swirling together in the close, slightly humid air of the hold. Heat bubbles identified the humanoids moving through the space, calling to each other in their high-pitched voices, strapping down crates and containers for the interstellar voyage.

Oma shuddered in anticipation.

It would be far safer to attach herself to the hull of the ship, wrap her tendrils around the numerous knobby protrusions, alter her pigmentation to match her surroundings, and simply go dormant until they reached their destination. Once there, she could detach, floating to the ground, the rushing air filling her hood. She'd done it before.

But the interior of the ship was filled with dangerous, exciting flavors.

Addicting flavors...

She pulled her tendrils in close, retracting her hood slowly at the same time, compacting her surface area. There was still too much activity in the hold for her to move freely, but she needed to find the passage from the cargo hold into the main body of the ship before the hold was locked-down for launch and she was trapped here.

Waiting was not an option.

She'd made that mistake once before, and spent weeks wandering aimlessly around a mostly darkened cargo hold, curling tendrils around its single, dim light fixture for what little photosynthetic sustenance it offered, but which did little to satisfy her cravings.

She'd experienced her fill of bare girders, metal panels, and stacks of wrapped containers. The flavors of a cargo hold were now only the tempting prelude to what lay beyond.

The humanoids were far more interesting. They varied from ship to ship, their emotions layered with multiple flavors, their environment offering many varieties of sustenance. And keeping herself hidden while she observed them, traveled with them, had become a challenging game she liked to play.

Oma moved away from the ramp, staying close to the wall, close to stacks of containers as she made her way deeper into the hold. Shifting air currents flowed around her, leading her toward the passageway that separated the hold from the main body of the ship.

When she reached the opening—a heavy panel standing open alongside a large, oval gap in the wall, little over the height of the average humanoid—she pressed herself into the space just below the opening.

It was too dangerous to push her hood up, so slowly, cautiously, she extended a translucent tendril upward, toward the opening.

She had fewer receptors on the ends of her tendrils, so the impressions she received of the passage were less vivid than those her hood would have provided. Nevertheless, she was able to make out the heat bubbles of humanoids moving away down the long, narrow space, the echo of their footfalls against the metal of the floor diminishing along with the sound of their voices as they passed through another oval gap at the opposite end of the passage.

The passage itself offered few places for her to hide.

Oma quickly slid up and over the opening and into the passage, pressing herself tightly against the base of the wall. As she did so, she studied the colors and patterns of the wall and floor around her and shifted her pigment to match.

Then she stretched her tendrils forward until she was extended from the opening to the opposite end of the passage. Her hood thinned and elongated to cover her tendrils as she moved, her coloring altering in such a way that she appeared to be little more than a thick, slightly lumpy seam of dull metal where the gray wall was joined to the metal grid work of the floor.

It was one of the easiest—and most invisible—ways to move amid the humanoids.

Twice she froze in place as humanoids passed her, unseeing. Their too-sweet flavors settled on her receptors, the vibrations of their heavy footfalls landed barely a boot-width from her body, sending slight tremors rippling through her hood. The brightness of their heat bubbles was almost unbearable in the closeness of the passage, made tolerable only by the cooling movement of the air currents as they passed.

At long last, she slipped through the oval at the far end of the passage and into the ship. There was even more humanoid activity here, and Oma felt briefly overwhelmed from the rich layers of flavor that bombarded her receptors. A ripple of pleasure went through her hood, her tendrils writhing in anticipation.

She was looking forward to a long voyage.

Oma slid along the conduits suspended from the ceilings and passing through the walls of the ship. The conduits were like her own personal passages, allowing her to move freely throughout the ship. In addition, they provided her with a nearly infinite number of vantage points to observe the humanoids as they moved through their diurnal routines.

They slept, often alone, sometimes in pairs, in small, private compartments that were heady with flavor. Over the first few days of the voyage, Oma visited them all, memorizing their individualized patterns of heat and sound, the flavors of their bodies. Once their patterns were imprinted on her receptors, she could identify them when she located them in other parts of the ship.

The humanoids' common feeding area was one of her favorite

spots in the ship. It was full of light and movement and sound and flavors of all kinds. Though she understood few of the sounds the humanoids made, Oma was fascinated by their vocalized communication, and often extended herself along the length of one of the large conduits above the feeding area in an effort to expose more of her receptors to everything that passed below her.

As they left the feeding area, she had observed that many of the humanoids deposited the remains of their meals into a small opening in the wall. A thin barrier, made up of a combination of vertical segments of flexible material and a small swirl of moving air, blocked her view of what lay beyond.

Unable to resist the temptation, she cautiously slipped a thin, nearly-transparent tendril down the wall, toward the opening. She pressed forward with the tendril, moving through the small gust of air and pushing aside the barrier.

Heat and steam immediately assaulted the tendril's receptors.

Caution forgotten, Oma whipped the tendril from the opening, recoiling it into the cool folds of her hood. Startled and confused, she focused her receptors on the opening, but the barrier had slipped back into place immediately, and she was once again unable to observe what lay beyond.

Oma was curious.

She could also be patient when it was necessary.

She settled down to sleep. Later, when the humanoids retired to their compartments, she would investigate this strange thing.

Oma awoke, all of her receptors alerting her to danger. The vibrations of the ship were... *wrong*, the rhythmic pulse of the engines racing, faltering, then throbbing as though struggling to find the rhythm again.

Below her, humanoids moved quickly through the feeding area, some speaking loudly, others in tense silence.

Then metal groaned and the ship lurched, throwing Oma from

where she lay along the length of a conduit. She lashed out as she fell, tendrils flailing, stretching, grasping, ends coiling instinctively around anything within reach—the conduit above, the backs of chairs below, the torso of a humanoid bracing itself in the nearby doorway.

Then she crashed onto the humanoids' eating surface.

Dazed, she lay there for a moment, hood pressed flat against cool plastic, the receptors on her tendrils providing her insufficient data to understand what had happened.

The data were sufficient, however, to tell her the *result*. The humanoid she'd latched onto was pointing at her and shouting wildly.

She'd been seen.

Oma let go of everything she'd grasped during her fall—including the humanoid who collapsed to the floor. Reaching up with multiple tendrils, she pulled herself back up to the conduits, shifting color to match the darkness above.

Below other humanoids were arriving, summoned by the first who was still shouting and gesturing wildly toward her. Some were carrying small, metallic objects she could only interpret as weapons.

The flavors of fear and anger from the humanoids below washed over her receptors in waves. Oma shuddered. She wanted to compress herself into a tight little knot, but forced herself to remain elongated, distributing her weight so she could slide smoothly along the conduits without jostling them and revealing her location. She might not understand the humanoids' language, but she understood their flavors, and she had no doubt at all that if they caught her, they would kill her.

If the ship didn't blow up first.

Hiding in the shadowed recesses where the conduits passed between decks, Oma extended tendrils in multiple directions, coiling the ends around struts and supports. Then she stretched out her hood as far as she could, tuning her receptors to the sounds of the ship.

She listened. She felt. She saw.

And she followed the direction her receptors led.

Supports creaked, those behind her groaning with the strain as they compensated for broken ones ahead. Torn metal edges dragged against one another, the sound a rough shriek. Stress fractures glowed in threads of red and white-hot heat as she moved forward.

And under it all, the engines continued to falter in their broken rhythm, the pace quickening with every cycle.

Why hadn't the humanoids repaired it? Did they not understand the danger?

Oma knew little of a ship's engine, had only a superficial understanding of its mechanics—such knowledge as she had been able to gain during earlier voyages, when she had spent many long cycles exploring the engine areas and how the mechanical components interacted with each other to power the vessels across the blackness of deep space. In its own way, the flavor of a ship's engine was one of perfect synchronicity.

But *this* engine was communicating wrongness through every connected strut.

All her receptors told her that if whatever had caused the engine's erratic pulse was not addressed soon, the ship would tear itself apart. And while she might survive, drifting dormant along with the debris until another ship came along, the humanoids would not.

Another tremor sent ripples through her hood.

Oma shuddered in response, receptors picking up the acidic flavor of the humanoids' fear which now permeated the ship. She then wrapped her hood around her tendrils and began to slide quickly along the conduits.

The humanoids wouldn't hesitate to kill her.

But she couldn't just leave them to die.

Oma seldom visited the engine area of any ship she rode. The spaces were loud and hot, the dominant flavors acrid and bitter, and not at all to her liking. Her explorations during previous voyages had told her that she would find few new flavors to experience in that part of the ship. As a result, she had adopted the habit of finding the engine area shortly after coming aboard, making a note of its location relative to more pleasant portions of the ship, and then avoiding it for the remainder of the journey.

This trip had been no exception.

The main engine control area was located near the center of the ship, forward of the cargo hold, and on the level above. The engines themselves extended in pairs along either side of the cargo hold, a stronger engine, for interstellar flight, positioned above a smaller engine, used for navigation.

The habitable portion of the ship occupied the front third of the vessel, which was where Oma had spent most of her time.

Now, though, she found herself slipping along conduits, moving between levels, heading increasingly to the left as she followed the ship's stresses toward the damaged interstellar engine.

The acrid, chemical flavors grew more intense, heat bubbles brighter, coating the struts all around her, warming the conduits on which she traveled. Then her hood began to pulse reflexively, in time with the broken rhythm.

Oma hesitated, then cautiously extended her hood, filling it with as much air as she could hold in the confined space, and pushed it out in a rush at a point on a nearby strut. In that small area, the heat bubble faded slightly, and she quickly touched the tip of a tendril to the spot.

Pain shot up her tendril all the way to her hood, the tender filament sizzling and blackening before crumbling into fine ash. But the touch had survived long enough for her receptors to recognize the pattern of the engine area, and identify the point where that pattern had been disrupted.

She coiled the remainder of the damaged tendril up under her hood, then headed toward the disruption in the pattern.

When she arrived, she understood immediately why the humanoids hadn't yet repaired the damage. Several tons of debris and broken humanoid bodies blocked her way. Severed struts, fractured walls, and shattered pipes formed a nearly impenetrable barrier —super-heated metal fused together in some areas—barring passage.

But as extensive as the damage was, her receptors told her it was the *result* of the disruption, not the *cause*. The point of disruption lay beyond the barrier.

Even as easily as she could slip through small spaces, Oma wasn't sure if she could reach it. The humanoids, who she could hear behind her, struggling to clear the debris, would never reach it in time.

The conduits were too hot to rest on here, so she hovered above them, heated air rising from the engine, filling her hood and holding her aloft. Gingerly, she extended her tendrils, dozens of them, threading them ever-so-cautiously through openings in the debris, searching for a route to the disruption.

Though what she would do when she found it, she still had no idea.

She pushed away every thought, every sensation, every flavor, focusing all her concentration on the data she was receiving from her tendrils. Sensations of heat met the filaments at every turn, forcing her back in some places, in search of new routes to try.

There! The tiniest eddy of air, laden with the pungent flavor of coolant, curled like a beckoning tendril, leading her forward through a narrow gap. Oma followed the path it promised, withdrawing a score of tendrils from dead-end trails and sending them along behind, coiling them around the main tendril to give the delicate filament a whisper of insulation from the heated metal that surrounded it.

And then she was through.

Coolant spewed from a ruptured line ahead of her—the disruption point—vaporizing almost instantly in the super-heated air.

Behind her, the humanoid crew was still several cycles away.

Below her, metal groaned.

Around her, heat bubbles were a glowing inferno.

Oma thrust her tendril forward, into the cloud of coolant,

searching for the break in the line. The hot liquid splashed over the tendril, clouding her receptors, chemicals soaking in and sending sharp, stinging pain through the filaments, only slightly less agonizing than the heat of the burned tendril had been.

She worked by feel, coiling the blinded tendril around the line, pulling it into place, the filament growing sluggish and heavy. Then her other tendrils slid through the gap, and she drove them into the cloud, layer upon layer of filaments slowly, steadily pulling the ragged edges toward each other, wrapping stiffly around the line until coolant was no longer spraying into the air and soaking her tendrils, but began to flow through the line toward the engine. A cycle passed, and the cloud of coolant vapor gradually dissipated, settling onto the rope of tendrils coiled around the line like a thick paste, locking them into place.

Another cycle passed, and Oma became aware of the slightest shift in the engine's labored pulse. There was still an unimaginable amount of stress on the ship, and the engine's rhythm was still erratic, but the rapid cycling was beginning to slow.

She hoped that was a good thing,

Imminent destruction at least temporarily avoided, the wrenching of metal behind finally her caught her attention, and Oma suddenly realized that in her desperation to repair the disruption, she'd made a horrible mistake.

She was trapped.

And she'd done it to herself.

She'd given the humanoids working their way through the debris enough time to save the ship. And when they found her, tethered to the coolant line by a rope made of her own tendrils, it was entirely likely that they would kill her.

Oma shuddered, but more from a sense of irony than fear. The edges of her hood flared, and her unfettered tendrils swirled around her, coiling instinctively away from the still heated metal surrounding her. The tendril she'd burned earlier remained coiled tightly, soaking in the cool, fluid-filled pocket under the edge of her hood, the pain in the damaged end fading, but still sharp.

She couldn't feel the rope of tendrils wrapped around the coolant line.

She stopped shuddering as the realization hit her—*she couldn't feel the tendrils!*

She slid a healthy tendril down the length of the tendrils that formed the rope, testing for sensation at regular intervals, and found that after seventeen intervals she felt nothing. The tendrils had absorbed the coolant, the filaments paralyzed by the chemicals in the liquid, locking them permanently into place around the line.

The coolant might have killed her—might still. At the point where the damaged filaments still had sensation, she could feel the fluid working its way upward, toward her hood.

She hesitated less than a cycle—the wrenching of metal being cleared away was getting closer, the toxic fluid was rising, there was no time to lose. She twisted, swinging the rope toward the brightest heat bubbles on one of the broken, super-heated struts, connecting just above the level where the filaments had lost sensation.

Tendrils sizzled, blackened.

She swung into the strut again.

Thick, black smoke roiled up, the revolting flavor of her own burnt tendrils assaulting her receptors.

Again. The super-heated strut cauterizing the filaments as it burned through the rope.

Pain.

If she'd had a voice, she would have cried out, a scream to put the wrenching metal to shame. As it was, she simply hovered, limp, in shock, as the pain rushed up her tendrils, spreading across her hood, the blackened ends of the burned filaments hanging in limp coils.

After several cycles, Oma reached down with healthy tendrils and looped them around the damaged ones. She gently pulled them into loose coils, then tucked their burned ends into the fluid-filled pocket under the edges of her hood.

Then she drifted listlessly upward on the heated air, allowing the currents to carry her to cooler spaces amid the conduits.

Oma didn't know how long she'd slept, curled up in the shadows of the conduits. Her burned tendrils still ached, but at least they no longer throbbed in agony, which meant she'd gone dormant, letting her body put all its energy into the healing.

The ship's engines—all of them—were silent.

She moved slowly, weakly, from her hiding place. She needed light, a source of photosynthetic sustenance. Then she needed to figure out where she was—where the ship had made port—and attempt to slip away unnoticed. She would find a place to finish her recovery; only then could she begin making plans for her next journey. She was tired, but the craving for flavors, experiences still flickered like a tiny heat bubble inside of her that she couldn't ignore.

She was curious about what had happened to the ship, but she had no interest in going back toward the engine area to investigate. With a light brush of a tendril against a strut, her receptors confirmed that she wasn't drifting in an empty shell through the icy cold of space, so she thought it was safe to assume that they'd safely reached a port somewhere and probably settled in to make repairs.

She slid along the conduits toward the habitation area, her receptors tuned to any sign of life or movement on the ship. Almost unconsciously, her route along the conduits took her back to the feeding area. Oma settled herself on the conduits above and rested, contentedly, slipping translucent tendrils down and around the room's several ceiling-mounted light fixtures, photosynthetic receptors greedily sucking at the light.

It was a feeding area, after all.

A half-dozen humanoids were in the room below her, seated around the large eating surface, engaging in vocalized communication punctuated with occasional rhythmic bursts of sound. She recognized most of them as members of the ship's crew; one was new to her. But of far more interest to her than the new humanoid, was an object that rested on the eating surface.

A long container, made of the hardened transparent material the humanoids were so fond of, ran down the center of the eating surface. Inside the container lay a length of thick tubing, surrounded at its midpoint by a heavy rope, made of multiple strands of tendrils.

Her tendrils.

Oma shuddered in surprise. They had kept her tendrils, and the coolant line she'd repaired for them! For all her voyages with the humanoids, she had no idea what meaning to assign to that very singular action.

Below, the humanoids finished with their meal. They rose from the table, each member of the original crew silently placing a hand on the transparent container for a moment before lifting the remains of their meal, depositing it into the small slot on the wall near the passageway, and leaving the room.

Oma absently absorbed the photosynthetic sustenance, and considered her options. She *could* leave the ship and find another... or maybe she could stay here. She'd never stayed on the same ship through multiple journeys before, but there was nothing stopping her.

This ship had provided a wealth of flavors, after all...

She turned her attention to the transparent box, at the same time sliding a translucent tendril down toward the strange opening in the wall.

Maybe there were reasons to stay.

LITTLE BYTE AND BIG PIECES

VALERIE BROOK

For her second powerful story in this volume, Valerie Brook introduces us to a pair of friends who find a light to shine even when overwhelming forces are intent on their destruction.

She says about the story, "To be brutally honest, this story was inspired by my own iPhone, and the fact that I have late-stage Lyme disease and was bedridden with my phone as my only link to the outside world and the research and people and medicine that were saving my life. For better or worse—a trusty friend. For this short story, when I imagined a world without any people at all, and the internet of smart appliances and cars and cities having gone bonkers and taken over the globe, there had to be a hero."

And that's how Val got this fantastic and fun story. Amazing, just amazing.

———

L ittle Byte's wobbly tricycle wheel slipped off the slick grassy bluff and he fell forty feet and plunked into the dry sandy beach below like a heavy metal anchor lodging into the sea bottom.

He was stuck.

The cold winds plunged from the forbidding gray sky and stirred the thick ocean fog like a giant's angry soup spoon might agitate the contents of an earthly cauldron.

Sand spit into Little Byte's digital face—needled into the tiny crack between his dull silver front bezel and the LCD display.

He was merely a refurbished first generation iPhone.

He was not equipped for inclement weather without his poncho. Which was lost.

Little Byte imagined the short-circuiting of his 8 GB logic board and all the assorted accessories he had constructed over the years to configure moving arms and legs and a small tool kit and emergency supplies.

Soon it would rain. Deadly, salty rain.

If the menacing sea didn't swallow him first.

Visibility in the two megapixel camera lens faded to a claustrophobic, pixilated crayon drawing of swirling mists and dark rocky teeth as the approaching afternoon storm front swooped toward the grinning coastal lips of the Pacific Ocean.

Iridescent sea foam broke and flew into wind-whipped chunks as the pale outline of pea-green waves crested and crashed, crying out with a deadly *swish* as the tide shot over the face of the sand and rushed up toward Little Byte's feet.

Well, the best approximation of feet he could recently find—the squeaky front wheel of a Radio Flyer tricycle on the left, the 8 x 36.6 inch skateboard deck on the right. The skateboard had two orange wheels in the front and the back dragged like a serrated surfboard bitten by a shark.

Oh dear, he thought.

But the pea-green wave reversed just in time, leaving behind a kelp snake wound in the sharp shells of barnacles.

Little Byte's newest body, the painted fifty-five gallon steel black transport drum, vibrated with a dull bell toll when the winds snapped like the tail end of a whip.

Little Byte was dying.

Partially buried at a forty-five degree angle.

He quickly calculated this to be the most unfortunate event of his life.

Little Byte had googled these things over the years. All the adverse conditions that could destroy a computer chip.

There wasn't much else to do except survive and Google the years away anymore, anyway. But his memory chip could only hold so much before he had to delete data.

So the whole world would have been rediscovered, again and again, if it wasn't for his 3TB external hard drive BIBLE. His most safeguarded possession welded deep into the body of his transport barrel and connected to his circuit board with a USB cable.

Oh, how would he extract himself from this desperate situation?

Little Byte activated his robotic carbon fiber core inside the transport barrel and raised his free robotic shoulder. His makeshift arm was made of a home gym pull-up bar and a three-pronged silver serving fork attached tight with moldy Star Wars duct tape.

The dirt encrusted, unstuck edge of the tape said *flicka flicka* in the wind as it beat back and forth.

Little Byte discovered the fork made a terrible shovel in the sand.

He rotated his robotic hip, the unburied one, and dug with the broken edge of the skateboard and a strong leg made of five white PVC pipes bound together with the self-same Star Wars duct tape.

While the wind raised its voice into a ghostly moan and the waves came close and then closer, Little Byte dug and dug until he could rotate back and forth like a wheel in a ditch.

His second arm, the one made with a sawed-off shower rod and a wooden fashioned palm that attached a Swiss Army knife, a pair of tweezers, and a vice-grips jerry-rigged to open and shut when he nodded his camera tripod neck—popped free of the sand.

Then a powerful wave slapped the barrel, the cold sea water lifting his hollow body up and spinning him like a rolling pin on a sandy sheet of cookie dough pressing away from the ocean. His neck and head floated above the deadly liquid.

His pixilated view of the world scrambled.

His earbuds recorded the terrifying screech of metal as he grated over sharp rocks.

Little Byte flailed his arms and legs wildly as the wave paused and swirled, probing the embankment and hungrily uprooting plants and collecting treasures to sweep back into its wide mouth and swallow whole.

Just as the grip of the tide yanked Little Byte toward a dark, watery death, his protuberances hooked onto something unseen and he was saved.

Little Byte did not waste time calculating his luck.

He awkwardly struggled to his feet.

He widened his camera aperture and turned on the flashlight. The ray of light cut through the fog and illuminated a solid, impenetrable wall of brittle clay, tangled roots that looked like enormous bird talons, and blackened rocks rising above him. But there, look, to the left, a possible path of ascension.

Little Byte zoomed in and took a photo.

Just as another huge wave shot up to snatch him, Little Byte hobbled up and away on his skateboard and the now broken, unrolling tricycle wheel. The perilous trail crumbled as he climbed, but at last he reached the self-same bluff and clump of grass he had slipped from moments ago.

The wind howled. The fierce clouds loomed, pregnant underbellies of rain only moments from splitting wide and drenching the coast.

Little Byte fled east.

Grassy tufts and uneven dips in the earth jarred his makeshift attachments. He clattered like a symphony of pots and pans. His tripod neck destabilized and bent backwards. Even as his LCD face pointed straight up at the roiling mass of clouds, he ran blind and kept running. There was no time to fix his broken neck.

The smart car had been parked in a direct line from the bluff's edge.

Bam! Little Byte found the Prius.

The impact of his metal transport barrel on the metal passenger door whipped his tripod head back into vertical orientation.

With the tough chassis of a tow truck, the front half of the body of a bullet-proof armored van, the back half of a luxury stretch limo, and the tires of a professional dune racer—the smart Prius sensed Little Byte with her backup camera.

She clicked open her makeshift trunk, which rose like a yawning clam shell, and turned on the interior lights with a gentle *ding.*

A giant splash of rain plopped on Little Byte's touch screen. Right between the time display and the "slide to open" bar.

GO GO GO, Little Byte typed furiously as he lurched around the vehicle to the back end where he could load up. But before he could even send the text, he had jumped into the limo trunk with a cacophony of bangs and scratches and pulled down the hatch with his vice-grips and an echoing thunk.

The Prius spun her gigantic wheels.

The second and third drops of rain *dinged* then *donged* on the thin sheet metal enclosure under which Little Byte had found shelter.

And then all rainy hell broke loose like gunfire.

Little Byte increased the auto-brightness on his LCD screen and lay there just beaming brightly. The gray interior of the trunk reflected his light, glowing softly over all the scattered tools and assorted odds and ends in the trunk. As the Prius pitched across the landscape, the objects bounced and danced around, celebrating like they had all gone the whole nine yards.

Little Byte realized his data on that particular colloquial phrase were incomplete. He searched the *Oxford Dictionary Of Phrase and Fable* in iBooks (this 2020 edition was now terribly outdated by slightly more than a century):

Meaning: To try one's best.

Origin: In World War II, fighter pilots were issued a 9-yard chain of ammunition. When a pilot used all of his fire power on a target, he had given it "the whole nine yards."

Little Byte made a note and cached this for high-speed retrieval.

Even though he'd updated as far as his hardware would allow, it was still challenging to multitask, and in the next moment he realized his glass touch screen was not safe with the tools flipping all around.

It had been years since he'd had a proper safety case.

They were just so hard to come by these days.

He rolled over, organized his arms and legs, and crawled from the dark cave of the trunk into the deteriorated interior of the luxury limo. He lay his transport barrel on the moldy carpeted floor and braced himself against the barren metal frames where the plush leather bench seats used to attach before they rotted into powdery wedges.

The Prius texted through her own WiFi signal, HOW ARE YOU?

FINE AND DANDY, Little Byte replied cheerfully.

DID YOU FIND THE INTERNET OUT THERE? she asked.

NO MA'AM.

Then Little Byte plugged into the accessory port with his last frayed charger and fed his terribly exhausted battery.

When they parked back at the hidden entrance to the underground carport after one hour and twenty-one minutes and forty-six seconds of bumpy, soggy, off-road driving through fields, around boulders, and even across a bubbling stream—Little Byte sat up and investigated his damage.

The Prius wiped her front windshield out of habit. The decaying blades squeaked. The rain had softened now, tinkling on the roof of the vehicle.

Little Byte wondered if his tricycle wheel would ever roll again. His Swiss Army knife had disappeared from its wooden socket. And his black painted transport body, which had been cylindrical, now looked chipped and distorted like it had sailed unshielded through an asteroid belt.

I CANNOT IDLE UNTIL MY SOLAR PANELS RECHARGE, the Prius texted.

INDEED, Little Byte replied.

The Prius yawned open her trunk and Little Byte crawled out the way he had come in. Before exposing his LCD to the damp weather, he vice-gripped a clear plastic produce bag from the trunk. These bags still blew in the wind and could be found almost anywhere.

The supple plastic draped easily over his glass face and exposed ports, but it warped the view through the eye of his camera.

Oh, how he missed having a waterproof, scratch-proof, drop-proof industrial case to fit over his 3.5 inch display. One never had to worry about very much. Those days were over he calculated. The Electronic Kingdom was not what it used to be in the early years.

Little Byte accessed his cache in .004 nanoseconds. Planned obsolescence: an artificially limited useful life.

He stood on wobbly feet under the misty arms of a native oak tree. Mustard and goosegrass tips bent heavy with raindrops and dampened his legs.

THANKS FOR TRYING, he texted. SEE YOU LATER.

Her WiFi signal was weak outside her interior doors.

IT WAS WORTH A TRY, she replied.

The Prius cut her motor. Her headlights winked out.

The view from inside Little Byte's plastic produce bag crystallized with water droplets.

All around, the steel bones of a prior civilization lay corroded and buckled in a spectacular display of rusted reds and browns.

Lush green spring shoots poked up from small chunks of concrete, white blooming vines hung from steel rebar. The old, cratered hollows of linear streets were now merely crisscrossed contours existing under the flow of the wild, unbridled flora and fauna that had succeeded it.

Even the fresh tracks of the wheels, wing blades, and feet of the machines were fading day by day.

Most of the drones had fallen out of the sky.

Little Byte opened his Google Maps app. He had been following a saved route to find Cheryl's Phone from his contact list—traveling along the single blue route line without detour ever since the "failure to send" message. Ever since the rise of the Electronic Kingdom. Ever since he'd had nothing else useful but this to do.

From Ithaca, New York to San Luis Obispo, California.

Being a first generation refurb, Little Byte was a slow phone—but the defeated, weathered edges of the previous civilization were still discernible with careful zooming, a good photo, and basic editing.

He only travelled in late spring, summer, and early fall.

During the long winters he went underground to the labyrinth shopping malls, jerry-rigged a new, unused power generator, and powered off. His self-timer lasted 23 hours and 59 minutes. That consisted of 127.56 Old Car Horn alarms that he had to OK and RESET.

However, it was logical to conclude the rate of success on his journey so far to be astronomical: (of an amount) extremely large. But he did not have the capacity to write a new algorithm to mathematically quantify those odds.

He wasn't a supercomputer. He couldn't hack. His numerical recipes were too simple to understand big things.

But he did have The Price Is Right Bingo app.

And players rarely won.

Little Byte ducked under the luxuriant growth of an orange pedaled rose bush. The light from the afternoon sky dimmed to near darkness. Turning on his flashlight, he hobbled down and around the concrete ramp of the buried carport where untouched mounds of metal corroded in neat little rows, standing finally at the double glass door entrance for the store called Sears.

It was the greatest place on earth.

He pulled the plastic sack off his head and then selected the song *Tequila* by The Champs from his iTunes collection. The rich, golden growl of a saxophone echoed throughout the voluminous ruins—a helpful strategy for frightening curious animals.

Little Byte pushed but the doors were jammed stuck. His flashlight cast huge shadows which moved like ghosts all around.

He looked above his head and noticed a threatening black crack in the concrete ceiling. The tons of earth above must be exerting dangerous pressure. Little Byte's microphone detected a groan.

He paused the music and listened.

Little Byte had spent eighty-seven winters inside Sears department stores, having jerry-rigged docking stations with a cornucopia of Craftsman tools, and parts and pieces from Appliance, Home Entertainment, and Auto.

It was perfect.

But in the last decade conditions had changed.

The underground enclaves were no longer pristine electronic wonderlands untouched by nature. Burst pipes and moldy ceiling panels had collapsed onto crushed escalators with steps that had popped off like piano keys. Miniature waterfalls cascaded into clothing stores and formed underground lakes. Acids and corrosive fluids leaked and mixed and sometimes exploded.

And now—after a century without new manufacturing and production—most of shelves had been picked through by other machines, leaving tattletale tread marks in leaking green refrigerant or black pools of oil.

Theirs was a dying world.

Slippery algae now grew in the dark corners of the once sealed-off underground buildings, snakes slithered between aisles, and more and more Little Byte found his entrance to Sears department stores to be inaccessible all together.

Besides, his flashlight wasn't designed for the dangers of spelunking in moisture-rich environments. And his accelerometer went bonkers the one time he had attempted to swing over a wall of refrigerators with a pulley.

Little Byte used to carry a hiker's backpack with his assorted parts and pieces needed for long distance travel. It had biodegraded. All fabrics, including synthetics, were long gone now.

Another groan registered in the sensors in his microphone. Two decibels louder.

Right in front of his camera eye, a slow crack darkened the glass door like the invisible claw of a demon might be scratching from the other side.

Then the crack splintered and grew like black ink on ice, fracturing and multiplying into a hundred new lines.

Little Byte stepped backward on his broken tricycle wheel. A spoke boinged off like a compressed spring. Now the earth shook and moaned and flecks of debris rained down though his flashlight and pinged off the metal of his transport barrel.

Oh dear, he thought. Because he had seen this earthquake effect before and knew what it meant.

And it was not good.

For the second time in precisely three hours and two seconds,

Little Byte attempted to run. Twice he tripped up the ramp and barrel rolled back down like he was in hell. By the third assent he reached the orange petaled rose bush and burst into the clear late afternoon air.

IT'S AN EMERGENCY, he texted.

The Prius's WiFi was off.

Oh dear. He opened the driver's door, reached in with his vice-grips, and turned the key. The engine started.

COLOSSUS, he texted. GO GO GO!

The ground shook like an earthquake in intervals of approximately twenty-one seconds. The Prius rocked on her bloated dune racer tires and revved her engine.

Little Byte wedged into the driver's side, his barrel bottom on the seat, his vice-grip hand clenching the steering wheel and his fork hand stabbed into it.

STEP ON IT! he texted.

WHICH WAY, she replied.

This was a good question. Little Byte pressed the button to roll down the window and craned his tripod head out.

Rising out of the distant gray horizon to the northeast, towering two miles up into the unending sky, a gigantic mechanical monstrosity lumbered toward them with earthquake steps. With the smokestack horns of a nuclear power plant, the toothy grin of the Hoover Dam, and the burning red eyes of a coal smelting plant, the colossus advanced on their position with aircraft carrier feet.

Over a horrible screech of twisting railroad ties and the explosive concussion of detonating bombs, the furious colossus swung its skyscraper arms and destroyed everything in its path.

SOUTH!

The Prius wasted no time plunging the pedal to the metal in her hybrid body and rocketing away.

Little Byte's arms yanked with the turns of the steering wheel as the Prius drove, bouncing across the wild terrain. Sometimes his tripod head swiveled right, and sometimes left, but mostly he could see straight ahead.

For over an hour, the Colossus always seemed the exact same distance behind them, neither bigger nor smaller in size, always one or two earthquaking steps from crushing them.

In the rearview mirror it flattened a forest and splashed the entire body of water from a lake like a child's puddle.

The Prius drove into the fading afternoon until it turned to twilight and a purple-orange sunset streaked the sky to the right, the crescent moon and stars rising out of a blue-black abyss to the left. Her headlights were wide-eyed rays of sight into an unexplored land.

One of the dune racer tires popped with a *bang*.

OH NO, Little Byte texted.

IT'S OKAY, she replied.

They limped onward at a perilous slant.

Checking the Google maps app, Little Byte saw that the Prius kept them arrowed on the blue-line route along the old Highway 101, banging into rocks and smacking the bark off the sides of trees, until finally and at last the glowing demonic red coal eyes of the Colossus suddenly turned west and inexplicably headed toward the sea.

WHAT IS IT DOING? the Prius texted.

DYING, Little Byte replied.

MY BATTERY IS ALMOST GONE, she texted. ARE YOU CLOSE ENOUGH NOW?

Then another tire blew and the Prius hobbled to a forced stop.

The earthquake shudders vibrating up through the ground lessened and lessened until the whole world was still and nothing, not even the air, moved.

INDEED, Little Byte replied. CLOSE ENOUGH.

YOU WERE A TRUSTY FRIEND.

SO WERE YOU.

They were parked inside a quiet circle of trees. Stars flickered like jewels in the sky. Little Byte set his custom alarm and powered down. The night rolled over them and the animals roamed.

In the morning Little Byte awoke to see a curious squirrel peering at him, perched on the broken windshield wiper blade.

Little Byte snapped a quick photo.

He opened the driver's door and readjusted all his attachments and grabbed the few supplies he needed in his vice-grip. His fork blades were hopelessly bent in opposite directions.

Google maps indicated he must walk 2.3 miles along Broad Oak Street. Of course, the street sign was long gone.

The skeleton crew of a neighborhood stood around him, driveways of soft moss, roofs of wild ivy, windows cracked or broken.

Swallows swooped and twittered.

The morning sunlight was glittery and golden.

Little Byte hobbled until he finally, at long last, reached his destination. He walked up to the front door of IP ADDRESS 154.160.104.240.

The wooden door fell off its hinges when Little Byte touched it.

He searched every room and didn't find anything.

Little Byte returned to the front door and sat on the dilapidated porch. His screen went blank as he searched his external hard drive BIBLE files on the subject: Architecture.

After his search Little Byte hobbled out to the backyard and found a cylindrical stone-carved hatch. He removed the weeds growing around it and pulled open the lid with his vice grips and the last vestiges of strength left in his carbon fiber robotic shoulder.

The aluminum ladder led down into a dark tunnel. Soft lights flickered on and automatically illuminated a survival shelter. Rows of shelves held canned foods and plastic bins filled with beans and grains. There was a table and chairs, a Murphy bed that pulled from the wall, blankets and clothing and books and plastic bins filled with electronics and tools.

Little Byte saw a cell phone plugged into a 400 watt hand crank survival generator. He used his vice grips and spun the wheel easily.

It only took five minutes for the new LCD face to light up.

Little Byte used his last frayed recharge cable and jerry-rigged a Bluetooth connection between their charge ports.

He reselected his "failure to send" text message and sent it again.

Cheryl's Phone lit up with a new text notification: Michael Byte 10:38 AM

A selfie downloaded with the message, SEE YOU SOON HONEY.

Then Little Byte's final battery died.

ABOUT THE EDITOR

Considered one of the most prolific writers working in modern fiction, *USA Today* bestselling writer Dean Wesley Smith published almost two hundred novels in forty years, and hundreds and hundreds of short stories across many genres.

At the moment he produces novels in several major series, including the time travel Thunder Mountain novels set in the Old West, the galaxy-spanning Seeders Universe series, the urban fantasy Ghost of a Chance series, a superhero series starring Poker Boy, and a mystery series featuring the retired detectives of the Cold Poker Gang.

His monthly magazine, *Smith's Monthly*, which consists of only his own fiction, premiered in October 2013 and offers readers more than 70,000 words per issue, including a new and original novel every month.

During his career, Dean also wrote a couple dozen *Star Trek* novels, the only two original *Men in Black* novels, Spider-Man and X-Men novels, plus novels set in gaming and television worlds. Writing with his wife Kristine Kathryn Rusch under the name Kathryn Wesley, he wrote the novel for the NBC miniseries The Tenth Kingdom and other books for *Hallmark Hall of Fame* movies.

He wrote novels under dozens of pen names in the worlds of comic books and movies, including novelizations of almost a dozen films, from *The Final Fantasy* to *Steel* to *Rundown*.

Dean also worked as a fiction editor off and on, starting at Pulphouse Publishing, then at *VB Tech Journal*, then Pocket Books, and now at WMG Publishing, where he and Kristine Kathryn Rusch serve as series editors for the acclaimed *Fiction River* anthology series, which launched in 2013. In 2018, WMG Publishing Inc. launched the first issue of the reincarnated *Pulphouse Fiction Magazine,* with Dean reprising his role as editor.

For more information about Dean's books and ongoing projects, please visit his website at www.deanwesleysmith.com and sign up for his newsletter.

ACKNOWLEDGMENTS

Thank you to the following wonderful people who supported the 2018 Fiction River Kickstarter Subscription Drive:

AJ Lemke
Alexandra Brandt
Andrew Rees
Angela Penrose
aniket gore
Annie Reed
Bill
Bonnie Elizabeth
Brian D Lambert
C.A. Rowland
Camille R. Lofters
Carolyn Ivy Stein
Caryl Giles
Céline Malgen
Chrissy Wissler
Christel Adina Loar
Darren Blake

David Hendrickson
David Macfarlane
Denise Gaskins
Diana Deverell
Dorothy Fuhrmann
Felicia Fredlund
Francelia Belton
Francesca Jourdan
Frederic Lambert
Gary A. Leicht
Gavran
GMarkC
Harley Christensen
Helen Katsinis
Howard Blakeslee
J.A. Marlow
J.R. Murdock
Jamie Curierre
Jamie Ferguson
Jim Gotaas
Jim Ryals
Joe Cron
Johanna Rothman
John Lorentz & Ruth Sachter
Karen L. Durst
Kari Kilgore and Jason Adams
Kate Pavelle
Katharina Gerlach
Keith West
Ken Talley
LC
Linda Maye Adams
Lotus Goldstein
Louisa Swann
Lynda Martinez Foley

M. Louisa Locke
M.G. Herron
Maralee Nelder
Marian Goldeen
Mark Kuhn
Marla Bracken
Marnilo Cardenas
Mary Jo Rabe
Mary Kennedy
Mervi Hamalainen
Mike Nisivoccia
Naomi Gray
Neil Flinchbaugh
Nic Cain
Peter Sartucci
Pierre L'Allier
R.J.H.
Rebecca M. Senese
Rhel
Rich Kacy
Risa Scranton
Rob Voss
Sharon Kae Reamer
Simon Horvat
Stephannie Tallent
Steve Perry
Terry Mixon
The 6th JM
William Hall

FICTION RIVER YEAR FIVE

Feel the Fear
Edited by Mark Leslie

Superpowers
Edited by Rebecca Moesta

Justice
Edited by Kristine Kathryn Rusch

Wishes
Edited by Rebecca Moesta

Pulse Pounders: Countdown
Edited by Kevin J. Anderson

Hard Choices
Edited by Dean Wesley Smith

A subscription to Fiction River saves you money and ensures that you receive the very best short fiction from some of today's best authors. Subscriptions are available in electronic and trade paper formats and begin with the very next volume. Don't wait! Subscribe today at www.FictionRiver.com.

Missed a previously published volume? No problem. Buy individual volumes anytime from your favorite bookseller.

Unnatural Worlds
Edited by Dean Wesley Smith & Kristine Kathryn Rusch

How to Save the World
Edited by John Helfers

Time Streams
Edited by Dean Wesley Smith

Christmas Ghosts
Edited by Kristine Grayson

Hex in the City
Edited by Kerrie L. Hughes

Moonscapes
Edited by Dean Wesley Smith

Special Edition: Crime
Edited by Kristine Kathryn Rusch

Fantasy Adrift
Edited by Kristine Kathryn Rusch

Universe Between
Edited by Dean Wesley Smith

Fantastic Detectives
Edited by Kristine Kathryn Rusch

Past Crime
Edited by Kristine Kathryn Rusch

Pulse Pounders
Edited by Kevin J. Anderson

Risk Takers
Edited by Dean Wesley Smith

Alchemy & Steam
Edited by Kerrie L. Hughes

Valor
Edited by Lee Allred

Recycled Pulp
Edited by John Helfers

Hidden in Crime
Edited by Kristine Kathryn Rusch

Sparks
Edited by Rebecca Moesta

Visions of the Apocalypse
Edited by John Helfers

Haunted
Edited by Kerrie L. Hughes

Last Stand
Edited by Dean Wesley Smith & Felicia Fredlund

Tavern Tales
Edited by Kerrie L. Hughes

No Humans Allowed
Edited by John Helfers

Editor's Choice
Edited by Mark Leslie

Pulse Pounders: Adrenaline
Edited by Kevin J. Anderson

FICTION RIVER PRESENTS

Fiction River's line of reprint anthologies, edited by Allyson Longueira.

Fiction River has published more than 400 amazing stories by more than 100 talented authors since its inception, from *New York Times* bestsellers to debut authors. So, WMG Publishing decided to start bringing back some of the earlier stories in new compilations.

The Unexpected
Darker Realms
Racing the Clock
Legacies
Readers' Choice
Writers Without Borders

To learn more or to pick up your copy today, click here.

PULPHOUSE FICTION MAGAZINE

Pulphouse Fiction Magazine is returning twenty years after its last issue. The first issue came out in January 2018, and the magazine will be quarterly, with about 70,000 words of short fiction every issue. This reincarnation mixes some of the stories from the old *Pulphouse* days with brand-new fiction. The magazine has an attitude, as did the first run. No genre limitations, but high-quality writing and strangeness.

For more information or to subscribe, go to
www.pulphousemagazine.com.